SONG OF
SUGAR SANDS

ENDORSEMENTS

Praise for
Joy After Noon—Sugar Sands Book One

Joy After Noon is the story of a woman whose multi-faceted personality offers an emotional connection to each of us who have ever loved, lost, and dared to love again. Whether you're a daughter, wife, stepmother, housewife, professional or any combination, Debra Coleman Jeter has created a character you'll embrace. As Joy matures, her decisions have consequences worthy of a team cheer for her, her family, and maybe even all the rest of us.

—**Jane Wells**, writer

The first book in a promising series … the author does an excellent job keeping the tension high, as the heroine, Joy, discovers that secrets can tear a life apart. The book had me in suspense to find out what would happen - give it a try, you won't be disappointed!

—**Jennifer Macaire**, blogger, reviewer

Sometimes the situation seems perfect, but underneath lie secrets and time bombs ready to explode. *Joy After Noon* is a story with depth, with characters who, in learning more about themselves and what they're capable of, discover nuances of relationships that will change their lives. Apart from the wonderful characterization, the quickly increasing pace of the plot, and the introspection, there are a scattering of lovely insights in the story.

—**Laura Hogg**, Author (AKA Lara MacGregor)

I give *Joy After Noon* five stars. I look forward to getting my hands on the next installment from the Sugar Sands series. I cannot wait to see what happens next.

—**Amy Booksy**, Blogger

Trying to take over as a stepmother is difficult enough, let alone trying to take the place of a mother who has passed away… Add in all of the other difficulties that pop up in her marriage and career, and life just gets even more complicated. Prepare yourself for a roller coaster of emotions in this one.
—**Andi's Book Reviews**

This was a thought-provoking, heart-stopping read. The family dynamics portrayed in this book were handled realistically yet respectfully … seeing how easily miscommunication can destroy a relationship and seeing the struggles to integrate into a previously formed family. I highly recommend giving this book a try.
—**Sharing Links and Wisdom**, Blog

Jeter's characters and scenery are so vivid and real that I felt I was right there sharing all their hope and fears. So looking forward to the next installment!
—**Jana Little**, Reader

Debra Jeter does a beautiful job creating realistic characters whose lives intertwine in an honest and purposeful way. I found myself still thinking about their stories once the book ended. A novel best enjoyed beachside, pool side or fire side. Once I started it, I couldn't put it down.
—**Katy Owen**, Minister's wife

Joy After Noon drew me in and I longed to see Joy make the right decisions and embrace God's plan for her life. My heart ached along with hers as I followed her struggles. I found myself relating to many characters in the novel--cringing sometimes and laughing at others.
—**Tracy Wilbanks**, Writer, Editor

I was instantly drawn into Joy's story. A beautiful story full of inescapably good characters - you get so pulled into their world that you miss them just as soon as the book is closed … this realistic and well written novel is sure to become an instant favorite to all who read it.
—**Paige Boggs**, Writer and Blogger

I thought this story was a very realistic take on some blended families nowadays and how they handled dealing with everything in their way. This was a beautifully written story about a blended family, dealing with day to day struggles. A new author for me, but I will definitely be reading more soon.
—**Enchanting Reviews**

I really liked the main characters. Joy, Ray, Marianne, and Jenny were easy to connect with and relate to. My mom was a single parent and I remember her dating and later re-marrying (and later divorcing). The tricks I played on those guys and the rude behavior I had towards them – they never stood a chance … It was pure entertainment when [the first wife] Carolyn's parents came to visit for Christmas. You could feel the awkwardness just roll off the pages.
—**Ally Swanson**, Blogger

Just finished *Joy!* Loved it so much. Carolyn is shades of Rebecca by Daphne du Maurier … Wasn't ready for it to end. Looking forward to the next book!
—**Joanna Sikes**, Minister's wife

This main character's integrity grounds her, but her racing thoughts often lead to false conclusions … Marrying into a ready-made family of teen-age girls whose mother died in questionable circumstances complicates an already complicated challenge. The author does a good job of keeping the reader involved and the action flowing.
—**Amazon Customer**

SONG OF SUGAR SANDS

Debra Coleman Jeter

PUBLISHING THE POSITIVE

ELK LAKE PUBLISHING INC
Plymouth, Massachusetts

Cover and Interior Design: Derinda Babcock

Editor(s): Linda Rondeau, Deb Haggerty

Author Represented By: the Steve Laube Agency

PUBLISHED BY: Elk Lake Publishing, Inc., 35 Dogwood Drive, Plymouth, MA 02360, 2019

Library Cataloging Data

Names: Jeter, Debra Coleman (Debra Coleman Jeter)

Song of Sugar Sands / Debra Coleman Jeter

302 p. 23cm × 15cm (9in × 6 in.)

Description: Young woman with self-esteem issues and who is not even sure there is a God marries a young man who is a preacher. Will she find her role in life?

Identifiers: ISBN-13: 978-1-951080-32-7-1 (trade) | 978-1-951080-33-4 (POD) | 978-1-951080-34-1 (e-book)

Key Words: Family, relationships, contemporary, women's fiction, beach read, marriage, self-esteem

LCCN: 2019948042 Fiction

DEDICATION

For my parents, Cliff and Marie, and my children, Nikki and Clay, who surround me with love and fill me with pride but also with humility. I learn from you all.

ACKNOWLEDGMENTS

I want to express my appreciation for the support, encouragement, enthusiasm, and helpful criticism of so many people. In particular, I thank my friends, my family, my publicist (Angela Johnson), and the terrific team at Elk Lake—Deb Haggerty, Linda Rondeau, and Derinda Babcock.

As always, I especially thank my loving and supportive husband, Norm, and my daughter, Nikki, who believed in this book and in me from the start.

Place me like a seal over your heart,
like a seal on your arm;
For love is as strong as death,
its jealousy unyielding as the grave.
It burns like blazing fire,
like a mighty flame.

Many waters cannot quench love;
rivers cannot wash it away.
If one were to give all the wealth of his house
for love,
it would be utterly scorned.

Song of Solomon 8:6–7
New International Version

PROLOGUE

I stand at the edge of the water, a deep aqua today, as I listen to the waves crash onto the shore. I think back to all the times I've stood here, all the moods we've shared this past year, the Gulf and I. Times when I was saying goodbye, convinced I could not survive another day in this life, in this place. Times when the water drew me in, embraced me, caressed and comforted me. And times like today when I gaze in awe at the magnificence of the vast waters before me, at their power and the power of their maker.

A girl crystallizes before my eyes, rising like a mermaid from the water. That girl would never in a million years have believed that Acadia Powers, at the ripe age of twenty-four, would find herself in this position. Not only in this position, but actually grateful to be here. That girl would have been appalled. For an instant, I can see her and feel her as vividly as if that time were yesterday, the scene in my head as real and as near as the sand beneath my feet.

Part I

The Courtship

November 1977

Where is the thatched roof village,
the home of Acadian farmers
Men whose lives glided on the rivers
that water the woodlands,
Darkened by shadows of earth,
but reflecting an image of heaven?

From *Evangeline* by Henry W Longfellow
"A Tale of Acadie"

CHAPTER ONE

Malibu, California

November 1977

My acne finally cleared up about the time I started college. By junior year, I had come into myself, into my comfort zone so to speak, and was having the time of my life. Or so I told myself. Then I met Peter. Something about him jarred me out of this zone so completely that, try as I might, I simply could not find my way back.

The first time I saw him, I was at an off-campus party. Bored, I looked around for a cute guy to talk to. With his long blonde hair, intense green eyes, and especially the way he laughed—as if all the joy of the universe radiated from him—he certainly fit the bill.

I made my way across the room toward him. The record player blasted "We Are the Champions" by Queen. Pretty coeds in miniskirts and wedge-heeled boots or knee socks were everywhere. Peter was absorbed in conversation with a classmate of mine named Greg and paid me no attention as I edged into his path of vision.

I'd recently learned the power of eye contact, having gained enough self-confidence to take risks—once my acne cleared up. Today, though, not only Peter, but Greg as well, seemed oblivious to my approach. Peter gestured with a wave of one hand to emphasize a point while Greg listened intently, his eyes on Peter. I was about to back away when Peter's words caused me to pause. "If you really believed in everlasting life or punishment, if any of us *really* believed, why wouldn't we do everything in our power every minute to ensure the one and not the other?"

Hadn't I once accused my parents of exactly that? Or maybe he was putting the words to something I had been trying but failing to communicate. "Are you saying they're all fakes?" I pivoted to confront Peter. "That nobody really believes at all?"

Both guys turned to gape. Greg's eyes flickered over me, taking in the details of my appearance in one practiced sweep. Peter, however, looked directly into my eyes. "No, that's not what I'm saying. I'm saying we're weak, and it's a good thing God has such a generous, forgiving spirit. Don't you think?"

I stalled, hoping he would keep talking so I wouldn't need to answer. He waited, his eyes intent on mine.

"I—uh …"

Greg saved me. "Acadia, pardon our manners. Peter O'Neil, this is Acadia Powers. She's a pre-med major."

"Pre-med," Peter echoed, holding out his hand and offering a lopsided grin. "Impressive."

"Only if I pass." I took his hand, and my heart performed a peculiar little leap.

"I get carried away sometimes," he said, "when I think about how awesome our God is. Forgive me."

Clearly this guy was some sort of religious nut and not my type at all. My best bet was to contrive a fast escape. My feet, however, seemed glued to the floor, cooperating about as well as my tongue. "O'Neil? Funny, you don't look Catholic," I said at last.

"I'm not." He smiled with his eyes. "I think I'll get some popcorn. Do you want some?"

I nodded. The food at these types of parties was all over the place. Kids with trust funds might have catered dishes like shrimp cocktail or fondue. Other times, like tonight, there was nothing fancier than chips and salsa. And, of course, the popcorn, which did smell tantalizing.

A couple of sorority girls approached, and Greg slipped away with them. Girls who looked like these two beauties still made me feel like my clothes were all wrong and my hands were put on backward.

All through high school, I failed to get so much as a date to the prom—though I was known to be the one to ask about rock bands *or* for help with homework. A lot of the kids called me "the brain," which wasn't true and definitely not a compliment. None of the cute guys ever came close to asking me out. By high school graduation, I wondered if anybody ever would. When I arrived on a college campus and started to get attention from the opposite sex, I gobbled up the change like a kitten with tuna fish.

The girls' eyes lingered on Peter as they moved off. He took my hand and steered me through the crowd.

"Acadia," he murmured as we worked our way toward the salty aroma. "I think I'll call you Cadi."

"Cadi sounds so much like Katie." I articulated carefully.

"Not to me," he said, as if the matter were settled.

The way Peter looked at me broke all the rules I thought I'd sorted out for myself. He did not appear to notice the way my crocheted granny skirt hugged my hips and legs right down to my platform sandals, or my lacy sleeveless top, or the crimson scarf I had wrapped around my waist. Instead he kept looking straight into my eyes.

"So, Cadi Powers, where are you from?"

"Kentucky. Can't you tell?" I exaggerated a hillbilly twang.

"Maybe, a little."

"I've been practicing my elocution in order to drop the accent." I replaced the southern drawl with my best British inflection.

"Why?" His eyebrows lifted.

"You know, the image thing—that we're all barefoot and chasing houseflies."

Peter laughed, the same joyous laugh that had first drawn me in his direction. His teeth were white and even, with a small chip off one front tooth. "That's ridiculous. You should be proud of your southern-ness. It's what made you who you are."

"How do you know that's something to be proud of?"

"Just a feeling." He placed a bowl of popcorn in my hand and guided me with a light touch on my elbow across the room to a couple of empty chairs. The tweed upholstery scratched my back, and I squirmed away from the itch.

"Sometimes, I'm not sure I have any faith at all." Where had *that* come from? I wanted to bite back the words as soon as they were out.

"We all have doubts," Peter said.

"Even you?"

"Sure. Did you know that when Jesus was on earth, he told his followers that if they had no doubts in their mind, they could tell a mountain to fall into the sea, and it would happen?"

"Yeah, but that's crazy," I said.

"Crazy, if you take God out of the picture."

"Nobody could do that."

"Nobody I know. Maybe that's because there's always a doubt. What I'm trying to say is … just because you have doubts, don't think you have no faith."

"Just not enough."

"Maybe not enough to move a mountain. Not yet."

"Why would anyone want to move a mountain anyway?" I tossed a handful of popcorn in my mouth, ready to switch to a lighter topic.

"Depends on what your mountain is. Could be you haven't encountered it yet." His smile was so disarming I couldn't help smiling back.

A pretty girl with legs as long as *Gone with the Wind* plopped into a chair nearby. She wore a coral pantsuit made of a crinkly fabric with a wide belt that accentuated her ridiculously small waist, one rivaling Scarlett O'Hara's. She crossed her legs and blinked thick lashes at Peter. "Hey, handsome!"

"Stacey. How's it going?" The magical smile veered away from me.

"Peachy." She leaned toward him and muttered something in a sultry voice so low I couldn't catch the words. The honey-colored hair swung forward, shimmering with golden lights even in the dimly lit room.

"See you around," I said, telling myself I'd just escaped a train wreck. Taking my nearly empty bowl, I tried to look casual as I sauntered off. As I edged away from Peter, my eyes searched for someone I might know while my ears stayed tuned to the tinkle of the golden girl's laughter. For a moment, I thought I heard, "Don't go." But I dismissed it as my imagination. I could envision Peter's face all lit up as he talked to the blonde. Jealousy ripped through me like wildfire, and then I spotted a handsome guy I'd gone out with a couple of times.

I caught his eye. "Josh!" I fought the urge to glance back over my shoulder. Was Peter watching?

For the rest of the evening, the same urge kept bubbling back—a need to locate Peter in the crowded room … just to see what he was doing … just to refresh my memory of his face. Without looking, I could somehow sense his position in the room, his eyes on me or on someone else, the timbre of his voice deep in conversation, the rich baritone of his laughter.

The party drew to a close and people began to leave. Peter headed my way, and my heart thumped so hard I thought I'd have a heart attack. "Can I call you? Maybe go out or something?" he asked.

Every instinct told me to flee, warned me this guy might be my undoing. "I'm pretty busy."

"Maybe just once?" His eyebrows squished together to form a question mark, and I squelched a laugh. One time, I thought. One time, and that's all.

CHAPTER TWO

"That might just be the best movie of all time." Peter's eyes glowed.

"No way." I rescued a dollop of hot fudge just before it slid from my dish onto the blue and white checkered tabletop.

"You didn't like it?"

"I liked it. For a science fiction flick, I liked it a lot. But I wouldn't say it's the best film of all time." To be honest, I did love *Close Encounters*. I loved seeing it with Peter. Still, I felt argumentative. Besides, I wasn't ready to put it in the category of all-time greatest movies.

"All right. So what is?"

"What is what?"

"*Your* best movie of all time?"

"My favorite or the best ever?"

"Isn't that the same thing?" Peter took a bite of his strawberry ice cream. How did he make strawberry ice cream, probably my least favorite, look so good?

"I doubt it."

"So what's your favorite—*Gone with the Wind? Annie Hall?*"

His tone mocked me, and I wanted to impress him by naming a film I loved which would appeal to men as much as women. I couldn't come up with one off the top of my head. *The Godfather* or *The Godfather: Part II* perhaps? Both great films, but in all honesty the ones he named were more to my taste. "Maybe."

"Which one?"

"Both."

"They can't both be your favorite." He grinned, and my eyes were once more drawn to Peter's chipped front tooth. I wondered how that happened and if I'd ever get the story.

"Let's talk about *Close Encounters*," I said. I'd always enjoyed analyzing movies, so I put Peter to the test. "What made this movie so great?"

"That spaceship coming over the mountain took my breath away," Peter said.

"That *was* pretty awesome. What did you think of the characters?"

"The characters or the actors?"

"Either."

"I think his wife should have stayed the course."

"No way!" I tapped the table. "Knowing what we know, as the audience, sure. But look at it from her perspective."

"I'm not saying she wasn't justified."

"So you admit she was?"

"Sometimes it's not about being right or wrong. Sometimes it's more about going on faith."

"Even if it's crazy?" Putting my spoon down, I challenged him, hands on my hips, the way I used to confront my parents.

"He wasn't crazy."

"She had no way of knowing that. It was easy for the Melinda Dillon character to believe him. She was caught up in it too."

"All right. I'll give you that. Surely, though, he and his wife had enough history together for her to know he wasn't crazy. I believe in the sanctity of marriage." Peter paused, and the strangest feeling washed over me—as if we weren't talking about the movie at all. "Don't you?"

I thought about my parents and their friends, about the values they gave lip service to and the opposite ones they sometimes lived. About free love and the values I'd embraced. Or pretended to embrace … I wasn't sure which. I twisted the Bulova watch on my wrist, trying to remember where I bought it and how much it cost. Trying to think about anything except the way Peter's eyes made me feel. "What else did you like about the film?"

"The way they were all drawn to something they couldn't explain. A magnetic force."

"May the Force be with you." I knew he'd recognize this quote.

Peter was not to be distracted. "Haven't you ever felt something tugging at you like that?"

"Nothing that made me want to build a mountain in my backyard."

Peter waited, his eyes solemn, and a shiver ran through me. "You mean like God?" I asked.

"Yes. Like God. Don't you ever feel him tugging at you?"

I shook my head.

"Never?"

I shook it harder, not ready to admit that sometimes I did feel pulled toward something undefined. Another couple had entered after us and ordered their ice cream to go. The sugary scent of their waffle cones trailed behind them, making me wish I'd ordered mine in a cone.

Peter reached across the table and stroked my arm ever so lightly—not the skin as much as the pale film of hair on it. I trembled under his touch, hoping he didn't notice. I had the feeling, though, that he noticed everything. "I think you might be right about the wife," he said. "It would be asking a lot for anyone to understand the way Roy was behaving."

I stared at him, surprised by his reversal, and rethought my own position. From the jukebox, Linda Ronstadt crooned that falling in love was so easy. "I wonder if there was a way Roy could have articulated his feelings better," Peter said.

"He didn't understand them himself." How had we switched sides?

"He could have tried—tried harder."

"It's not easy to communicate when you're frustrated yourself." I fiddled with my spoon, scooping up the melting bits of ice cream around the edges.

Peter nodded. "Everyone gets frustrated at times. I know I do. Let's not let that happen to us."

"What?"

"Miscommunication. Lack of communication. Whatever tears couples apart."

I tingled at his words, at the idea that there was an *us*—that we were more than just a casual date. I thought of the long-held anger I'd felt toward my parents. Then I thought of some of the things I'd done, not so much because I really wanted to ... rather because I knew how much my parents would hate my actions if they'd known. Things Peter would never approve of.

"You look way too serious," he said.

"Maybe that's one of the things I didn't totally love about *Close Encounters*. Sometimes, I just like to watch a movie that's fun—you know, that makes me crack up."

"And you expected *Close Encounters* to be that kind of film?"

"I don't think I knew what to expect," I said, feeling a little peeved.

"You don't watch a lot of sci fi, do you?" Peter's green eyes glinted with amusement.

"Why do you say that?"

"Because, compared to most science fiction, *Close Encounters* is a walk in the park."

"A walk in the park?" Now *I* was amused.

"Warmer and lighter."

"Lighter?"

"You know, less dark."

"I know what lighter means!" I wasn't certain whether I was annoyed or just pretending to be.

"Are you sure?"

"No, I guess not. I give up. It was a masterpiece." I exaggerated the word to make sure he caught my sarcasm.

"Finally."

"I bet you're the kind of guy who always has to get in the last word."

"No, I'm not." He reached over and took the last bite of ice cream from my dish. "I do, however, relish the last bite."

"Hey, I was saving that!" I reached for his dish, but it was already empty. "That's not fair."

He burst out laughing, the hoot of a young boy crowing over winning a footrace. "Want another one?"

"Nope. I wanted *that* bite."

"Sorry." He rose to throw away the plastic dishes. I stood too, and he took my arm. My annoyance melted away at his touch. To hide my confusion, I blurted out the last thing I'd meant to say. "When are you going to get off this religious kick?"

Dropping my arm, he turned to look squarely at me as we stepped outside into the moonlit evening. "It's not a kick."

I felt chastised and didn't know what to say next. After a moment, Peter spoke again. "One thing that bothers me about a lot of the movies I see is the way they portray religious people. Like we're all fanatics or something."

"Aren't you?"

"Not the way they show it. As soon as a character shows up sharing the Word or reading a Bible in a movie, you can pretty well figure that character is going to turn out to be the killer. Or a pedophile or something else disgusting."

"Or both." I'd noticed the same thing. "Why do you think?"

"It's a form of stereotyping. It's not cool to show all the professionals as men or the secretaries as women, or the housekeepers and janitors as black. But it's just fine to assume all religious types are either unethical and manipulative, or else irrational and out of control."

We were at the car now. I leaned against it, breathing in the cool night air and watching Peter's facial expressions. Gone was the teasing glint. He was serious now.

"My parents are the first type," I said.

"That's an awful thing to say. You really think they are unethical and manipulative?"

I nodded. "That's why I'm here."

"Your parents manipulated you into going on a date with me?"

I laughed. "Not that manipulative. No, I meant that's why I'm here at Pepperdine instead of Berkeley."

He opened the car door for me, and I placed my Gucci bag on the floorboard. Had I offended him? I should be hoping I had. He was probably too nice to ever say a harsh word against his parents, which was exactly why this had to be our first and last date. I thought again of those things in my past I could never tell Peter. Why torture myself by spending time with someone I could not be totally honest with? I buckled my seatbelt with a decisive snap, flushed at the thought, and wondered how Peter would react if I uttered my feelings out loud.

Peter slid his key into the ignition and turned his warm gaze on me again. "Well, all I can say is—good for them. If that's what it took to get you here. Pardon the cliché, but sometimes God works in a mysterious way."

CHAPTER THREE

I worked my spoon deep into the bottom of my bowl for a mouthful loaded with hot fudge. Even the chocolate, which never failed to please, tasted a little bland. "So," I said, "what did you think of the play?"

When Dave suggested the same ice cream parlor Peter had taken me to on our first date, my initial impulse had been to say no. But why? So here we were. Tonight, from the jukebox, Crystal Gayle's voice fretted that her brown eyes were being made blue.

Dave rolled his eyes—dark brown with heavy lids. Bedroom eyes, my friend Cynthia would call them.

"What a downer!" Dave made a fake gagging motion. This was our second date. Though the first had been less than thrilling, I'd decided to give him another chance. Anything to take my mind off why Peter hadn't called. I had been so sure he would.

I nodded, waiting for him to say more. When he didn't, I prompted, "Weren't you familiar with the storyline?"

After all, *The Glass Menagerie* had been his idea, not mine. After auditioning for the play and failing to get a part, he'd wanted to see what the competition had that he didn't.

"Not really. I read some of the play before the audition, but mainly I just concentrated on the parts I figured I'd be reading."

I digested this but wasn't ready to drop the subject. "Are you still sorry you didn't get the part?"

"Are you kidding? Night after night of rehearsing that crap!" He rolled his eyes again.

I always found it annoying when people rolled their eyes a lot. I stifled a laugh at hearing Tennessee Williams's masterpiece described as crap, especially by a theater major. "I remember the first time I read the play," I mused aloud. I'd hated the plot too, but my reason was different. Seeing

Laura's hopes rise, and then die, hurt too much. Her humiliation made me cry.

I had cried again tonight, at the exact moment Dave inched his arm around my shoulder. He stroked little circles on my upper arm, working his way under the lacy little flap of sleeve of my nearly sleeveless white top. For an instant I thought he was experiencing the heart-wrenching pain of the moment, was reaching out to share and offer comfort. When I turned to look at him though, the grin I saw had nothing to do with the story.

He snorted now. "That chick was pathetic."

"Yes, she was." I had no desire to explain to him how close to becoming Laura I had once been. Like Laura, I'd been unpopular and too proud to admit my longings. Turning in on myself, losing myself in a world of the imagination seemed like my best bet for a long time. Dave took his popularity for granted. How could he possibly understand loneliness?

Then, in a habit I was trying to shed, I thought of Peter. He was also a guy to whom popularity would come easily. Still, I suspected he would have understood. At least, with Peter, there would have been a real conversation—about the characters and the fragility of the human spirit. *Why* was I thinking of Peter again, seeing his disheveled blonde hair and crinkly green eyes in the chair across from me? I forced myself to focus on the moment, to give Dave the benefit of the doubt. "What about Williams's other plays—*Cat on a Hot Tin Roof* or *A Streetcar Named Desire*, for instance? Do you have a favorite?"

"Not really." He shrugged. "To tell the truth, I'm not much into reading plays."

"I figured that was the main thing you did when you majored in theater."

"There's always Cliff's Notes. You'd be surprised how many of those classes you can pass without doing the reading." He laughed, revealing teeth that were spectacularly white against the bronze of his face and aligned so perfectly I figured he must have worn braces at some point. Had he ever had acne a day in his life? I tried to picture him in braces with his face covered in blemishes but failed.

"Don't you like to read? Other stuff besides plays, I mean?" I asked.

"Sure, it's all right. But there are only so many hours in the day. When the surf's up and you've got to make a choice, that's an easy one. You finished?"

I spooned out the last little bit of fudge and ice cream and tried to savor the flavor, tried not to remember Peter's howl of laughter at stealing the bite I'd been saving.

"There's still time to go to Chase's," Dave said. "Plenty of time in fact. I imagine the party's just warming up."

When I said nothing, he added, "If you don't want to go, of course, we can always do something else."

He peered at me through remarkably long lashes. His look made me think of a little boy being nice to his mother on Mother's Day—offering to eat a salad bar instead of pizza, or to wash dishes instead of going outside to play.

"I'm pretty tired." I yawned. "Why don't you take me back to the dorm and go to the party without me?"

"All right, if you're sure." As if afraid I might change my mind, he propelled me toward his car, a glossy black Jaguar. I pictured Peter's beat-up Plymouth and wondered for the umpteenth time why he hadn't called by now. I had even practiced how I would turn him down. Dave tapped his fingers on the steering wheel to the rhythm of Jimmy Buffet's "Margaritaville," which blared from the car radio.

Dave parked the car near my dorm, and with practiced ease, reached for a kiss. Despite the vaguely unpleasant feel of his fingers against the back of my neck, I allowed the kiss.

"You're lovely," he murmured and this, too, sounded practiced. When his kisses became more intense, I pulled away. "Thanks for the play and the ice cream," I said. "I had fun."

"Don't mention it." He looked peeved, but I didn't care.

He walked me to the door of my dorm, and already my mind was elsewhere. I suspected his was too. "See you around," he said.

I forced a smile.

He walked away without looking back, a slight strut in his step. I stared after him, pictured him on a surfboard. A guy almost any girl at Pepperdine would swoon over. What had I been thinking? Did I forget all I'd learned in the past two years about how to hold a guy's interest? Why had I cringed at his touch, pulled away from his kiss, allowed the thoughts of another guy to enter my mind?

Had it been the play? Most likely. *The Glass Menagerie* always made me feel weird, ever since I first read it. I sped to my room, my head spinning with unwanted memories. I thought of Laura and of the self I'd been then, of the reasons I deliberately revamped my image from a shy, unpopular girl to an independent freethinker who didn't care what anyone thought. By the time I reached my dorm room and threw myself on the bed, I was no longer the self-assured girl I believed myself to be. I was right back in the eighth grade, riddled with self-doubt, acne, and, at times, loathing.

The year is 1971, and I'm fourteen years old. A time of Bob Dylan and James Taylor and Michael Jackson. Jim Morrison is found dead. I cry at *Love Story* and croon along to "Maggie May" and "Knock Three Times" and "Me and Bobby McGee." At school, I'm lonely. So lonely, for reasons I can't fathom, not having figured out yet that popularity has little to do with logic.

"Acadia, why don't you read the part of Laura?" Ms. Cartwright asks in PASS class.

PASS—Program for Academically Superior Students—lasts one period a day and is mostly a joke. Supposed to challenge gifted or talented students, the class seems more like an easy way for a teacher to get a break. All Ms. Cartwright does most days is distribute a few brain teasers or mind benders, which are basically glorified crossword puzzles. The class is easy for the students too, because Ms. Cartwright doesn't give a flip whether we apply ourselves or just pretend interest while whispering with friends.

On this particular day, though, we are actually doing something as a class. We are reading *The Glass Menagerie* out loud. I meet Ms. Cartwright's eyes. When she asks if I will read the role, I accept, trying to sound bored. My heart thuds with excitement.

PASS is usually torture for me because I have no real friends in the room. So I actually attempt the puzzles and brain teasers. Perhaps because she feels guilty over neglecting us, Ms. Cartwright gets up from her seat … where she's usually reading a fashion magazine or doing her nails … and wanders around the class to peer over our shoulders from time to time. When this happens, several students will suddenly become my friend … just long enough to copy a few words or figures onto their blank pages.

As we begin to read the play, the kids without roles go back to their usual whispering. Their voices fade into the background as the storyline grabs me. I *become* Laura, and the becoming is so painful I can barely breathe—let alone read aloud. I am totally humiliated for Laura when her mom, Amanda, begs her brother to find a nice gentleman caller to bring home for his unpopular sister. When he does … and the *gentleman* turns out to be someone Laura's had a crush on all through high school, my heart pumps furiously. I am, in equal parts, excited for and annoyed at the mother, as she insists Laura make herself more attractive by adding "deceivers" to her dress … like a padded bra, I figure.

"All pretty girls are a trap, a pretty trap, and men expect them to be." Sara Truman, who is reading Amanda, titters. I barely notice, as the words play in my head. The snickering spreads, and I wonder vaguely if they are laughing at me or at something totally unrelated. Yet, mainly I am absorbed, transported to Williams's world. To Laura's world.

I breathe a sigh of relief when my turn ends. Still the play does not release me. I shut out my giggling classmates the way they've been shutting me out. I read ahead. I've got to know what happens, even as I sense that nothing good is in store for this fragile girl. The gentleman caller ignites Laura's hopes, and I long with all my being for things to work out for her. At the same time, I fear desperately that they won't. Why does Laura's fate feel so personal? Somehow everything has changed for me in the last couple of years. There are cliques now. The eighth-grade class is small … twenty-seven kids total … and there are really only two categories: those who are *in* and those who aren't. The ones I thought to be my friends are so busy *staying in* they can't risk their status by taking a chance on the nerdy girl with the bad complexion.

The girls obsess over two things: boys—who pay me no attention, and parties—to which I am not invited.

I ache for Laura, and I ache for myself.

I think of Laura's line: *Oh, be careful—if you breathe, it breaks!... You see how the light shines through him?* I picture her holding her favorite glass figure, the unicorn, so different from the others.

I weep when the gentleman caller Jim breaks Laura's treasure and then, after kissing her, tells her he's engaged to a girl named Betty.

Is the mother the smart one after all, with her focus on being *perceived as pretty*? Is Laura, who seems so much wiser, merely confused? For in the end, just as I fear, her hopes are dashed. Not through any fault of her own so far as I can determine, except shyness and being less than physically perfect. Or is there a deeper flaw, something Laura and I share, something that eludes us both?

What is Tennessee Williams's point?

When I picture Laura, I do not see a crippled girl. I see a lonely one. I don't envision her physical infirmity as a great one, no worse really than a bad case of acne.

Tears slide down my face, and I don't care who sees. I cry for Laura and for myself. In that moment, I do not care if the laughter erupting around me is directed at me or at something else.

I cannot … will not … become Laura. Of course I cannot *will* myself to become pretty, but I can find a way to be striking.

Stealthily, so my parents scarcely notice what's happening, I accumulate the materials to create my new look. I don't really need mascara since I've been blessed with dark, nearly black lashes. Still, I use a heavy eyeliner to draw attention to my eyes, which are large and slightly slanted at the corners, though of an odd gray-blue shade. When this gets no one's attention but my parents', I decide more extreme measures are needed. I thumb through magazines, looking for eye-catching ideas. Although the hippie movement has been underway for several years now, the ideas have not made significant inroads in our conservative Kentucky small town. Identifying with the rebellion, I decide to throw out my bra and embrace the California fashion scene before the trend either catches on or dies out.

If no one appreciates me as I am, I will become someone else. *I will not be Laura.*

CHAPTER FOUR

I began to think I'd never hear from Peter. When he finally called, I realized only a few weeks had passed since our first date … though it felt much longer. I tried to sound offhand, as best I could with my heart hammering in my chest. "I'll have to check my calendar," I said.

I spent an unusually long time choosing my clothes for our date—simple but flattering jeans and a striped, turtle-necked bodysuit in Pepperdine's blue and orange. I told myself the fuss was because I wanted to be the one who tired of him, not the other way around.

"So, what have you been up to lately?" I tried to ask during a lull in the noise of the basketball game. I wasn't just making conversation—I really wanted to know. The din of the fans rose at that moment and drowned out my words.

"What did you say?" Peter shouted.

"Never mind!" I yelled back, shaking my head and laughing.

Making my way through the crowd to the ladies' room at halftime, I realized there was a skip in my step, a skip having little to do with the basketball score. No one really expected Pepperdine to pull a win over Gonzaga.

I decided to buy us each a soft drink on my way back to the stands, and Peter's eyes warmed with appreciation at the small gesture. The crowd's cheering and excitement mounted throughout the second half.

As the clock ran down, Pepperdine trailed by only two points, a much closer game than anyone expected. When my favorite player—a small wiry guy with quick hands but more heart than skill—stole the ball, there were less than three seconds left on the clock. He raced toward the goal, tossing up an off-balance shot from somewhere between half-court and the three-point line. The ball swooshed through the basket right at the buzzer, and the fans went wild.

Peter and I hugged, and the scratchiness of my throat told me I'd been screaming my lungs out. Outside the gym, Pepperdine supporters of all ages moved and chattered with the thrill of an upset over a higher ranked team. Peter took my hand, and his was warm and dry and comfortable against my skin. "That was some game," he said hoarsely, trying to clear his throat.

"Sure was," I croaked back. The realization that we both lost our voices in the excitement struck us as hilarious, and we hooted with hoarse laughter.

The guy behind the counter at the Malibu Ice Cream Shoppe remembered us from before, and Peter gave him a play-by-play account of the game. He rewarded us with extra generous portions. Over ice cream sundaes, we talked and talked until our strained voices were little more than whispers. Unperturbed, we croaked on.

Peter sighed. "My dad would have loved that shot. He used to eat and breathe college basketball."

"He doesn't anymore?"

"I don't know."

"Aren't you and your dad close?" For a second, I was afraid I'd forgotten something important I was supposed to know, like whether Peter's dad was dead.

"Not really." A cloud passed over his green eyes.

"Why not?"

"I don't know really." He frowned. "That's not true exactly. My dad drinks. I've been trying to reach him, ever since my conversion. I know he needs help. I don't think he can quit by himself. He needs the Lord, but every time I bring the subject up, he pushes me away."

"What about AA?"

"He won't admit he has a problem. He's not the kind of drinker who gets sick or passing-out drunk. His problem is more subtle than that. He just drinks more and more all the time."

"Are you sure he has a problem then?"

"It's not just the drinking that worries me. That's bad enough, but I worry about his soul too."

I was not comfortable with the direction of this conversation, so I made no comment.

He pushed his empty ice cream dish aside and leaned toward me. "What if he got drunk and died in a car wreck or something?"

"Or hurt someone else ..." The remainder of my ice cream was turning to slush, so I spooned a mouthful before realizing I'd lost my appetite.

"Exactly." Peter's eyes welled with tears. Most of the guys I knew would have been ashamed to be seen crying, but Peter made no move to hide his emotion.

I stirred my melted ice cream and waited, not knowing how to comfort Peter.

"I just get so scared for him sometimes."

"You have to trust in God to take care of him." I wondered where these words of encouragement came from. They certainly didn't sound like me.

"You're right. You're exactly right."

"No, I'm not," I said, suddenly ashamed, convinced now of my insincerity. "I'm a hypocrite."

"Why do you say that?"

"I don't know. Something about you makes me feel hypocritical."

"That's a back-handed compliment if there ever was one." Peter's eyes were sparkling again. There was a hint of concern in them though, in the way they crinkled at the corners as if unsure whether to make a joke or an apology.

"I don't mean it that way." How had our evening mutated from fun to serious?

"What *do* you mean?"

I carried our paper dishes to the trash, stalling for time. Should I turn the conversation back to something pleasant and non-threatening ... or try to answer honestly? After all Peter had shared tonight, and especially after seeing those unshed tears, I had no choice.

"My motives aren't as pure as yours," I said. "The way you care about your dad. The way you really care about people."

"And you?"

"Me?" I hesitated ... how could I answer him without sounding mean? "I'm always critical, especially of my parents."

"In your mind, you mean? I do that too."

"Not just that. I've not exactly been respectful. In the past."

Peter shrugged. "The past is the past."

"Is it?"

Later that evening, when I was alone, I pondered our conversation. "The past is the past," Peter had said.

On an impulse, I reached for my phone and dialed the familiar but not often used number. I hung up before they could answer. They were probably in bed. I'd call in the morning.

By morning, though, I had forgotten.

Peter and I had been seeing each other for a couple of weeks by the time I finally made the call. For some reason, being with Peter brought the impulse back. I caught myself thinking about his words on our first date. *Pardon the cliché, but sometimes God works in a mysterious way.*

My parents and I didn't agree on much when I was in high school, but we agreed on one thing: I would go to college. They'd made this expectation clear to me for years, and I was eager to try campus life myself. The problem was we had different sorts of campuses in mind. I pictured a school with students from all kinds of backgrounds—different nationalities and religions and races and political beliefs, as different from western Kentucky life as I could get.

"We think you should go to a Christian college," my mother informed me. She glanced at my father for confirmation, and he nodded.

"You've got to be kidding me! You want me to go where everyone *looks* the same and *thinks* the same and *believes* the same. I'm sick of sameness." I glared at them.

"That's enough." Dad glared back.

"It would just be an extension of high school," I said, desperate for my parents to see my point. "I want to expand my horizons—I want to spread my wings."

"You can spread your wings just fine in a Christian environment," Mom said.

"You don't understand me at all!" I fled the room, trying to calm myself but already planning my strategy to get what I wanted.

After days of debate, they had finally agreed to visit a couple of state universities in California on condition I also visit the campus at Pepperdine University in Malibu. Not their first choice but an acceptable alternative.

So here I was.

She picked up on the first ring.

"Hello, Mom?"

CHAPTER FIVE

"Are you seeing anyone special?" she asked after a few awkward pauses.

I hesitated, remembering how my mother saw college—mainly as a pricey way to find the right kind of husband. "There is someone, actually." The second I spoke I knew I shouldn't have. Still, *special* seemed to fit Peter so perfectly.

"Oh?" Mom's voice lifted, and I could imagine the raised waxed eyebrows, the pursed mouth, the piqued interest in the round gray eyes. "Is it serious?"

I tried to undo the damage. "No, I didn't mean it that way. He's just—different."

"Different how?" A frown in the voice, brows drawn together, eyes skeptical—I could see as much as hear her. Different was not to my mother's liking.

"It's hard to explain." *What had I been thinking?*

"Try."

The silence dragged on. Finally, I blurted, "For one thing, he's pretty religious."

"That's good." My mother sounded relieved, even pleased. "What does his father do?"

"I don't know," I admitted. I do know he's an alcoholic, I thought of adding. *Like father like son*, Mom would have concluded … and a perverse streak urged me to go that route.

Instead I said, "When I say he's religious, I mean *really* religious. Not just religious on the surface … religious down deep."

"I'm not sure I understand the difference," Mom said.

Of course you don't.

"Are you saying he's a religious fanatic?"

"No, of course not." *Was* Peter a religious fanatic? What did that mean anyway? A bad thing, in Mom's mind. In mine too, maybe.

I needed to end this conversation, which was going from bad to worse in a hurry. "Just remembered," I lied, "I've got a meeting. I'm late already."

As I hung up the phone, frustration burned my stomach. I was annoyed with myself as much as I was with Mom. Annoyed with Peter, too, as if he'd deliberately placed me in this position.

Irritation still reigned when I saw Peter the next day. We'd signed up to work the booths at a Pepperdine fundraiser for an orphanage in Mexico. Although neither of us could find time in our schedule for the upcoming trip to Mexico, we could help out by selling T-shirts and tickets for a dinner show.

I'd slept poorly, after waking up in the middle of the night with cramps. My conversation with Mom kept replaying in my head. By the time I met Peter, I felt bloated, crampy, and very grouchy. I sucked in my stomach, not wanting Peter to think I looked fat in my denim granny skirt. The overcast sky and rolling clouds—a rare occurrence in Malibu—mirrored my mood.

Peter took the booth with the dinner show tickets, and I started out with T-shirts and caps. "Is the writing going to peel when it's washed?" asked my first customer, a skinny girl who squinted as if nearsighted.

She held up one of the Pepperdine shirts—brilliant blue with an orange wave and *Pepperdine* scribbled almost illegibly in bright orange. *Save the Children* was printed more clearly on the back.

"How would I know?" I said, and Peter shot me a glance. "I mean, I doubt it. For $10.99, you'd think they would be well-made."

"Well ..." The girl crooked a brow, then squinted to read the label on the inside of the shirt. "I can't make out what it says."

I sighed, picked up a shirt and read the label out loud. "Machine wash, cold, with like colors." I met her gaze. "It doesn't say anything about drying. To be on the safe side, maybe you should keep it out of the dryer."

"Do you have an extra-small?"

I sorted through the stack, though I was pretty sure we did not. "No." I wanted to yell *Why didn't you ask me that first?* I managed to restrain my misdirected frustration. "The smalls are in short supply, though we do have several mediums, and an abundance of large and extra-large shirts."

"It's for a good cause," Peter said, smiling at the girl.

"That's true." She nibbled on a fingernail for a second, then smiled back, revealing a slight dimple. I felt a wave of something like jealousy or impatience as a line formed behind her.

"So do you want the shirt or not?" I asked.

"Okay." She was still looking at Peter. "It is for a good cause after all. I'll take a small."

"Hey, Acadia." The voice belonged to Tom Greene, a good-looking guy with dark curly hair and mischievous brown eyes. I'd been on a couple of dates with him during my freshman year.

"Hey." I swallowed my frustration and turned on my charm, acutely aware of Peter's presence beside me and of two or three girls who were flirting openly with him. "What have you been up to lately?"

"This and that. Where have you been keeping yourself?"

"Did you lose my phone number?" I countered, hoping Peter had overheard. A peal of high-pitched laughter in response to something he just said told me he hadn't.

"Why don't you write it down for me?"

"You'd probably just lose it again," I chided, with a look intended to take the sting out of my words. "It's in the directory."

"All right." He held a medium T-shirt to his chest. "How much is it?"

"$10.99, but it's for a good cause."

"All right, I'm sold." When we completed the transaction, he sauntered off with the shirt, turned and smiled. "You'll be hearing from me."

"What was that all about?" Peter asked.

"Just an old friend."

"I see." He turned to explain the dinner show to the next group of students in his line, but some of his sparkle had faded. I thought without satisfaction he was, after all, a little daunted by my banter with Tom.

Hours passed before both lines slacked off to the point where we could carry on a conversation. When they did, though, we fell silent. "I called my mother yesterday," I said, perhaps to fill the void.

"How did that go?"

"Not well."

"Why not?"

"I'm not sure. She wanted to know about you."

He grinned. "How would she have known of my existence unless you mentioned me first?"

My cheeks heated. I'd been told often enough that blushing made me splotchy—not a becoming look, and one I tried to avoid. "All right, I guess I mentioned you first, but don't go getting all cocky on me. She wanted to know what your father does."

"What he does …" he echoed. "Like watching football on television and drinking one beer after another?"

"You know what I mean."

"What did you tell her?"

"I told her I didn't know."

Peter bit his lower lip, swallowed, then asked, "Does it matter?"

"Not to me."

"He works in a factory. Would your mother disapprove?"

"Probably."

"What else did you tell her about me?"

"I told her you were religious …"

A couple of girls approached Peter's booth, and I waited for him to turn his attention to them. But he was looking at me, and the girls strolled off.

"And—?"

"And she wanted to know if you were a fanatic." I met Peter's gaze and waited for his reaction. His expression gave away nothing. "Are you?"

"I don't know. What do you think?"

"I don't know either. I just don't understand how you can be so sure about all this Jesus stuff that you want to push it on other people."

Peter's face was thoughtful but not offended. His answer was ready, his face earnest, and I knew he wasn't merely mouthing platitudes. "Because I want them to know the joy I've found."

"How do you know what would make them joyful? Maybe they're joyful enough the way they are."

"I don't think so."

"But how do you *know*—how can you be sure? Maybe you'll just upset them, throw them off balance."

"Is that what I've done to you?"

"No—maybe."

"Sometimes a person needs to be off balance for a while before they can get on the right track."

"The right track!" I shook my head in exasperation. "That's what's so annoying about you—you assume your way is the *right* way. Maybe it's not the right way for everybody."

Peter nodded. "Maybe not. I have to do what I believe is right. Isn't that what we all have to do?"

"What if a person is better off *not* knowing your way? What if learning about your Jesus just puts them in a worse position with God than if they never knew?"

"That's a tough one," Peter said. "We know Jesus told the apostles to go into all the world—"

"And preach the gospel," I finished. "I know, I know. I grew up hearing that stuff, but I can't make sense of it all. What happens to the kids in Africa who die without hearing? Besides, who made you an apostle?"

A pair of sorority girls with straight platinum blonde hair and blue-green contact lenses had approached while we talked and were staring at us, their turquoise eyes wide. I stared back for a second before remembering they were scheduled to relieve us for the next couple of hours while we took our lunch break.

"It's all yours," Peter said to the girls. We collected our belongings and moved a safe distance from the booth before we turned to look at each other. His eyes glowed with amusement, and I began to giggle.

He joined in, and we fairly rocked with peals of laughter. "Did you see the expression on those faces?" I gasped.

"I think they got there just in time to hear you say, 'Who made *you* an apostle?'" Peter's imitation made me laugh harder, even though I knew beneath the laughter lay some serious unanswered questions.

"I don't know why you put up with me," I admitted to Peter when our mirth finally died down. I was ashamed I'd flirted with Tom to get even with Peter ... though I was pretty sure he hadn't really been flirting with those girls. He was just being friendly.

"I don't know either," he said. I punched him on the shoulder, and he punched me back. Not really hard but hard enough to make me flinch.

"Hey, I bruise easily."

"So do I." Suddenly serious, Peter looked at me with an expression so intense I felt as if his eyes bore straight through to my soul. "I really like you, Cadi."

"Heaven help us … I like you too," I said, the perverse streak in me refusing to let up.

"Are you bothered that I'm … so—"

"So committed," I said. "Yes, I guess I am. Maybe because I don't really understand why."

We walked while we talked and found ourselves in the Student Commons. "Hungry?" Peter asked.

I was, so we made our way through the cafeteria line, ordering chili and grilled cheese sandwiches. Watching Peter eat, I was amazed at how quickly and efficiently he devoured his food. "You've got a big mouth," I said.

"Thanks a lot—I like yours too."

"You take such big bites."

"No, I don't. Only in comparison to you. You're a nibbler."

He made his food look delicious, and he wasted no time. Like his attitude toward life. Big bites. No fear of the risks. I was more hesitant, afraid of burning my mouth or dribbling chili onto my top. The result was that he finished his food while I was less than halfway through mine. I concentrated on catching up.

Peter talked while I ate, first about the fundraiser and then about a paper he was writing for one of his classes. Still I had the feeling he wasn't saying what was really on his mind.

When he paused abruptly in the middle of a sentence, I looked up, spoon midway between my chili bowl and mouth. "What?" I asked.

"I've been wanting to tell you about my conversion." He leaned toward me, his eyes bright with earnestness. "But I haven't known how to bring up the subject."

"I guess you just did." My mouthful of chili tasted cold and greasy, and I felt less hungry all of a sudden.

I put down my spoon and waited.

CHAPTER SIX

"I was eleven years old." Peter's eyes clouded over as he spoke of his past. I followed him back to a time when he was a younger version of the Peter I knew. The same mischievous grin, the same flashing green eyes, the same thick blonde hair, a Peter without the serious streak that troubled me.

"This friend of mine, Mike Gerard, invited me to spend the night at his house, and his parents made us go to church with them on Sunday morning. Mike was really ticked off because we got up early to spy on this teenage girl next door. She always dressed in front of the window before she went to work at Wal-Mart. Mike's family didn't go to church much, but they were having a revival meeting that week. Mike tried to talk his mother into letting us off the hook. 'We're right in the middle of a game,' he told her.

"Mike's mom glanced around the bedroom, looking for evidence of a game, and I could see a bulge where we shoved the binoculars under the bedspread. I tried not to look in that direction, though it didn't really matter. She'd already made up her mind we were going with her.

"For the first part of the service, Mike and I weren't paying any attention. We scribbled notes to each other and laughed behind our hymn books. Then this big guy with a bushy beard went down front and started talking about his life, how he was converted, and what a difference Jesus had made for him. He wasn't all that old … in his twenties maybe. He'd already been into drugs and alcohol in a bad way. This was what caught my attention— especially because of my dad." At the mention of his father, Peter seemed to snap back to the present long enough to see if I was following.

"I started listening real close then. I knew this kind of turnaround he was telling us about was what Dad needed. Then I got to thinking about some of the lies I'd told, like how we tried to trick Mike's mother that very morning and what we'd been planning to do. And other stuff that was even worse … and I started to think I needed a turnaround myself." Peter's voice, as he told the story, took on a lilt that brought the eleven-year old Peter even more to life.

"When the guy with the bushy beard went to sit down, the preacher talked to us again. And this time I listened. I was sitting on the edge of the pew, my heart beating all fast and excited, like something was happening or about to happen. He said Jesus could help us make the changes we needed in our lives, just like he did in Jack's—that was the guy's name with the bushy beard. Some people were going down front, and I started to get up." For a second, Peter started to rise from his chair in the cafeteria, as if forgetting where he was. Then he sank back into his seat and continued his story. "Mike looked at me funny, but I wasn't paying him any attention. He grabbed my arm and said, 'What are you doing?'

"I remember thinking he'd heard everything I had, and so he should've known what I was doing. So I didn't say anything. Then I remember wondering why there weren't more people going down than there were. Salvation sounded so easy. All this was running through my head while I was walking down the aisle. All of a sudden, I got scared. I wondered if there was some kind of catch. My legs shook, and I almost turned around. I was nearly at the front by then, and the preacher came down the aisle and met me and reached out to take my hands. He had this big warm smile on his face, and he asked me what I wanted to do, and I tried to explain what I was feeling.

"Then the big guy, Jack, came down and talked to me too. He said I could be baptized into Christ right then, that very day, if I wanted to—and I could be forgiven of all my sins, and all I had to do was ask. Then Jesus would be my personal savior and would help me to be the person I wanted to be.

"The preacher asked me if I was ready, and I told him I was. It was the best day of my life. It was also the day when I knew what I needed to do with my life."

"What? What do you mean?"

"To share the news, to spread it … to let others in on the joy I have."

"Like—preaching?" My voice rose to a squeak. "You don't mean—to be a preacher?"

Peter's eyes burned. "I do." He reached out and took my hands in his, and I didn't know what to say. I was both stunned and not stunned. I had known. Of course, I had. Down deep, I must have known such a life was what he wanted, but I'd been in denial.

"What about your dad?" I said at last. "Did he understand your decision?"

The joy in his eyes abruptly faded. "No." He released my hands. "I'm still trying to figure out how to get the message to him."

I stared at Peter for a moment, moved by the anguish there, wondering if I'd deliberately erased the joy I couldn't understand. A group of students at a nearby table rose suddenly, and I thought of the time. I glanced at my watch. "Oh, Peter, we're already late getting back to the booths."

We rushed back, out of breath and laughing by the time we arrived, all serious topics put aside for the moment. Thunder crackled, and fat raindrops splashed down. The sorority sisters turned their blue-green eyes on us, and their mouths formed O's of surprise, perhaps because we were still together and laughing amiably now. I could tell they were glad to escape before the rain forced us to relocate indoors.

For our next several dates, Peter and I seemed to have agreed to disagree. We went bowling and roller skating. We played handball, and we swam in the frigid California ocean. Whatever we did, I felt supremely alive and could no longer deny the reason was because I was with Peter. We did not speak of anything heavy, and I could almost forget the one thing I saw as a blemish in Peter's person—or in my own.

After a time, Peter started to seem like any other guy to me, and I grew in the certainty that I could turn him from his faith ... or at least from devout commitment to something I couldn't fully understand. I flirted and teased, stretching my wings as a temptress, and he responded. Guilt nagged at me from time to time, but I didn't care. All those interminable years in high school—when the other girls were stretching their sexual wings—I'd been so lonely and felt so undesirable I wasn't about to give up my new role, not before I did some serious growing up.

When we kissed good night, I knew he longed for more. Under the star-studded indigo blanket of the Malibu sky, I let him sense my desire as well, my regret upon our separation. Our kisses grew deeper and sweeter, and the longing I let him see was not an act. Still, I knew Peter's conflict was far greater. He told me he was praying about his struggle, and this admission infuriated me.

"You're what?"

"I'm taking it to my Father. I need his strength."

"I thought your father was an alcoholic and a weakling." I flushed with shame at my mean words.

"Not that father."

"How many fathers do you have?"

"You know what I mean, Cadi." He took my face gently between the palms of his hands, and I resisted the temptation to turn my mouth to his hand and kiss his palm. "Why do you get so upset that I pray about our relationship?"

"I don't know," I said. "It just seems too personal to let someone else in on what's going on between us."

"I agree," Peter said, "but I'm not talking about just anyone here."

"I know—I know." I moved out of his reach.

"What *is* going on between us anyway, Cadi?" Peter reached out for my hand and drew me back to look into my eyes. We were standing outside my dorm under the large palm tree that had become our usual spot to say good night.

"That's a good question." I pulled away, waving to another couple who passed by as I contemplated my reply. "A really good question."

I was going to have to face the issues beneath the surface of our relationship whether I wanted to or not. As I saw it, I had three choices. One: I could turn Peter away from his conviction somehow. Two: I could find in myself the kind of peace that Peter had. Or three: we would have to go our separate ways.

The first two choices seemed pretty farfetched. "Maybe," I said slowly, "maybe it's time for us to try it apart for a while."

"Date other people, you mean?"

I drew a shaky breath. The suggestion appalled me. But I said, "Yes, that's what I mean."

Peter's eyes clouded over. "All right. If that's what you want. Should I call you?"

I had not expected him to acquiesce so easily. I shook my head and raced to the door before he could see me cry.

Next, I dated Warren. Warren was a senior, and exactly the kind of guy I'd been looking for all my life. Funny and good looking, well-read and irreverent, athletic, too, which was an added bonus.

We arrived at the beach on a Sunday morning with his surfboard in tow. I reached up on my tiptoes to kiss him. "Knock 'em dead!" I said, and he shot me a quizzical look. Probably the wrong expression—better, though, than *break a leg*.

I watched him in the distance. He bobbed in and out of my path of vision, waiting for the right wave. The water was a misty blue gray with patches of white where the surf broke and tumbled. Warren was one of many surfers out this morning. Yet, when he caught a wave, his style set him apart. I marveled at the way he could choose just the right wave and the right moment to take the longest, most glorious ride of any of the surfers.

I flushed at the thought that Warren would be as skilled a lover as he was a surfer, though for some reason I consistently resisted his advances in that direction. The reason was not something I wanted to think about, though my mind didn't always go along with my wishes.

My mind kept drifting to Peter. And each time I thought of him, the pain in my chest gave fresh meaning to the concept of a broken heart. I wondered who he was with, whether he was seriously dating anyone, whether he ever thought of me. My friends told me that he had been spotted with other girls ... that he was looking happy or distraught ... that he was completely over me or still mine for the taking. I didn't know what to believe, and I didn't want to care. Yet I couldn't help listening as if my very life hung in the balance.

He was, most likely, at church this morning. I pictured him on the same pew where we had sat together. Being here on the beach instead of in a church, surrounded by worshipers, made me uneasy in a way I couldn't quite grasp. I certainly didn't want to be in the same building as Peter, watching him with another girl, smiling at her or touching her arm or her back. I wouldn't hear a word of the sermon with my imagination working overtime.

If there was a God, he was every bit as likely to be with me here, in the midst of his own magnificent creation, as in a church full of hypocrites and fanatics. So why did I feel misplaced? I smoothed my blanket and reached into my bag for a tube of suntan lotion, resolving to enjoy myself. Though the sun was barely visible through the dense morning fog, I knew from experience how easily I could burn.

Still, I had managed to cultivate a deep golden tone on my arms and legs. I would never be one to tan a deep bronze, but I liked a little color on my skin. A kite floated high overhead, trailing a long tail with a series of bows. Higher still, birds dove and pumped, coasting above the kite, as if wondering what pathetic man-made creation could ever compete with their effortless command of the skies.

I breathed in the tang of seaweed and salt, telling myself how peaceful I felt. Still the restlessness and unease persisted. Finally, I rose to take a plunge in the cold water. There were only surfers on the side of the pier where Warren waited for the next wave. On the other side, a few body-boarders popped in and out of view, along with a couple of less experienced surfers, and a few children playing at the edge of the water.

Summoning my courage, I ran to meet the cold sea. The initial shock jarred every fiber of my body. I dove into a wave, coming up breathless and invigorated. I shook my head and dove again. For a time, I was lost in a state of mindless harmony with sea and sky, surf, and sun. I relaxed on my back, peering up into the brightening morning sky, until a large wave dunked me.

Surfacing and shaking the water from my hair, I discovered the ache had returned to my chest. For a moment I couldn't think why. Then, I remembered playing in the water on a day like this with Peter. My longing for him was so sharp I cried out loud, "What have I *done?*"

Shivering suddenly, I swam to the shore and wrapped myself in a towel while I waited for Warren's return. A woman and her three children had settled onto a nearby blanket. I smiled, trying to picture myself married to Warren and managing a family of blonde-haired kids. Impossible.

She smiled back in my direction but was immediately distracted by commotion from her kids. "Mommy!" the oldest of the three was crying. "Help me. I can't—can't—can't make this work."

"Well, you're going to have to. Can't you see I'm busy?"

I studied the trio of youngsters. The oldest boy stacked a series of sandcastle molds haphazardly, crying out in frustration when they toppled, while the two younger children tumbled into the sand as the mother rummaged through a large beach bag. The pretty dimpled girl ... about three ... announced, "*Firsty*. Me *firsty*."

"I asked before you. Get mine first, Mommy," shouted her brother, who appeared to be a couple of years older than the girl. There was a gap of several years between these two and the oldest boy, who looked to be around thirteen or fourteen. Too old to be building clumsy sandcastles. His behavior, as well as his facial features—something about the eyes—suggested he was mentally much younger.

"Say," I offered. "Would you like me to help you with that?"

The boy's eyes lit up, and he nodded eagerly. The mother smiled gratefully.

"What's your name?" the boy asked.

"I'm Acadia. What's yours?"

"George."

"Nice to meet you, George." I shed my towel, and we worked away together. Soon he was happily hauling buckets of saltwater to and from the ocean.

Before long I realized my efforts to construct a castle from sand were only marginally more successful than George's. This didn't seem to perturb him. He was delighted with the attention.

The mother—who told me her name was Mildred—was spreading out sandwiches and snacks for the four of them when Warren emerged from the water and headed toward shore.

"Can—can—can 'Cadia have a sandwich, Mommy?" George tugged on his mother's arm. I shook my head at the sandwich Mildred offered and returned to my own blanket.

"Thank you so much for your kindness toward George!" she said.

"It was my pleasure. Really."

"Bye, 'Cadia," George said, waving a bit sadly at my departure. "Can we play together again?"

I smiled. "Maybe next time we're both at the beach."

I watched Warren wriggle out of his wetsuit. He managed to make even this awkward process look graceful. He grinned broadly, apparently pleased with his prowess on the waves. "Did you catch that last run?" he asked, oblivious to the water dripping from his wetsuit onto my towel.

"Sorry. I think my mind was wandering there at the end, but I saw plenty of amazing runs earlier." I didn't mention my preoccupation with George and his sandcastles.

He pouted a little, then reached down to kiss my mouth. "You taste like salt. You've been for a swim, haven't you?" he said, taking in my water-soaked hair.

"It was nice."

"Not too cold?"

I shook my head, and he flopped down beside me on the wet, sand-covered blanket. "So what has you so deep in thought?"

"I was feeling guilty about not being at church this morning," I said. "Isn't that silly?"

"I didn't realize you were religious." He vigorously rubbed his arms and legs with a large towel so that the fuzz of golden hair stood up on his skin like an odd halo.

"I'm not. That's why it's silly."

"The way you were brought up?"

"No, it's not that. I guess I've just been thinking about things. Do you ever wonder if there's a God? And if there is, whether he has a plan for your life?"

He stared at me for a moment and then laughed, shaking water droplets from his hair onto my face and arms. "I think you've been staring into the sun too long. Let's go get some breakfast."

Over pancakes, I marveled that I had actually brought up the subject of faith with Warren. I suddenly pictured myself as an aging spinster, sitting alone and devout in a church pew. *The ultimate irony … me as a woman of faith. Without Peter.*

CHAPTER SEVEN

I was at a men's volleyball game with Cynthia, my roommate from the previous year, when I saw Peter again. I'd broken up with Warren shortly after our day at the beach, not for any good reason except that being with him didn't ease the pain in my heart. During the weeks that followed, I'd started spending more time with my girlfriends while I tried to sort out what was going on inside my mixed-up head.

Cynthia and I had been really close once, back before she started dating Henry and they became practically inseparable. She played a big part in my transition from moth-to-butterfly in my freshman year. Tonight Henry was studying for an important exam, so I had Cynthia to myself.

"How did you know he was the *one*?" I prompted. I had no doubt asked her this question before, but I couldn't remember the answer. This time, I really wanted to know.

She chewed on the end of her dark braid. She had woven bright blue and orange ribbons into the single thick braid, and I noticed how the orange ribbon ran out before the bottom of the braid. Freshman year, I would have braided the ribbon into her hair, would have made sure the ends matched up perfectly. Strange, how important something like that would have seemed to us then, and how trivial now.

The little strap of Cynthia's tank top slid off one slender shoulder. "I just knew," she said at last.

"And you never changed your mind?" I had once been certain the fire between her and Henry would die out soon enough, as her previous relationships had. Her feelings for Henry seemed too intense to be genuine. That had been before I met Peter.

"I wouldn't say that exactly." She hesitated and adjusted her strap. "We almost broke up a few months ago."

"Really? I didn't know."

"I don't think anyone did. Except me and Henry."

"What happened?"

"It started with a silly quarrel. I don't even remember what about. I think the real problem was the way our future was pressing in on us. We were both scared. I could see us turning into my parents, or even worse, into his parents."

I thought of Mom and Dad and wondered if one of the reasons I was attracted to Peter was because he was so totally different from them. With Peter, at least, I wouldn't have to worry about us turning into anybody else. "And then?" I urged Cynthia to continue the story.

"And then we made up, and we're closer than ever." Cynthia's voice broke on her last words, and suddenly, the tears were streaming down her face.

"What?" I said. "What is it?"

"I lied. We haven't made up. That's why we're not together tonight. Henry didn't have an exam. At least I don't think he did, but he wouldn't have told me if he did. We haven't exactly been communicating." She buried her face in my shoulder.

I patted her back awkwardly, trying to think what to say. Cynthia pulled away and smiled through her tears. "I'm just being silly. Don't mind me."

"You're not being silly at all. I know how you feel about him." Reaching for her hands, which were tucked out of sight, I thought back to the days before Henry, when the two of us were having a blast as we tried to find our way through college life. At least in the beginning. Then there was that period where … things went wrong for a time for me, things I pushed way down in the recesses of memory. Like now. I preferred to focus on the positive.

During our first year on campus, Cynthia and I traded makeup secrets and clothes, attended parties together and flirted with the best-looking guys. That was the year I learned that being really different—too daring or too striking in clothes, hair, makeup, whatever—was more likely to scare guys off than to attract them. Cynthia and I puzzled over how to be just different enough to draw attention without being so different the attention was negative. We tried dozens of variations on eye contact and smiles or semi-smiles. We practiced for each other and in front of the mirror until we fell on the dorm floor, laughing hysterically. Eventually we came up with our own unique strategies to attract the guy we wanted. When we compared notes and demonstrated our techniques, we discovered that what worked best for me wasn't even close to what worked for Cynthia. The whole thing felt so ridiculous, we laughed till the tears flowed.

Now, unexpected tears stung my eyes. I dabbed at them, not wanting to ruin my makeup. I hadn't realized how much I missed her. I actually saw Henry more than I did Cynthia these days because we had a class together. Henry and I didn't talk though, not beyond a quick hello.

"The sad thing is … we're engaged … or we *were*," Cynthia said.

I looked down at the hand I held. It was plump, faintly dimpled, and I saw she still chewed her nails. "No ring?"

She shook her head. "We hadn't told anyone yet. We were trying to sort out how to break the news to our parents."

"Would they be upset?"

Cynthia's smooth forehead puckered. "Henry's for sure. They wanted him to finish medical school before he even thought about … you know …"

I squeezed her hand. "You'll work it out. You and I can talk all night if we need to."

"Thanks. Let's talk about something else now though. I need to take my mind off Henry for a few hours. So tell me what's going on with you and Warren."

"Nothing."

"Nothing?"

"Nothing is what's going on with me and Warren."

"Why ever not? There isn't a girl on campus who wouldn't die to have a chance with him. He's so dreamy."

A couple of cute guys carrying popcorn and soft drinks squeezed past us and shot interested glances our way. I was more intrigued by their popcorn than by them. The salty, buttery smell made my mouth water … and made me think of Peter and the popcorn we almost shared on the day we met—before some sorority girl spirited him away.

"Let's go to the concession stands." I changed the subject. "I think I need some popcorn."

"All right, but you're not getting off that easily. I still want some answers."

"All right, all right." As we stood in line to order, I tried to explain to her what felt wrong about being with Warren without mentioning Peter.

When I paused, she said, "So … you're still hung up over that other guy. Aren't you?

"What do you mean?"

"You're not fooling anyone," Cynthia said, "except maybe yourself."

"I don't know what you're talking about."

"Yes, you do. Why did you break up with him?"

"Break up with who—with Warren?"

"No, the other one. Peter. Why did you break up with him?"

The girls in front of us turned around to listen, and I pasted on a faux sweet smile. "I don't know what you're going on about." Under my breath, I added, "We'll talk when we get back to our seats."

By the time we returned to our seats, the game was underway. And the roar of the crowd drowned out any effort at serious conversation. I wasn't going to shout about Peter. I shrugged and mouthed the word "later."

We watched the game for a while, though my mind tumbled with Cynthia's questions. A tall guy in front of me blocked my view. I craned my head, first one way and then another, still unable to see past his broad shoulders and thick neck. Cynthia jabbed me in the side as she whispered something unintelligible.

"What? I can't hear you."

"Isn't that him?"

I followed the direction of her gaze, and my heart lurched.

Peter was making his way up the steps toward us, looking directly at me. I glanced away, tried to get my bearings, and then lifted my head and met his eyes.

His eyes, his mouth, his entire face radiated his gladness to see me … and I felt mine answering back. Cynthia scooted over to make room for Peter and elbowed me again. After that, the game passed in a blur with the warmth of Peter's presence so near, his thigh next to mine.

"How long has it been?" Peter asked during a lull in the action.

I smiled up at him. "An eternity."

After the game, we stood outside in the cool evening air. A full moon loomed enormous, pale gold and perfect, hanging low in the sky over our heads. I turned to Peter, and he turned to me at the exact same moment.

Then his arms were around me, and our hearts were pounding together. "Let's go somewhere," Peter said, "so we can talk."

Cynthia. For a second, I thought she'd slipped off. Then I found her standing nearby, chatting with a mutual friend. Her eyes were sad though.

"I'm sorry," I told Peter. "I can't. Not tonight. I should be with Cynthia. She needs a friend."

"Okay," he said. "I understand." Now *his* eyes looked sad. Why did I feel like I'd be disappointing someone, no matter what I did? He walked off, his shoulders drooping a little.

Cynthia and I walked to the dorm together, and we talked into the wee hours that night. She and Henry made up the very next day. I didn't hear from Peter, though. Had I blown my chance with him?

A few evenings later, he called, and my heart fairly leaped from my chest in gladness. When I hung up the phone, I fell back on the bed, basking in the joy of the moment.

Less than an hour later, we were together, outside the Malibu Ice Cream Shoppe. "I've missed you so," I murmured, and then he kissed me. In the sweetness of that kiss, I was certain not only that I had never been kissed like this before, but that no one else had either. When we pulled apart, we began to move inside as one soul, merged together ... though only our hands touched ... during the most beautiful night in the history of Malibu.

Our usual soda jerk, the one who always chatted with Peter, wasn't there. The new girl gave us smaller portions. I didn't care. Sucking the smooth hot fudge off my spoon, I tried to remember the last time I was here. Was it with Warren or Roger or someone else? Their faces faded into one blurry image. All I could remember was how empty I'd felt while with the other guys ... how differently from the way I felt now—as different as rich hot fudge was from thin pale chocolate sauce.

I drank in the aroma of sweet waffle cones, I ran my fingers along the cool plastic of the blue and white checkered table, and I scanned the selections on the jukebox. Every song seemed to speak to us—too directly, too personally. I ruled out Leo Sayer's "When I Need You," ... Streisand's "Evergreen," ... Barry Manilow's "Looks Like We Made It," ... and Carly Simon's "Nobody Does It Better." I finally settled on "Dancing Queen."

All my senses vibrated. We talked about everything and nothing, smiling into each other's eyes as we ate our ice cream. Then, abruptly,

Peter's mood seemed to shift, and the smile vanished from his eyes and mouth. "I've been thinking a lot," he said.

I shrank with dread.

"There's something I need to ask you."

"What?" I swirled my ice cream as I contemplated what was coming. Of course. Peter was worried about my soul. I was sure *that* was his issue and equally sure I didn't want to think about the condition of my soul.

"Do we have to discuss this now?" I asked, as I polished off the last bit of ice cream and scraped my bowl for the final traces of hot fudge.

"No, I guess not." Peter put down his spoon and smiled at me. He drew a breath, started to speak, then pressed his lips together.

I sighed. "All right. Go ahead and say it."

Peter laughed, his face lighting up with apparent amusement. "That's not exactly the reception I was hoping for. What did you think I wanted to say?"

"You tell me."

Peter drew another shaky breath, and I thought he was going to clam up again. Then he said, "I'm hoping you think—that you'd consider—that you would do me the honor …" He broke off and grinned—the old Peter grin—but his face was bright red. "I'm making a horrible botch of this—I mean, I think we should get married."

I gulped. "Did you say …"

If I hadn't already swallowed my last bite of ice cream, I might have spewed it in astonishment.

"Marry me," Peter said. He reached across the table and took my hands. "I love you, Cadi."

His words and the touch of his hands against mine stirred me so much I could not think. I drew back, and hurt flickered in the green eyes.

"I'm just—I'm just really surprised," I said.

"Me too. I mean I didn't know I was going to say this today. I didn't even know I was going to see you today. But surely you know I'm crazy about you."

"How was I supposed to know that?" I couldn't prevent an accusatory note from creeping into my voice. "Until tonight, I thought you were completely over me."

"I'll never be over you, Cadi."

"You don't know that."

"I knew the first time I saw you. Crossing the room in that little denim skirt with a red scarf tied around your waist."

"No way. You didn't even notice me until I was right up on you." The night we met came back to me in a flash. The melodious ring in Peter's laugh, how rapt he was in his conversation with Greg.

"Are you kidding? I saw you when you came in the door—before you even started in my direction. And you know what popped into my head?"

I shook my head.

"An old song." Peter sang the lyrics to "Some Enchanted Evening" as unabashedly as if he were alone in a shower.

I stared in astonishment. "I didn't know you could sing like that."

Peter laughed. "I'm pouring out my heart to you ... and that's all you have to say?"

I sang a lyric from the song. Very softly, and probably off key.

"Oh, Cadi," Peter breathed. "You know it too."

I went on, dodging the real issue. "My parents took me to see *South Pacific* on stage that awful year when I was in the eighth grade." I'd told Peter a little about that year. Not everything, but some.

Peter squeezed my hands. "So, will you?"

"Will I what?" I stalled.

"Marry me."

My heart pumped furiously at the love I saw in Peter's eyes.

Still, I hesitated. There were so many reasons why I had to say no, so much I could never tell Peter. "Don't you think this is kind of sudden?"

"It doesn't feel that way to me, because I've been thinking about us so much. But I can see how you might think so." Peter's eyes were bright with hope again, blazing with emotion. "You don't have to answer me now."

I had to look away. As I did, I noticed the girl behind the counter watching us with curiosity. I'd almost forgotten she was here while Peter and I were belting out show tunes. "Maybe we should go."

Peter nodded.

My head spun as we exited the shop. Once outside I faced him. "Why can't we just—you know—keep on dating? I mean, we don't really know each other that well. I haven't met your family, you haven't met mine, and ..."

If I didn't stop myself, I'd be ranting about our backgrounds and sounding exactly like my parents.

Peter pulled me into his arms, and I breathed in the delicious male scent of him. "I said you don't have to answer tonight." He kissed my lips and my nose. "You can have all the time you need." He pulled me still tighter.

I pressed my body against his, yielding to the sensations sweeping through me. Almost imperceptibly, Peter eased away from me. "Whew!" he said. "It would be so easy to get carried away."

"Would that be so awful?"

"That's one of the reasons I want to get married," he said.

Shaken by the intensity of our mutual longing, I was still rational enough to pounce on this statement. "That's a foolish reason for getting married!" I pushed him further away. "Surely you see that."

Peter's jaw tightened. "I disagree. I mean that's not the only reason—I told you I love you."

"Yes … that's what you said, but maybe what you're feeling is just lust. How do you know it's not?"

"I know—that's all." Every line of Peter's face expressed stubborn certainty.

The evening soured, and we moved apart. I was ashamed of how I'd handled my first marriage proposal, but I also blamed Peter. He should have prepared me better, perhaps chosen a more romantic setting or presented me with a ring. He should have waited until I was ready. *Would I ever be ready?*

CHAPTER EIGHT

Alone in my dorm room, I replayed the evening—my joy at seeing Peter, the rightness of being with him again, the shock of his proposal. One voice inside me wanted to shout, "Yes, yes, yes!" A second voice kept insisting I think long and hard about the future.

I struggled to envision my life, either with or without Peter. I simply couldn't. I gave up, wanting to sleep.

"Just lie still," Mom used to say when I was little and complained I couldn't fall asleep.

"My brain won't lie still," I'd say.

"Try counting sheep."

I tried my mother's formula to end sleeplessness, though not certain how the process worked. White sheep, with an occasional black one for spice, darted across my mind's screen. Then the thought of Peter's spicy aftershave skittered across, telling me that adding spice was a mistake. I willed the black sheep away and filled in a background with rolling green pastures beside a delicate creek threading its way down a slope …

Suddenly, the landscape was threatened by an ominous presence, and the dark shape of the wolf was all too familiar—achingly, cunningly familiar. Making her way stealthily toward the rear of the stream of white, gentle-faced sheep, the wolf lured one sheep from the flock. Looking into the trusting eyes, the wolf took no pity but grinned her hideous, seductive smile and pounced. A kindly young shepherd with green eyes, also achingly familiar, appeared. The wolf sidled into the distance. Tenderly, the lad embraced the blood-soaked sheep, burying his blonde head in the white and crimson wool.

Watching from the distance, the wolf began to cry, huge, ripping sobs of remorse. I recognized the wolf and woke up, my face contorted, my cheeks wet, my heart hammering against my ribs. I bolted upright. Sleep, it seemed, was a treacherous escape. I collapsed back onto the narrow dormitory mattress and stared at the ceiling, fearful to close my eyes again.

My lids grew heavy, and I rested them for a moment. Gradually two figures emerged in my dream ... me and Peter. "Don't you see—that wolf was me," I said. "That's why I can't ever, ever marry you."

"It's just a dream, Cadi," Peter said. "A silly dream."

"No, it's not!" I screamed, consumed with the desperate need to make him see the truth. "I'm the wolf, and you're the shepherd. The good shepherd."

"No," Peter said. "Jesus is the good shepherd. I'm just a sheep."

"So you do believe me!"

"I'm not saying I believe you. You're not the wolf. I promise you're not."

Then I was in his arms, beating his chest with my fists until my grief subsided as he held me, still wanting me. I was comforted and happy... so happy.

This time upon waking, I got up and wandered aimlessly about the room, arranging my books, sorting my laundry, rearranging my jewelry box, anything to keep my mind occupied. When I ran out of tasks, I sank back onto the bed and allowed my thoughts to spin—back over the recent months, to the time before Peter, to middle school, to high school, to my first two years in college. How could Peter ever love me if I told him everything?

And, yet, could I move forward without telling him?

How I wanted someone to talk to. If only Cynthia were here ... Cynthia, who loved to talk into the wee hours. Though I had been thrilled to get a room to myself this year, tonight I longed for a roommate like Cynthia.

I saw the problem all too clearly: Peter was good, and I was not. Not evil exactly, but definitely not good. And perhaps *not good* was, in some insidious way, the same as evil. Or worse. What did Jesus say about being lukewarm? The question was whether I wanted to be good, or simply for Peter to be *less* good.

How much could you learn from a dream? Thinking back to the Bible stories from my childhood, I had to believe dreams meant something. There was Joseph, who interpreted dreams for the Egyptian Pharaoh after his brothers sold him into slavery. Then there were the dreams of his father, Jacob. If my dream meant anything at all, the message was bleak. I'd tried—

how I had tried—to ignore Peter's religious inclination. But I had to face reality. His God was too much a part of him to be ignored.

What terrified me was my potential to destroy... to destroy Peter and his faith as surely as I had destroyed and broken him in my dream.

And yet, even in my dream, Peter believed there was hope for me.

He believed I could find his kind of peace. A part of me wanted desperately to trust in his vision. What I couldn't sort out was whether that part of me just wanted Peter, or whether some tiny seed of good inside me might somehow take root and grow into something strong and lasting and real. I thought of the parables in the Bible about seeds... the faith of a mustard seed. Did I perhaps possess the faith of a mustard seed? How much faith was that anyway?

I figured I'd give prayer a shot. Phony as I felt, I kept trying for a long time. *Help me,* I pleaded, *to know what to say and what to do when I answer Peter. If you're there, help me to know that you are, and to feel you ... to find peace. And, please, let me sleep without awful dreams. Just a little sleep ...*

As I drifted off, the thought rumbled like distant thunder in the back of my brain that God might feel slighted if a person fell asleep in the middle of a prayer.

Peter parked the car and turned off the engine before turning to face me. "Well?"

"Well," I echoed.

We'd driven in silence to this quiet Malibu beach, and I knew he was as anxious as I was. My nerves were totally on edge, like a diver on the very end of the board, gripping it with his toes. I'd agreed to meet Peter after my last class today to put an end to this state of indecision. Perhaps clarity would miraculously descend on me as we talked.

"Do *something* even if it's wrong," my dad used to say when we were playing Scrabble. I loved the game, and I would beg him to play with me, and occasionally, he'd agree. Sometimes the three of us would play, my mom forming words like *crux* and trying hard to get the *x* on a triple letter score. The crux of the matter, I thought, the crux of the decision, the crux of a person's life.

Peter's expression told me he was trying to read the answer in my eyes. I averted my glance. "Let's walk," I said.

"Okay, let's walk."

"I don't know where to begin." I reached down to steady myself as I climbed onto a pile of rocks near the water's edge.

"How difficult is it to say yes?" He reached out to help me, and I noticed how his hand trembled. He dropped onto a flat rock.

"More difficult than you'd think." I perched on a rock nearby, only dimly aware of the rock gouging into my right hip.

"Why?"

"Because I'm trying to be rational … for both of us."

"That's no fun." Peter's tone was light yet edged with seriousness.

"No, it's not." I chewed a ragged cuticle while I thought how to say what needed to be said. "The thing is—I know myself better than you know me, and I know just how horrible I'd be as a preacher's wife."

"Does that mean you're ready to try?"

"No, no, that's not what I'm saying!" My choice of words had been all wrong. "I'm saying I don't want you to spend the rest of your life regretting your decision."

"Let me worry about that," Peter said.

"Are you?"

"Am I what?"

"Worried."

"No, I'm not." Peter seemed to think he was on solid ground, as if he needed only to reassure me of his faith in me.

"That's the problem," I blurted. "You need to be worried. You need to face the realities of this—this mismatch."

Peter clenched his jaw—a trait I'd noticed whenever he was upset. "Is that how you see us? A mismatch?"

I wanted to reassure him, to soothe the hurt in the green eyes, dark as the forest in this moment. Instead, I said, "Yes—in some ways, yes."

"In what ways are we a mismatch?"

"In matters of faith. Yours is so strong, and I'm so full of doubts."

"Apparently so." He grinned as he spoke, and I knew he was referring to his faith in us as a couple … although he knew I was not. He added, more soberly, "Do you think I haven't thought this through? Do you think

I'm just acting on an impulse, Cadi? Do you think I haven't prayed about *us*?"

"I don't know what to think." I sighed. "I've prayed too. Last night I kept praying and praying for God to send me a sign so I'd know what to do."

His smile was so full of hope and confidence, I wanted to smile back in spite of myself. I knew he was pleased to see this prayerful side of me. Still I knew, too, this wasn't the real me. So I continued, "But he didn't, Peter! I got nothing from God. And then I thought *What did you expect, Acadia?* If you pray without being sure he's hearing you, how can you expect him to answer?"

"You might be surprised." Peter leaned toward me and tucked a strand of my wind-blown hair behind my ear.

"What do you mean?"

"You're not the only person with doubts, Cadi. Everyone has some doubts, if they're honest."

"Not like me! You just don't know me. Even when I'm trying to be devout, part of me is looking down and laughing at the other part and saying, 'Who do you think you're fooling?'"

"Faith grows with time. That's part of maturing in the Lord."

"What if it doesn't, Peter? What if it doesn't?"

Peter was silent for a long moment, and my heart lurched. He was seeing now. I had succeeded in my mission, and I longed suddenly to take back my words. I only wanted him to take me in his arms and shush my doubts with his certainty and wisdom, with his vision of a glorious future for us together. Instead, here he sat on this rock, seeing his future with an infidel for a wife while the sky turned brilliant hues of purple and coral before us. He was envisioning the portrait I'd forced on him. My eyes filled with tears, and I rose before he noticed.

I climbed down from our perch on the rock. Blinded by my tears, I stumbled. "Oh!"

Peter caught me in his arms. They were still trembling, but he pulled me firmly against his chest. His heart pounded through his thin shirt.

With the sun sinking into the horizon, the temperature had dropped. I shivered. He held me closer, drying my tears with his fingertips. "So what are you really saying?" he asked.

"I'm saying... if you still want me, I'm yours."

Like a burst of sunlight, his face exploded with joy. He swung me around and around to the applause of the surf. Together we splashed through a tidal pool, abounding with life, not minding that our shoes and socks were soon soaked, oblivious to the problems that would build over the upcoming months until they seemed insurmountable. I knew only how much more alive I felt with Peter than I could ever again feel without him.

Part II

Love and Marriage

Oh, God, thank you for this beautiful hour of love. My dear is asleep now, but I am too filled with the wonder and joy of it to sleep just yet.
Marjorie Holmes

CHAPTER NINE

"Cadi—a variation of Katie, is it?" Peter's father beamed at me. "That's a good Irish name."

"No, it's Acadia actually. Cadi is just Peter's name for me, spelled with a C. Everyone else calls me Acadia."

"Acadia," he repeated, looking as if he preferred Katie. "Odd sort of name, isn't it?"

I was used to this reaction, and I nodded. "Yes, it is. My parents went to New Orleans on their honeymoon and fell in love with Cajun cuisine. I guess Acadia was the province where the Cajuns came from, which seemed romantic to them at the time."

"You can call me Gerald," he said, without commenting on my explanation. The floor squeaked where we walked, and I couldn't help noticing the worn fiber of the carpet. Nor could I keep from contrasting it with my parents' polished hardwood floors.

"We're tied to them," Peter had said, to convince me to visit both our families. "Whether we like it or not. Tied to our families with bonds as strong as any on earth."

Bonds as strong as any on earth. A thrill passed through me at the very memory of these words, a thrill of fear as much as joy, at the idea of Peter and me forming such a family.

"You must be tired after that long drive," Peter's mother said. I admitted I was. She showed me to Peter's old bedroom and handed me a towel and washcloth in case I wanted to wash up. "Call me Elinor, please."

I soaked in the atmosphere of this room which had been Peter's. His poster of the seven original astronauts was still on the wall, his train set on the dresser. The room held a strange blend of the child and the teenager. I leaned into the bookcase on the headboard to read the titles. *Hardy Boys, Tom Sawyer, A Tale of Two Cities, Grimm's Fairy Tales, The Red Badge of Courage.* I felt faint and dropped onto the bed, thinking of all the hours he had spent within these walls, hours before I even knew he existed. How strange that our lives had come together, this boy from Kansas and this Kentucky girl. Had mere chance brought us here, or design?

Coming to my senses some time later, I wondered how long I'd lain there. Had I dozed off? I jumped up and headed to the bathroom to splash water on my face, thinking everyone was probably anxious for my return.

They didn't seem to have noticed my absence at all, so perhaps I hadn't been gone long. The men talked while I watched Elinor bustle around the kitchen, finishing the preparations for dinner.

"Smells yummy," I said, though in truth, the heavy smells of frying fat and meat and onions made me feel slightly queasy. "Can I help?" I offered. When she declined my offer, I drummed my fingernails on the stained tabletop, nervous about not helping but also nervous about helping. "Are you sure I can't do something?"

If I were more like my mother, I'd have jumped in without being asked. I wasn't very useful in a kitchen, though, and I didn't want to be in the way.

Elinor looked like a feminine, older version of Peter. She had the same luminous smile and the same facial patterns. On her, the nose was a little longer, the teeth not quite so straight. Her ash-blonde hair, pulled into an old-fashioned twist, was threaded with silver. I thought her attractive. Yet, tired lines around her mouth and under her eyes gave an aura of resignation, like a visual sigh.

A teacher of mine once told our class, "One thing you'll discover, as you grow older, is how much you're like your own parents. Very often you'll find yourself acting just like them—doing the very things that used to drive you crazy. Mark my words." My classmates laughed out loud at this, but I was shaken—shaken and determined to prove her wrong.

Curious about Peter's family, I had persuaded him to visit his before mine. His father, I suspected, held the key to Peter's true self. Peter might never be able to unravel the tangled web of emotions he carried around as the result of his dad's alcoholism. I was drawn to the mystery of how the hurt and fear had combined to create the vulnerability that made Peter so lovable but also drove him to a higher power. On the other hand, I wasn't at all keen on sorting out my own past, the role my parents played in making me who I was.

"Where's the wine?" Gerald said as we sat to eat.

Elinor gulped. "I didn't think we needed wine." She glanced at me. "You don't drink, do you, dear?"

I shook my head.

"I know Peter doesn't, and I ..."

Gerald scowled. "Well, I'll want some. And these kids might drink a glass if you offered. Get the wine." Elinor complied, though her sidelong glance spoke volumes.

Peter's dad became increasingly talkative as the evening progressed and the bottle emptied. A wedding photo on the wall—I assumed to be Peter's parents—revealed a handsome man and lovely bride. I could easily see why Elinor had fallen for the younger version.

His nostrils were reddened and enlarged now, and his eyes threaded with pink. A maze of blood vessels was visible in his face, even in the jaws, which still showed signs of having once been sculpted and lean. Despite the physical signs of alcohol, Gerald was a charmer, with traces of an Irish lilt and eyes that sparkled with humor and goodwill. His amusing stories brought characters to life, and his thick brogue evoked the essence of another time and place. I laughed in appreciation, and he lifted his glass in salute. "I'd like to drink a toast to Peter's lovely fiancée, Katie."

In a beautiful baritone, he sang, "K-k-k-Katie, she's the only g-g-g-girl that I adore. When the m-m-m-moon shines over the cow barn, I'll be waiting at the k-k-k-kitchen door." I blushed, but I was not displeased. I did not remind him that Peter's name for me was Cadi with a C, not K.

If only the evening could have ended then. Sadly, his stories became muddled and a bit maudlin. I was embarrassed for Peter and his mother. But mostly, I was embarrassed for Gerald. After the meal, Elinor and I carried the dishes into the kitchen while Peter and his dad retired to the screened-in back porch. I hid my surprise that she had no dishwasher.

Having grown up with one, I'd missed out on the camaraderie of talking while one person washes and the other dries. "Peter's always been a good boy"—she said, handing me a glass to rinse—"though hard on himself ... especially after his conversion. Whenever he got into the usual schoolboy mischief, he'd blame himself afterward for being weak."

Caught up with the drying, I waited for the glass she held in her hand while she talked. "Afraid of being weak like his father. That's what I think."

The far-away look in her eyes, clouded with regret, told me more clearly than words how much it cost her to say this.

Snapping back to the present, she handed me the glass. I dried the outside, then set it down on the dish mat. "He's such a dreamer," she said.

"Who—Peter?"

"No, Gerald. Peter, too, now that you mention it. They're alike that way." In motion again, she was handing the dishes over more quickly than I could dry. "Peter's a good boy even if he is a dreamer. He's got the folks here in Wichita believing in him—that's for certain. The church pays the balance of his tuition, you know … the part his aid package doesn't cover."

I hadn't known, and I wondered if this admission was painful for her as well. For Peter, too, which could be why he'd never mentioned his financial situation.

"But I was talking about Gerald. He wanted Peter and me to have things—things I didn't care about but *he* wanted us to have. Especially when we were first married. Then he believed the world was fair and full of promise … that if you worked hard enough, anybody could make it big in America. When we struggled just to pay the bills, he got to trying all those get-rich-quick schemes."

Having always been an American—and with American roots that went back multiple generations—I didn't think about the American dream—the notion that anyone could become a millionaire. Could they really? I thought again of what Peter said about the ties that bind families together, and I wondered how his grandparents' experience—emigrating from Ireland to America—had affected Gerald and might also have affected Peter.

With no more room on the dish mat, I eyed the cupboards. While Elinor continued talking, I moved the cups and glasses to the cupboard. Elinor appeared not to notice.

She gave a slight shake of her head, as she continued to wash and talk. "I tried to talk sense into him. I had a sixth sense those harebrained money schemes would never work out. He got angry, accused me of not having any faith in him. So I shut up and let him try." She sighed. "That was my mistake. I should have kept on reasoning with him. When I turned out to be right, it nearly killed him. Still, did he wise up?"

I waffled between feeling pleased that Elinor had taken me so readily into her confidence and surprised she had done so. What would my mother, who was so careful about impressions and privacy, have thought? The men's voices drifted in from the back porch. I paid little attention to what they were saying, too intent on Elinor's revelations.

"He just figured he'd chosen the wrong scheme. So, he tried another one, and another. That's when he started drinking—I mean, when he started drinking too much. He always had enjoyed a drink or two each evening, just to relax. Soon, one or two became three or four." She looked apologetic, as though asking me to forgive her for her husband's failings and her own. If Peter was like his dad in being a dreamer, perhaps he was like his mother in being hard on himself.

"There's nothing wrong with being a dreamer," I said, wondering where she was going with this. Did she think Peter was setting himself up for failure too?

"No, of course not …"

Gerald's harsh words vibrated off the walls, penetrating our space. "Will you lay off it? My soul is my own concern and none of your business or anybody else's!"

Peter said something I couldn't catch.

"Haven't I told you not to bring up that crap again? When are you going to get over this religious nonsense?"

Again Peter's words were too low for me to hear.

"Hasn't she cured you yet of those fool … fool nations—I mean, fool notions? She looks like such a sen … sensible girl."

We left soon after, despite Elinor's protests. "Surely you'll spend the night," she said. "It's too late to be heading out."

"Actually, I prefer to drive through the night," Peter said. "There's hardly any traffic, and Cadi and I can take turns driving and sleeping."

"Not at the same time," I joked, but no one laughed.

I could tell how much Elinor hated to see us leave, and I didn't like disappointing her. Still, I was anxious to get away. Peter's dad staggered a little on his way to the car. "Goodbye, Dad. I'm not giving up on you," Peter said.

I looked back as we drove off. Red-faced, Gerald was calling something after us. I rolled down my window, not sure I wanted to hear, afraid of more angry words. But the words sounded more like an apology. "I didn't mean to run you off—I just …"

I waved cheerily, trying to give the impression of a successful visit. Elinor stood on the porch, her head bowed.

We rode in silence. I glanced at Peter. His jaw was set in unfamiliar lines, and I read disappointment in every one. I could almost imagine being the mother of a little boy, Peter's son, and seeing that child crushed by the cruelty of thoughtless playmates or bullies, or by life. I searched my brain for a safe topic.

"You know what?" I tapped Peter on the shoulder. "I think I'm going to change my major."

His jaw was clenched, and he appeared not to have heard.

"What are you thinking about?" I asked.

"Nothing. Why?"

"I said I might change my major, and I guess I expected some sort of reaction."

He faced me, his jaw relaxing in astonishment. "Why? To what?"

"I don't know yet. Just something besides pre-med." For a while now, I'd been daunted by the prospect of going to school for another four years after graduation, not to mention internships and residencies and so on.

Peter was reluctant. "I don't think that's such a good idea."

"Why not?

"I just don't. You have worked hard to get this far, and you've succeeded when a lot of others dropped out."

The debate continued through the night as the miles rolled away under us. We'd drop the subject for a while, try to pick up a radio station for a few miles, then resume the discussion when all we could get was static.

We stopped at a diner for soup, and Peter took up the topic once more. "I don't want you to look back some day and think … I could have been a doctor."

"I could have been a contender," I quipped. He laughed, and I knew he recognized the quote from *On the Waterfront*. We both were Marlon Brando fans. I went on, "I don't think there's any danger of that. I'm more likely to look back and think, I could have been a doctor—what a narrow escape!" I took a large spoonful of soup and burned the roof of my mouth.

"What do you mean?"

I swished soda to cool the burn, letting my soup cool before I took another spoonful. "For a long time now, I've dreaded my future as a doctor … emergency calls, the long hours, how I'd feel if somebody I was responsible for died. I don't know if I could handle that."

"What would you study instead?"

"Now there's a good question." I didn't have a clue. I was mainly just relieved to have distracted Peter from whatever he'd been dwelling on. "Maybe we should make a list of majors and draw straws."

Peter sketched a drawing of a striped straw on his napkin in blue ink. "Like this?"

"Ha. Very funny."

"And just about as helpful as your idea."

Still, I could tell he was beginning to acquiesce. "How do you research choosing a major?" I pushed my soup aside and started on my slice of apple pie.

"Don't know ... there are probably books on the subject."

"What subject? Choosing majors?"

"Maybe. What I was thinking was more on career tracks—that is, if you want a career. Do you?"

I shivered with the realization ... how little we knew each other—how little I knew myself. "Yes, I do. I've always believed I should be prepared just in case I never married, or in case my husband decided to dump me for a younger woman ten or twenty years from now."

"I would never do that."

"I had a teacher who warned us not to say what we would never do. She said we would probably find ourselves doing that very thing someday."

"All right," Peter said. "I will *try* not to ever do that—unless, of course, she's really, really gorgeous."

I punched him on the shoulder as we rose to leave.

Our waitress, a petite brunette girl, smiled broadly at him. As the familiar blend of pride and jealousy flashed through me, I realized I would have to get used to this. Preachers probably had girls and women of all ages seeking comfort and counsel, not to mention those who flirted with them just to see if they could get a man of God to respond. I would have to rise above petty jealousy if I was going to be a preacher's wife.

A preacher's wife. Those words frightened the daylights out of me. I was okay most of the time with the thought of myself as Peter's wife, and even with the thought of Peter as a preacher. But, myself as a preacher's wife—never!

Peter held the door for me, and the simple gesture strangely moved me. I imagined Peter and me in our old age—me with frizzy gray hair and him with a cane, his smile as mischievous as always and still holding the door open for me. I slipped my arm around his waist and pressed my head against his shoulder. By the time we reached Malibu, all I could think of was the prospect of sleep in a real bed.

A couple of evenings later, we headed to the campus library and stood in line at the reference desk. When our turn came, I searched for the words to frame my question.

"What kind of career are you interested in?" asked a sour-faced librarian with a sparse but distinct mustache above her upper lip.

"That's just it," I said. "I really don't know."

She lifted one dark eyebrow, the corresponding side of her mouth curving downward. "Then I'm afraid I don't know how to help you."

"Thanks so much." I smiled, wondering if she detected my sarcasm. As soon as we were out of sight, I tried to mimic the simultaneous eyebrow and mouth contortion. I couldn't manage the maneuver.

"What are you *doing?*" Peter shot a quizzical look in my direction.

"I'll tell you later."

We moved over to the card catalog and searched for *careers* only to be bombarded with a plethora of choices. Overwhelmed, I was about ready to give up when a phrase leaped off one card, and the answer came to me. "Careers in mathematics," I said. "I've always loved math. I should be a math teacher."

"A math teacher?" he echoed. "You mean like a professor?"

"No, I mean like an elementary school teacher. Or maybe middle school."

"When did you come up with this?"

"Just now, though it makes sense. When I was in elementary school, I was certain I would be a teacher someday. When I was in third grade, I was sure I would be a third-grade teacher. Then when I was in fourth grade, I figured fourth was better, and so on."

"How long did you keep this up?"

"I guess I stopped around seventh or eighth grade."

"I can see that. Kids that age are no picnic." He glanced at the card I held in my hand. "Is this a book you want to look at?"

I was lost in thought, remembering my eighth-grade year. How different my junior high and high school days might have been if I'd had one teacher who sensed what I was going through and reached out to me. Or maybe not. "They're still impressionable, though," I said.

"Hey, kids *our* age are still impressionable." Peter wrinkled his brow. "See how impressed I am by your career choice?"

I laughed, and the stern-faced librarian shot us a nasty look. "Is that the expression of you being impressed in a good way or in a bad way? I can't tell."

"Impressed by your naïveté," he said, "if you think eighth graders are going to be impressed by anything mathematical."

Taking my hand, Peter led me out of the librarian's sight, then pulled me toward him and kissed me softly. "I like your naïveté."

This section of books included some old volumes, and I inhaled their musty scent. I pushed away the memory of the eighth grader I had been, preferring the naïve one Peter believed me to have been.

"You shouldn't judge all fourteen year olds by yourself," I teased. "I'm not sure I want to know what was on your mind at that age."

"I don't exactly remember, but I'm pretty sure it wasn't mathematics. What do you want to do now?" He pulled a volume of poems from the shelf and flipped through the pages. I leaned against his shoulder and read to myself.

Banners yellow, glorious, golden
On its roof did float and flow,
(This—all this—was in the olden
time long ago):
And every gentle air that dallied,
in that sweet day ...

Peter started to turn the page, and I put out my hand to stop him, so I could read on.

Along the ramparts plumed and pallid,
A winged odour went away.

"I love Poe," I said.

"Don't you find him depressing?"

"Not really. I just love the sound of the words and the rhythm of the lines."

"And you don't think about what he's saying?"

"Not all that much, I guess." I was like that with songs too. If I liked the sound and the beat, I could hum or sing along with a song for months without ever really hearing the lyrics. How could Peter not know this about me?

"So," Peter said, "do you want to look for the book on that card you found?"

I shook my head. "No, I'll sort things out later."

"When I was in elementary school," Peter said, "we had the same teacher for everything. Are you sure they even have math teachers in the lower grades?"

"I think so. Definitely in private schools and gifted programs." My mind reeled—pre-med to teaching in a flash—more like changing shirts than career paths. *What was I doing?* My life was spinning like a tilt-a-whirl at a county fair.

"Let's get out of here," Peter said, and I nodded.

The hostile librarian followed us out with her eyes. I turned back to smile at her once more. "Thanks for all your help," I called. Both dark eyebrows shot up, one slightly higher than the other. By the time Peter and I stepped outside into the cool evening air, we were giggling like grade-school children.

CHAPTER TEN

"So-o—when are we going to meet *your* parents?" Peter asked on the way to my dorm.

"I've already met them," I said. "Didn't you know?"

"Ha-ha."

A small brown and white dog bounded across the lawn and onto the sidewalk. "Hey, pup, where did you come from?" I squatted to pat his head, and he licked my hand.

An elderly gentleman shuffled into sight, scolding breathlessly. "Bad dog, you know you're not supposed to run off like that." He chuckled affectionately.

I gathered the dog's leash and handed it over. "He's adorable. What kind of dog is he?"

"Just a mutt. A little of this and a little of that. He's a she though," the man said.

"I don't know why I always assume all dogs are boys."

"Better than assuming that all boys are dogs," Peter said, but today his wit did not make me laugh. Did Peter even like dogs?

"Do you think we could get a dog someday?" I asked, my eyes on the dog, who seemed to be leading her owner rather than the reverse.

"I don't see why not, once we're settled," Peter said, "but stop avoiding the issue. You never answered my question."

"Which question was that?"

"About your parents …"

Unable to divert him, I sighed.

"Why is visiting your parents so … so …?"

You'll find out soon enough. "Are you going to be *that* kind of husband?"

"What kind is that?"

"The kind who's always harping on something, the kind who just can't stand to let a subject drop?"

Peter laughed. "Isn't the wife the one who does that?"

"Apparently not."

When we arrived at my dorm, a tall freshman entered just ahead of us. She held the door for Peter and me. "A bunch of us are going to watch a movie in the lounge," she said.

"I'm pretty tired," I told Peter, yawning to prove my point.

He took the hint and told the girl, "No, thanks," and then we kissed good night.

After he left, I went to bed but struggled to fall asleep. As I drifted off, visions of me and Peter visiting my parents haunted my dreams. The images were disjointed, almost cartoon-like, with their reaction to my engagement ranging from hilarity to outrage. I woke up, my heart pumping furiously at their reaction. The fury raised another question. Was I afraid they were right?

Peter and I both had hectic schedules the next day. We didn't see each other until late that evening. We met outside the science building after my last class, a lab lasting from six to nine, which sometimes flew by but that day felt like an eternity. I was wearing a pair of gray flared-leg pants I'd bought recently to wear with this gray geometric-print knit shirt. The problem was the pants were too long to wear with flats, so I'd been wearing these ridiculous platform shoes all day. What had I been thinking?

"Let's get away from campus." Peter took my arm, and I leaned against him.

By this time, I was crashing badly from my restless night of disturbing dreams and equally disturbing hours of lying awake. I said as much to Peter, who looked fresh and cheerful as usual. I didn't mention my aching feet, as I didn't want him to tease me about being vain.

"Maybe you need an ice cream pick-me-up," he said.

"Are you thinking of me or yourself?"

"I need the ice cream," he said. "You probably need the hot fudge."

To prove him wrong—and drawn by the tantalizing aroma of waffle cones—I ordered a cone instead. Peter's friend was working the counter. "No hot fudge today?" He looked up at me through long brown strands of hair that fell across his forehead.

I hesitated. "You can't put hot fudge on a cone—can you?"

He shrugged. "We can try. I'll give you a bowl in case the fudge slides off. What do you think?"

"Sure. Why not?"

Soon the ice cream and fudge were doing their job, and I was chatting away—about my day and classes and assignments, about a band I liked called the Cars, about pretty much everything but us. I felt so glad to be off my feet.

"Why did you have such a bad night?" Peter's tone of voice and the abrupt question struck me as more anxious than solicitous.

"I had a lot on my mind."

"Such as?"

"Oh, crud," I said. My ice cream was melting into the warm fudge and dripping onto my hand and making its sticky way up my arm.

"You're having second thoughts, aren't you?"

I said nothing.

"You can tell me about them. I don't ever want you to feel like you can't tell me what's troubling you." Peter's voice was low and gentle … but there was another quality beneath, almost a trembling, that belied the calm surface.

A glob of hot fudge slid off my ice cream cone and onto my hands. I licked the side of the cone and then the side of my hand, and Peter laughed. He went to get more napkins.

By the time he returned, I was a sticky mess. Decisively, Peter took the cone from my hands and turned it upside down into my bowl. Then he broke the cone into several pieces and scooped a bit of my ice cream and fudge onto a piece of the cone. He'd finished his ice cream, and together we ate mine chips and salsa style.

I looked at the pieces of cone and sighed. "I keep trying to see our life together, and I just can't. I'm afraid I'd make a mess of everything like …"

I pointed to the puddle of melted ice cream and chocolate on the slick blue-and-white tabletop.

"And I can't see my life *without* you in it," Peter said. "Or maybe I just don't want to."

"That's probably it." I pounced. "You just don't want to because you're not thinking clearly right now. You're too—too infatuated."

Peter laughed. "You think you've exercised this power you have over guys, and I've come running under some spell or delusion—is that it?"

I flushed, surprised and not exactly thrilled to hear my power over the opposite sex spoken of so dismissively. "No, I don't think that—of course not."

"I hope not," Peter said, "because I'm not infatuated. I see you pretty clearly, and I still love you ... with all your insecurities and vanities and—"

"Stop with the compliments. I can't take any more." I wiped at the dribbles on the table with an already soiled napkin.

"You don't need to be perfect for me. I'm in love with you, Cadi, as much because of your flaws as in spite of them."

"I just don't understand, Peter."

"What? What don't you understand?"

"What you see in me. What drew you to me in the first place?"

"The truth, Acadia? Do you want the truth?" His use of my full name warned me. Warned me I might not want the truth. Still I nodded.

"There was a sadness in you, beneath the façade. I think the sadness was what drew me to you."

I sat quietly for a moment. Then I rose to carry my dish, spoon, and pile of wadded napkins to the trash. The tilt-a-whirl I'd been riding was spinning out of control. "I just can't see myself as a preacher's wife," I said when I returned. "I actually *failed* convocation because I missed too many meetings. That's the kind of person I am. I don't want to destroy you, Peter."

"Is that all?"

I looked at him sharply to see if he was kidding, making light of something so serious. But he looked almost relieved.

"I think I know you better than you know yourself."

I thought of scoffing at this claim, of laughing at his sureness or his ego. Something stopped me. In truth, his words resonated deep inside me, the way they had when he spoke of the ties that bind families. Still I protested, "How can you say that? How can you possibly believe that?"

"I'm not saying God speaks to me the way he did to Moses, or anything like that. Still, sometimes I feel very strongly he's sending me a message. There are times when I argue with him and times when I doubt what he's trying to tell me. This time—about you—the message is too clear for me to argue. I know you're the person I'm supposed to share my life with. Even though I can't see what our life's going to be like any more than you can, I see us together."

"Bu … but …" I stammered, overcome by the certainty in his voice and more than a little frightened. Was Peter as special as he seemed, or was he some kind of lunatic? As much as I wanted to believe in him, I could not rule out the possibility that he was simply deluded.

"I don't know, Peter. I just don't know."

A bark of laughter coming from the vicinity of the ice cream counter reminded me that we weren't alone. Before I could suggest moving outside, Peter started to talk … his face so earnest I couldn't interrupt. "I don't have to be a preacher," he said. "There are plenty of other ways to serve the Lord. Not everyone who loves the Lord is meant to be a minister."

"But you were—you are. You've known for a long time. You can't give that up on my account."

"Yes, I can. And I will—before I'll let you walk out of my life. Because as sure as I am about my mission for the Lord, I've even surer about you."

In the background, a family with small children deliberated over their ice cream choices. I thought with awe that someday such a family could be ours. Out of the jumble of emotions overwhelming me at Peter's commitment to me, unworthy as I was, came one certainty. I could not let him give up the ministry for me.

Or could I? The thought was tempting. For a moment, I could almost envision us as a normal couple—Peter coming home from the office with his briefcase, a new BMW in the garage, myself in a state-of-the-art kitchen. With a start, I saw this picture through a different lens: my parents. Was that what I wanted?

"I will do anything in my power to keep from losing you," Peter said, the fire brighter than ever in the jade-green eyes.

I tried to hush the wicked little voice inside that congratulated me on trumping Peter's commitment to his Lord, on getting him to make such an offer. Was I already contaminating him, drawing him away from his God? Was this just that much more evidence of how wrong I was for him?

"Don't say that," I said. "Makes me feel guilty or something."

"What I meant was that I would be in the wrong to force you into the role of a preacher's wife. I can't be that selfish. I don't have to be a preacher to proclaim the glad tidings."

I did not laugh at Peter's archaic choice of words as I once would have. "If you weren't a preacher, what would you do?"

"We could figure it out together."

The enormity of what he was suggesting washed through me, leaving me so weak with shame I knew what my answer had to be. Then again, I was contemplating a change in my major. Still, my switch from pre-med to math was nothing like Peter's would be. Not the same at all.

"I can't let you give up your dream," I said.

"So?"

I took a deep breath. "So, I will marry you and we'll sort out the rest."

Peter scooped me in his arms and, with a quick wave to his friend behind the counter, herded me out the door. Once outside, we kissed … and kissed … his kisses sweeter than ice cream or chocolate or anything I had known before.

CHAPTER ELEVEN

Over the next few weeks, I walked up hills and down, covering every inch of Pepperdine's campus. I scheduled appointments with advisors and professors about changing majors. I ate and slept. I attended classes and daydreamed. I studied and wrote papers. And I kept finding reasons not to visit my parents. Still, Peter refused to surrender the idea. I finally gave in, steeling myself for their disappointment, their opposition to the match, and, worst of all, their conviction their rebellious daughter would never survive as a preacher's wife.

When we arrived, my mother was digging in the front yard, the rolled-up sleeves of her white blouse dirty, knees and hands grimy, her face more radiant than I remembered seeing in a long time. This passion for growing things was new but not really out of character, apart from the grime. She would typically get fired up about some new hobby or cause every couple of years. They never lasted long but, while they did, the new passion was all-consuming. A flash of pride for this woman, who was both familiar and foreign, was edged with misgivings. I braced myself.

"I lost track of time." She beamed at us. "That's one of the things I love about working outside, in the soil, away from clocks and appointments. You know?"

Peter nodded as if he often experienced the very same joy, and I gaped at him. It wasn't like Peter to be hypocritical. Why was he nodding like a puppet? Had he actually gardened, or was he too nervous to admit he hadn't?

"You must be Peter." She offered an elegant hand, then withdrew it. "I'm sorry. I'm still not accustomed to the dirty hands that come with gardening." She rubbed her hands against her dirty trousers.

Peter smiled and squeezed my mother's hand. "I don't mind a little dirt."

"Come on in and make yourselves at home while I wash up." She led us inside, and I entered with the oddest sense of seeing everything for the first time.

The heavy dark furniture glowed with fresh polish as did the wood staircase railings. Peter set our small overnight bags down at the foot of the stairs and looked around, his eyes bright with admiration. The aroma of freshly cut flowers mingled with my mother's signature honeysuckle perfume.

Back in the days when I resented Mom and Dad so intently, I'd shrunk from the smell of Mom's perfume, a fake front to cover the sour spirit inside. At fifteen, I'd blamed everything wrong in my life on my parents. At school, I'd gained a reputation for being artistic and original. I started writing poetry—dark poems about despair and death and hate.

I suspected they were mostly crap. Sometimes, I felt like a fraud even as I wrote them, as if I were a child of sunshine and light pretending to be more disturbed than I was. And yet a fear grew inside me that if I pretended long enough, I might turn into the dark creature of my poetry.

Deep down, I longed to return to church and to my parents' good graces. More than that, I wanted their respect. To Mom and Dad, I was neither artistic nor original. I was just difficult—a disgrace—and I saw their disappointment every time they looked at me.

Too proud to relent and dress their way, I watched in scornful disbelief when they left me behind yet another Sunday. How could they let me quit church with so little debate?

Don't get me wrong—there was plenty of debate between me and my parents, just not about that particular decision. "Can't you ever see me for who I am?" I'd screamed one day.

"I see you all too clearly," Mom said. "What I don't see is a string of boys clamoring to take you out on a date. Or a bunch of girls imitating your new sense of fashion." She paused—her lips taut with disapproval. "If this isn't about popularity, Acadia, I'm sure I don't know what it *is* about."

Oh! That had stung so bad I wanted to shriek. Possibly the worst thing about Mom was her knack for cutting right to the quick. Did she deliberately try to hurt me?

Now, experiencing everything with Peter, sensing my old world through him, I wasn't altogether certain. Still. I waited for what I knew must be ahead.

"So"—Dad said at the dinner table, drawing the word out into two syllables—"you've changed majors, have you?"

"Yes. I couldn't really see myself as a doctor."

"And you can see yourself as a teacher?" Mom asked, stirring artificial sweetener into her iced tea. She always made two pitchers, one sweetened with sugar for my father and the other unsweetened for herself. "I hear some pretty grim stories of how kids treat their teachers these days."

"I'll try to get to them before hormones kick in," I said. They were probably thinking of the years when mine were in turmoil, and I prayed they wouldn't bring up anything too awful in front of Peter.

"From the look of some of the kids, that's getting younger all the time," Dad offered. I was grateful he wasn't turning to the personal. At least, not yet.

"This tea is delicious." Peter poured himself another glass from the pitcher of full-calorie sweet tea, waving off Mom's gesture to do it for him.

"It's one of the things we're famous for in the South," she said. "Of course I never touch the stuff myself. Too many calories."

"I don't really think of Kentucky as a southern state," Peter said. "Do you?"

"I suppose I do." Two faint lines appeared between Mom's waxed eyebrows, as always happened when she was puzzled or thoughtful. "Kentucky was one of the divided states in the Civil War, with families split down the middle and brothers sometimes fighting against each other. Still, the people in our families considered themselves to be Southerners mainly."

As Dad nodded his agreement, I noticed the faintest hint of sagging around the jowls. He looked good, though, tanned and trim, as if he'd been working out with renewed vigor to compensate for the effects of gravity. "Where are you from, Peter?"

I tensed, ready for the conversation to progress to his background, his father's line of work, and the type of ministry—meaning the level of wealth—he aspired to. I prepared for the lifted eyebrows. Peter, however, dodged all bullets and managed to answer each question truthfully without raising a single eyebrow. By dessert—my mother's light-as-a-feather chocolate cake—the conversation had shifted back to my decision to teach.

"How much extra time is this going to take you at Pepperdine?" Dad asked.

Trying to gage his tone, I steeled myself for his rebuke or, perhaps, refusal to foot the bill any longer. "Not that much, not if I take a heavy load and some summer school classes." Maybe this would pacify him.

"Are you counting the student teaching?" Dad polished off the last of his cake and collected the remaining crumbs on his fork.

"Yes."

"You're sure about that?" he said. "If you'd gone on to medical school, we would have been looking at another four years anyway."

I breathed my relief. "That's right—and that doesn't even include all the internships and specialty training and stuff."

"Although you'd probably get paid for that part." Mom put down her fork between dainty bites. She was still working on her slice of cake, which was only half as thick as the rest of ours. Perhaps any resistance would come from her, rather than my dad.

"True," I said. "Some, anyhow." I hadn't given a lot of thought to finances, and I wondered how much teachers were paid. More or less than interns? I had no idea. I waited for her to ask more pointed questions, to zero in on my failure to think things through—the way she always managed to put a finger right smack on the weakest point in my arguments. But she said no more, and the moment passed.

After dinner, she offered to show Peter a few photo albums. Soon their two heads were close together, intent over the old photos. For a second I envisioned these same heads together over the years—Peter's tousled blond one and my mother's permed and frosted to cover the gray, looking at photos of our own children as they grew from infants to high school graduates. With something of a start, I realized this union might actually come to pass, that my parents were going to do nothing to prevent or even discourage us.

Was I relieved or disappointed?

Laughter rang out as Mom told stories about my childhood. I could tell Peter wasn't simply being polite. He actually liked my parents.

Then Mom told a story I'd nearly forgotten. As she talked, I was a kid again, wanting more than anything in the world to ride a real pony.

I'd always loved riding the carousel. I thrilled to the music and the ornate décor, the faces of the ponies, friendly and smiling, the up and down rhythm of their motion, so exciting and yet safe and predictable. I longed for something more ... I knew these ponies, with their smiles frozen in place, weren't real. If only I could ride a real live pony, the thrill would be even greater. Not so safe, not so predictable, and all the more exciting. So I pleaded with my parents.

Then, one day, they found a man at the carnival with real ponies, and they placed me on a warm, live back. With my dream now a reality, I panicked. After all my begging, I craved only the safety and predictability of the carousel.

"No!" I cried. "No!"

"What's wrong?" Mom's face had been wreathed with lines of concern.

"I want off!"

"But you wanted—you pleaded—"

"It will be fine. You'll have lots of fun," Dad said. He'd already paid the man for the ride.

I almost believed him. Then the pony lifted his head and let out a long, protracted whinny. Did the pony really, as in my memory, twist his head around to glare at me—his nostrils flared, his large yellow teeth bared, pink gums exposed? I shrieked. Mom lifted me off the pony, her face soothing, her arms safe.

She cradled me in her arms. "It's okay."

"We thought you wanted to ride," my dad said.

"This one said moo!" I cried, unable to replicate the pony's whinny.

I glanced toward Peter as Mom finished her version of the story, and his lips curved upward. I wondered if he realized he was, in so many ways, that pony.

When they reached the next album, which should have chronicled my teenage years, most of the photos were of Mom and Dad with some of their friends. I was conspicuously missing. I stiffened at what my absence might tell Peter, but neither he nor my mother seemed perturbed. Was there something ominous in Mom's lack of negativity?

Foreboding swept through me. Clearly, my parents were softening Peter up while they waited. As in some movie I couldn't quite place, they would catch him off-guard and pounce, forcing me to see for myself how impractical and how completely wrong a life with this sweet guy would be.

The phone rang, and Dad answered. He held the receiver out for my mother. "It's for you ... the Foundation woman."

I could hear Mom's distraught voice on the phone in the next room, though her tone was low. "Oh, no," she said. And then, "Don't let her do that. Tell her you've found a way to give her a raise. Or an advance."

After a pause, she added, "Yes, I can bring it tomorrow."

I glanced toward my father, who ran his hand through graying hair. He must have sensed my confusion. "I don't know if you'll remember Doris Eddington, the lady who cleans the church building."

"The one with the leg brace?"

"Yes, that's her. She had polio as a child. Anyway, she's had some financial difficulties, and she's trying to keep her grandkids in the church preschool program. She's raising them herself, you know. She's too proud to ask for assistance. Your mother has been trying to help Doris without her knowledge."

"I see." I sat quietly, taking this in. I was having trouble reconciling this new side of my mother with the woman who dismissed me so casually because of the way I dressed.

Still, I waited for the other shoe to drop. Not until Peter was hugging my mother goodbye and shaking hands with Dad did I fully grasp what had happened—the confrontation was only in my own head. Peter had actually won them over, or perhaps they didn't care enough about me to fight.

"Do you have any idea how incredible you are?" I murmured as we left, and I linked my arm through Peter's.

Nothing was in our way now. Nothing except my own reservations, and even those were rapidly melting away.

CHAPTER TWELVE

The weeks and months flew by, and Peter and I became increasingly comfortable as a couple. Girls who had once flirted with him remained openly friendly but with a difference. They no longer expected him to break up with me any day. They, too, were becoming comfortable with the reality of Peter and Cadi ... Acadia and Peter ... Peter and me. My life before Peter assumed a distant unreal quality, as if destiny or some other force intended us to be together always.

Occasionally, I wished time would slow its pace so we could savor these carefree days a bit longer. Yet time marched on, and soon Peter and I found ourselves in our final semester at Pepperdine. No longer could I avoid the decisions that would shape our future. Still, I longed to be able to fall asleep in Peter's arms night after night, and this longing assuaged my terror at what lay ahead.

While Peter looked for openings in churches around the country, I began my student teaching. My mentor, Mrs. Eugenia Roberts, was not at all what I'd anticipated as a role model. With a brief introduction, she turned the first class of the day over to me. "It's all yours," she said, then left me to conduct the class.

Thirty some-odd eleven and twelve-year old faces looked up at me with varied expressions of curiosity, boredom, and expectancy. I stammered a few words of greeting and almost immediately felt their interest wane. They had just returned from Christmas holidays. Within a matter of seconds, they were turning to their neighbors to catch up. A growing buzz filled the room, roaring in my ears like an oncoming tornado.

Mrs. Roberts sat in the back of the room, and I looked to her in my helplessness for guidance. Where were the useful tips, the wealth of experience, the eagerness to share her wisdom I'd been counting on? Deep in a paperback novel, she seemed oblivious to my dilemma. Her bent head, its sandy wisps of hair thinning to near baldness in spots, faced me. I was indeed on my own.

I cleared my throat, and the buzz grew louder. In the front row, a girl with frizzy red hair and wide-spaced blue eyes met my gaze. She frowned and turned around in her seat to address her classmates. Putting a finger to her lips, she hissed a loud "Shhh!" Miraculously, the room quieted. The girl turned back to face me, a slight smile lifting the corners of her mouth.

I was grateful to her but also abashed that a sixth grader could accomplish what I could not. Still I knew I had to take advantage of this quiet moment. I squared my shoulders and assumed my most authoritative voice. "All right. I know you've got some catching up to do. So let's take ten minutes now to get it out of your system. Talk all you want to. But when the ten minutes are up, I'm going to lift my hand like this"—I demonstrated—"and then, we're going to get down to business." After a moment of stunned silence, they took advantage of my offer.

My legs trembled during the ten-minute period, and I hoped no one noticed. Occasionally, a student would look up at me, either to see what I was doing or to see if the time was up. Trying not to worry what I'd do if they ignored my uplifted hand, I filled the board with math problems. When I finished, I stared back at the ragged numbers, as shaky as the hand that drew them. I returned to the board and erased one of the less legible, only to find the trembling had worsened. By the time I raised my hand, I was certain the students could see me shaking. Whether out of sympathy or respect, or mere curiosity, they quieted. Silence washed over the room.

"All right," I said, smoothing my skirt over my hips. I hesitated and then I repeated "All right." I cringed, telling myself not to say "all right" again, not to let it become my buzz word.

I remembered only too well how the kids in my class, myself included, had made fun of teachers who had a word or a gesture or even a noise that identified them. I had once thought to gain the respect or camaraderie of my classmates by making snide remarks. We actually tabulated the number of times our history teacher cleared her throat in an hour every day for a week, making wagers to see whose guess was the closest. I was paying for this now … and how.

"The first thing I need to find out is what you already know. I'm not trying to embarrass anyone. I just want to get a feel for where we need to start." I pointed to one of the simplest problems. "Who will volunteer to come to the board and try to solve this problem?"

To my immense relief, several hands shot up. I called on the girl with the frizzy red hair—Carol was her name—and moved on to the next problem. Soon several students were scribbling away on the board. The other students, having lost all interest, chatted among themselves.

Unsure what to do, I pretended not to notice. To my dismay, the noise level in the room grew so loud I feared we could be heard in the hallway. When Mrs. Roberts rose reluctantly from her seat in the back of the room, I knew I must act or my credibility would be destroyed.

I lifted my hand again and waited for a silence that didn't come. Since only a handful of students so much as glanced at my upheld hand, I strained my voice to be heard over the chatter. "I need all of you to attempt the problems on the board. See how many you can finish and whether you agree or disagree with your classmates' solutions."

By the end of the hour, I was exhausted. As the students filed toward the door, I called after them. "See you tomorrow, and don't forget your homework!" I sank into a chair—something I hadn't had the chance to do even once during the past hour—and kicked off my heels. The realization dawned that I had four more classes to face.

When the last period finally drew to a close, I felt as if I had been on my feet for days instead of hours. While I massaged my aching feet, I reflected over the day. *What a fiasco!* At least, I had learned a few things. For one, I'd learned to wear more comfortable shoes. For another, I'd learned that no two classes were quite the same, that the upheld hand that worked rather well with one group might have no effect whatsoever on another. I'd learned that one smart aleck firing rude questions at me could rub off on his classmates until their giggling and scoffing brought me to the verge of tears. I had not cried, though. At least I had that.

Perhaps the most valuable lesson of all came from a tiny girl who came to me at the end of the most difficult class of the day. She had pointed to a problem on the board. "Why couldn't you just skip these steps," she asked, "and go directly to this one?"

When I looked at her blankly, she picked up the eraser. "Do you mind?" she asked shyly.

She erased a string of steps and explained the logic that enabled her to do so. "You could," I said, astonished. "You could—absolutely."

I remembered teachers who demanded problems be solved their way or counted wrong. I vowed never to do that, not if the logic was sound. She had stood there with her feet pointed slightly inward, and I noticed the way one of her big toes poked through a hole in the end of her worn tennis shoe. From her, I got my first real taste of the joy of teaching.

CHAPTER THIRTEEN

Peter had an interview at last, and he wanted me to go with him. I tried not to let him see how terrified I was. The town was Sugar Sands, Alabama. The church was right on the beach, which sounded to our classmates like a dream come true. I wasn't so sure. The congregation was small, and the land had been a donation long before beachfront prices skyrocketed. There was a condition to the donation: the church had to remain on that plot.

The town of Sugar Sands had been recently decimated by hurricane Frederic, and the townspeople were still recovering. The church building was among those hit, and the congregation had been forced to meet elsewhere while it was being rebuilt. In the meantime, a fair number of the locals had transferred membership to some of the churches further inland and thus more stable. This congregation depended on its locals for a steady inflow of collections, though they also welcomed the tourists. They were back in their old location but not back to their previous numbers.

Come as you are, the sign read. *You're always at home here.* The idea of targeting a market for a church had never really occurred to me before, and I realized how much I had to learn. Churches were, in some ways, businesses. The small church stood precariously on stilts, like a delicate, long-legged bird. You could see straight through, from the entrance to the spectacular view of the ocean behind the pulpit.

Parking the rental car, Peter took my unsteady hand and pressed it to his lips. I pulled away, fidgeting with my handbag, before he could notice the tremor. "You're going to do fine," he said. I knew I had not fooled him for a moment.

"Aren't you nervous at all?" I asked.

"Are you kidding? I'm so nervous, I'm just hoping I can remember my name."

We climbed from the car, and the magic of the setting made me momentarily forget my qualms. The day was glorious—the sky clear and blue with just a few fluffy white clouds and the bright sunshine softened by a gentle breeze. I thought what a wonderful time Peter and I might have if we were here on vacation instead of a job interview. Within moments, we were surrounded by a group of elders and other members. They were all men except for one woman, who stood a few steps behind the rest. Several of them spoke at once, and I figured out that they were apologizing for not having met us at the airport. Apparently, there had been so much confusion about who should be the one to meet us, the decision was reached to let us drive here on our own.

Had I been a trifle more perceptive, I might have sensed the seeds of division right then and urged Peter to tuck his tail and run. Peter, of course, was being his usual positive self. "We enjoyed the drive," he said. "Honestly, it wasn't a problem at all."

"We are easy to find," said a tall, slightly stooped man with thick graying hair. "Just stay on the road until you're about to drive into the ocean and take a right. I'm Barry Davis."

The other men introduced themselves, and hands were shaken all around. Marlon Nichols ... Ray Jenkins. After the first couple of names, I gave up on trying to remember them, convinced I would stink at being a preacher's wife.

The woman in the group turned to me and took me by the arm. "Let's leave the men to it," she said. "I'll show you around. I'm Maude Davis." She wore thick pale makeup, nearly white—which looked as if it might crack if she smiled—and bright red lipstick. The lipstick had slipped into the creases around her mouth and onto her front teeth. I resisted the temptation to offer her a tissue, asking instead about the hurricane damage and the risk of another.

"We *had* to rebuild," Maude said. "We're the only church around that's convenient for the beach set. Do you have any idea how few people will make the effort to seek out a church on their own when they travel?"

I shook my head, not sure if she expected a reply.

"Very few," she said, disgust in her voice. "Very few indeed."

"But if the church is right here, then they'll come?"

"Some of them—yes. Most of them—no. A least it makes them feel guilty if they don't."

And that's a good thing?

Maude and I completed our brief tour in about five minutes, and I was not thrilled at the prospect of spending more time with her. Somehow, she made me feel young and ignorant and altogether out of place, which of course I was. As the present preacher's wife, Maude was not at all pleased about welcoming a younger couple into her domain. And she made no secret of her feelings. "The decision has been made by the elders," she said. "A definite error in judgment, though not the first. You'd think the congregation would appreciate all we've done for this place, practically building the work from the ground up. You'd think they would be ready to kiss our feet, but are they? No indeed. They think new blood is needed, *young* blood. They think the church needs a boost of energy."

Maude's knees were bothering her, so we settled onto a pew in the back row. The seat was extremely hard and uncomfortable, but I managed to keep from looking at my watch. "Do you have children?" Everyone liked to talk about their children, surely.

"No." Her tone was clipped, and her lips pursed.

No idea how to respond. *Sorry?* Maybe she didn't want children. Best to change the subject. "Are there lots of good restaurants here? I just love fresh seafood."

"You'll find that fresh seafood here isn't cheap. It's hard to afford on a preacher's budget."

I sighed, waiting for her to speak. She didn't. Silence stretched out like a thin, useless blanket. I opted to end the awkwardness. "What are your hobbies?"

Without children, she was bound to have lots of hobbies. I thought of my mother and her series of passions—crocheting, needlepoint, painting, and now gardening.

"Oh, I don't have hobbies," she said, the word falling from her lips as if she had tasted something rotten. "You'll find there's really no time for them. Being a preacher's wife is a full-time job in itself."

Perhaps, at this juncture, I should not mention my plans to teach school. I sighed again, trying to formulate one of the many questions I really needed to ask about the duties of a preacher's wife. Here was my chance, and I was blowing it. A small, sturdy woman burst upon us just then. She had very short strawberry blonde hair and glasses too wide for her narrow face. "I'm so sorry I'm late," she said, a bit breathless. "I'm Beatrice Wood."

Something about Beatrice made me smile, and I found myself beaming at her. "I'm Acadia."

She grinned back before turning to my companion. "Hello, Maude." She offered the preacher's wife a conciliatory smile as she added, "I'll take Acadia off your hands now. If that's all right with you."

"All right, I guess," said Maude. "I was just letting her know that— well, that she doesn't have a clue what she's taking on if she comes here, bless her heart."

"How about a walk on the beach?" Beatrice looked quite fit, like someone who walked regularly and had no knee problems. Flat sandals exposed slender toes with coral nail polish matching her outfit.

"I'd love it." I'd been staring at the beach through the window behind the pulpit for some time now, wishing I were there.

"I'll leave you to it then," Maude said. "I'm not that fond of sand in my shoes."

Rising from the pew as Maude did, I took in Beatrice's coral-colored cropped pants and sandals once more and glanced down at my hose and closed-toe pumps. I had pondered over what to wear and finally settled on an outfit my parents would have thought appropriate, with the result that my attire was closer to Maude's than to Beatrice's. "I'm not exactly dressed for the beach," I said.

Beatrice indicated my stockings with a tilt of her head. "I always walk barefooted myself. You can just take those off if you like."

I slipped into the bathroom and removed my hose with a sigh of relief. Already I felt better. I stuffed the hose into my handbag and carried my shoes back to where Beatrice waited. A few grains of sand stuck to the bottom of my feet despite the freshly scrubbed appearance of the bathroom tile.

Outside, a cool ocean breeze caressed our faces. "Is every day like this?" I asked.

"Like what? Pleasant, you mean?"

I nodded.

Beatrice removed her sandals, grunting a little as she bent over to work the buckle. "The old bones are getting a little creaky."

I considered remarking how youthful and fit she looked but dismissed the idea. I could tell she wasn't looking for compliments, and I wasn't any good at giving them. Somehow, they always seemed to sound phony despite my sincerity.

"To answer your question—no, it's not always like this." She lifted her face to the topaz blue of the sky. "It gets really hot by the middle of the summer. But when you're on the beach, there's almost always a breeze."

We listened to the tide for a few seconds, watching the waves break in the distance. "This varies too. Sometimes it's as calm as a lake. Other times, especially when it's about to storm, the Gulf roars like a beast."

Today the surf was not furious but not exactly gentle either. I inhaled the salty tang of the sea air. As school was in session this morning, the beach was mainly empty, dotted here and there by a few couples with small children and a smattering of older, probably retired couples who reclined in loungers. Sugar Sands seemed to be a place for couples, and I wondered about Beatrice. Was she married? Was her husband one of the men with Peter?

"Is there ever enough current here to surf?"

"Not right here, but there are a couple of places not too far—one toward Florida and one just the other side of that pier." She pointed. "You'll see the surfers when the waves are up. And there's often enough right here to get a good ride on a belly board. Boogie boards, they call them. They sell them in all the neighborhood stores."

I fell silent, struck by the potential reality that loomed—of myself, not as a tourist shopping for the right boogie board, but as a permanent citizen of this community.

"You're terrified, aren't you, dear?" Beatrice asked.

"Oh, no," I said, shaking my head in denial. Then, looking into the warm brown eyes—eyes slightly magnified behind the large lenses—I nodded.

"You're smart to be a little nervous." Beatrice bent over to pick up a sand dollar. She held out her palm to show me. "Usually they're not whole like this. This one's perfect." She offered it to me, and I took it. I stared down at the imprint of what appeared to be a five-pointed star. Its perfection seemed an omen of something, but I wasn't sure what. I traced the imprint with my fingertips.

"Being a little nervous," Beatrice went on, "means you're thinking about things. You shouldn't come here without knowing what you'll be facing."

"What do you mean?"

"You're not the first young couple to interview here. The others have been scared off."

"How?" Misgiving flooded my every pore. "Why?"

"Couldn't you tell that Maude Davis was on a mission?"

"Oh." I wondered how much loyalty Beatrice felt toward the current preacher and his wife. "Are she and her husband planning to stay on after the new preacher arrives?"

"I'm pretty sure they are. He'd have trouble finding a new post at his age, and I don't think anyone will ask them to move on. Maude and Barry have done a lot for the community over the years. We owe them a great deal, but we need a fresher viewpoint if the church is going to grow."

Beatrice and I took a detour around a young father with a small girl, intent on designing an elaborate sandcastle. The man was doing most of the work, while the little girl splashed in the moat he had installed around the castle. Tourists, most likely. Beatrice smiled at them and commented on their creation but didn't call them by name.

"Maude's not a bad person, not really. She's just feeling threatened … which isn't the whole story," Beatrice said as we moved past.

"What is?"

"There are two schools of thought in the church here. One group thinks tradition should rule, and everything about the worship service should stay the same as when they were young. They are invested in the age-old programs, many of which they established themselves. The other group sees the young people drifting away and wants to find a way to invigorate the congregation—to grow it. And that means changing things."

"Wow." I was pretty sure I didn't want any part of this war. It brought back too many painful memories of my childhood, of my battles with my parents over clothes and hair and everything else that had alienated me from them and their God. We passed a couple about my age and a small toddler wobbling alongside. The little girl suddenly darted toward the water. In one motion, the man reached out to scoop her up and tossed her into the air. The child squealed in delight, and I thought of Peter. He would make such a good father, but could I see myself in the role of a loving mother?

"Don't get me wrong," Beatrice said. "There are good people here, plenty of them. Still, some of their minds are not as open as they could be.

You'll be surprised at whose minds are closed—not always the old. There are young people with old minds and old people with young minds."

Her words confirmed what I already suspected—Peter and I had no business hanging around long enough to be surprised. I liked Beatrice, and I had the feeling she and I might have been friends in another setting, under other circumstances. But not here. I simply was not up to this sort of challenge. Sweat trickled down from my armpits. For someone who complained of creaky bones, Beatrice certainly walked at a brisk clip.

"Would you be working—outside the home and church, I mean?" Beatrice asked.

"I'm doing my student teaching now. I want to teach math."

Beatrice nodded her approval. "I think it's a good thing to have something to occupy yourself with—besides church work, you know. I'm in real estate myself, and I'm so thankful Ron taught me the business before he died. If I hadn't had that to keep me from feeling sorry for myself, I don't know how I'd have survived."

I was intrigued. This woman was a widow—and a businesswoman. In this community of couples, she was as much of an exception as I was. "Are there plenty of opportunities for math teachers?" I asked, not wanting to mislead her, but suddenly curious.

Beatrice chortled. "I wouldn't say plenty. In a town this size, there's not plenty of anything. Except sand. Still, we can probably find something for you—if need be."

Somehow, Beatrice made me feel as if she and I would be a team if Peter and I came here. I felt I had to be honest with her. "I just don't think this is the place for us," I said. "Being a preacher's wife is going to be hard enough for me without—without the challenges you're describing."

Beatrice stopped walking and turned to face me. She gave me a long look. "I hope you change your mind. There are going to be challenges anywhere, you know. That's what keeps life interesting."

I smiled at Beatrice, but I knew I wasn't going to change my mind. As we headed back toward the church, I hoped Peter had reached the same conclusion I had. When we arrived, one look at the men's faces—all wreathed in smiles—dashed my hopes. I could see how much they liked Peter and how mutual the feeling was. The only anxiety I read in Peter's face was for me and my reaction.

He grinned at me, his eyes lit with an inner fire that told me unmistakably how excited he was about the opportunity. Most of the other openings were for youth ministers or campus ministers. Not many congregations were willing to risk hiring a young preacher right out of school. Apparently, this congregation no longer had a separate youth minister, and they were looking for Peter to fill both roles. This felt to me like way too much for him to take on.

Could I convince him to turn the job down? *Should* I, even if I could? Or should I pretend to be as excited as he was?

I saw him then. Barry Davis, the tall, slightly stooped man who had greeted us first. Maude's husband. He was staring, almost glaring at Peter. When he caught me watching, he forced a strained smile. His facial muscles reminded me of the way I felt when I had a headache, and I wondered if he had a migraine. The knot in my stomach grew a little tauter.

CHAPTER FOURTEEN

"I thought having a big wedding with all the fuss and all the trimmings was every girl's dream," Peter said. He sounded faintly amused.

"Not this girl." I felt a little annoyed at being arbitrarily grouped with every other girl. In truth, I wasn't sure how I felt about having a big wedding. I had never dreamed about a huge wedding, nor had I ever been one to picture myself in a white dress with a long veil. Well, maybe a time or two when I was about ten but definitely not on a regular basis. I certainly didn't want to feel any more like a fraud than I already did.

I lay on my belly in my dorm room, talking to Peter on the phone and nibbling at a ragged cuticle. It was already past midnight, and I was tired. Student teaching, I'd discovered, was infinitely more tiring than being a student yourself. And being tired always made me grouchy.

"If you don't want a big wedding, that's more than all right with me. You might say that *not* having a big wedding is my dream," Peter said. He waited for me to laugh.

I did not. "I didn't say I didn't want one. I just said I wasn't sure I did want one."

"Isn't that the same thing?"

"Not at all."

"All right, all right. So do you want one or not?"

"Do I have to decide tonight?" I sighed loudly. "I'm really tired."

"Of course not." As always, I was surprised at how he took my mood swings in stride without reciprocating in kind. "Get some sleep, Cadi. We'll talk about everything later."

As I hung up the phone, I thought how easy he was to love. He hardly ever rubbed me the wrong way like my parents did at every turn. He always saw me in the best possible light, whereas they never did. I suspected my reticence about the wedding choice was due more to Mom and Dad's inclinations than my own. They saw my marriage as a great opportunity to put on a big, impressive spread and show off their affluence to all their acquaintances. While Peter and I could undoubtedly use the wedding gifts—or at least some of the more practical ones— dread filled me at the prospect.

Squeezing my eyes shut, I saw the elaborate reception Mom would plan. I saw myself at that reception, trying to live up to my parents' images but wondering what was being said behind my back. Would their friends be saying I'd turned out better than they ever expected? Or remarking quietly to each other that I would never survive as a minister's wife? By the time I finally dropped into a fitful sleep, I knew a small, quiet ceremony would be better all the way around.

A few days later, when I broke the news to Mom and Dad over the phone, I thought I was prepared for their disappointment. What I wasn't prepared for was the way their disappointment affected me, almost persuading me to change my mind. Was I being selfish? Should I do this one thing for them? I could see their faces—Mom's in the kitchen, Dad's in the rocker by the television—synchronized in their expressions of dismay.

Still, it was my wedding. Not theirs. Wasn't it? "I'm sorry, Mom. It's my choice." I heard the click as Dad hung up the extension.

"What about Peter? Doesn't he get a say in this?" Mom's tone told me she was almost ready to give up, and this mention of Peter was a last-ditch effort.

"He really doesn't care. I think he's relieved, to tell you the truth."

"Very well. As you say, it's your decision."

Her words were crisp, and I knew she would cry when she hung up the phone. I wondered if Dad would comfort her, or if they would unite in a barrage of vindictive words about my self-centeredness ... about how they simply could not understand their daughter and her peculiarities.

Peter and I settled on a little chapel in Gatlinburg, Tennessee, for the ceremony. Once the decision was finalized—and Mom and Dad informed—I started getting excited. What I wasn't looking forward to was the move to Sugar Sands.

The offer had been conditional upon Peter's word that he would begin taking graduate courses within the next two years. A local university offered a Master's in Divinity, which would be acceptable to the elders and within easy commuting distance. I had managed, with difficulty, to hold my tongue about my misgivings. Peter had said yes with little input from me. Did he really not know how I felt, or was he choosing to ignore my fears?

I did express one reservation. "What about Barry Davis? Didn't you sense some ... er ... hostility there?"

"I wasn't going to worry you," Peter said. "But since you picked up on it ... yes. In fact, when the elders called to make me the offer, they were pretty blunt about him. I suppose that challenge is something we'll have to face once we're there."

The congregation at Sugar Sands was anxious for us to be situated before tourist season. Peter agreed to a date that left us with less than a week after our wedding to honeymoon and move. Again, I bit back my protests.

"Don't you think the wedding should be either truly tiny or fairly big?" Peter said. "Because if we just invite a few of our friends, someone else is going to feel slighted."

"What about aunts and uncles?" I asked. As two only children, we'd be down to six people total, including us, if we just invited immediate family.

"I don't know," Peter said. "Do you have any you're especially close to?"

"Not really." I thought of my Aunt Norma, of whom I was very fond. "There's one," I admitted, "but then the question of cousins—"

"And great aunts and uncles," Peter added.

"Somebody's bound to feel left out," I said, knowing this was what Peter thought. I wondered if there was more to his desire to keep things simple than he was letting on. "All right, we'll keep it simple. Just our parents."

The wedding ceremony went smoothly, though my heart was beating at about twice its normal pace. There was still a part of me questioning the whole marriage decision, a part of me that wanted to run as far away as I could go. I wore an inexpensive, cape-collared long dress the color of champagne with an empire waist and gathers in front. Peter said I looked beautiful, but one glance into his joyous green eyes told me who truly glowed. He looked so handsome in his three-piece black suit. But, more than that, so good—so truly good—I knew I was the luckiest girl alive. His certainty reassured me, and the somersaults in my stomach ceased. The kindly minister conducting the ceremony shook our hands fervently and wished us the best. I wondered if the size of our group and the color of my dress had convinced him I was pregnant, though I was as thin as I'd ever been. The jitters in anticipation had somehow accomplished what dieting never seemed to do.

After the ceremony, my parents presented us with a full set of china and a check. Peter's dad handed him an envelope. My spirits surged upward. Surely everything was going to be all right. At dinner, Peter's dad was effusive. Soon everyone was chuckling at his stories. Dad had selected the steak house, which was rustic but expensive and nestled among ancient trees across the street from our wedding chapel.

The steaks were scrumptious, and I began to relax. As the third bottle of wine was ordered, a look passed between Peter's parents. I tensed. Elinor's gaze, eyebrows drawn into a sharp line, was a distinct warning to her husband. The look he shot back was just as clear. He was not in the mood to be told to stop drinking. He was enjoying himself too much.

After that, I winced each time he reached for the bottle to refill his glass, his stories becoming increasingly meandering. No one else at the table seemed to be taking more than an occasional sip of wine.

"I am so proud of that boy—I can't begin to tell you just how proud," he gushed at one point. "And I know you feel the same way about your lovely daughter. Let's drink a toast to the happy couple. Have you ever seen a finer looking pair?" He burped softly.

Unexpected tears welled in my eyes, and I blinked them away. My parents so rarely told me they were proud of me. What was I thinking—*rarely*? The truth was I couldn't remember the last time either of my parents said such a thing about me.

Dad pushed his glasses up a notch on his nose. He and Mom exchanged a look I couldn't read. "We should be going," Dad said.

"There's no hurry," my mother disagreed, rather to my surprise. She and Elinor seemed to have hit it off, and they were chatting together as though oblivious to the possibility of Gerald's falling on his face. Maybe I was overreacting. Maybe he was fine.

When Dad reached for the check, Gerald's hand shot out and covered my dad's. "Let me get it."

"Absolutely not. I chose the restaurant, and this one's on me," Dad said.

Apparently, Gerald did not recognize the finality in Dad's voice. "I know you don't think I could afford a plate … I mean, a … a place … like this … but I assure you you're wrong." He jerked the bill from my father's hand.

Gerald rummaged through his pockets for a time, and my father discreetly placed his credit card on the table. When Gerald spotted my father's credit card, he swiped it off the table with one quick stroke and triumphantly produced his own card.

Dad bent to retrieve his credit card. Silence had now fallen over the entire table. After the waiter took the credit card, our mothers made an effort to resume conversation. The waiter returned and mumbled something into Gerald's ear. Silence fell again, making it impossible to miss the gist of the exchange.

"Try it again!" Gerald's face grew redder. "I know that's a good one."

Once more my father offered his credit card, this time directly to the waiter. Dad glanced pityingly at Gerald, and his expression was a study of condescension and disgust.

I excused myself to go to the restroom. As I approached, I overheard a couple of waiters talking and laughing. "Try it again." Our waiter mimicked Gerald. "I know that's a good one."

I whirled on the waiter. "Unless you get back out there and make nice to every member of our group and especially to that man you found so amusing, I'll see to it this advice is the only tip you get tonight."

Once in the parking lot, Peter made sure his mother was driving. We waved goodbye to the two couples, then turned to each other in relief. This idyllic setting had turned into a nightmare.

"Will we ever be like that?" I asked.

Peter looked startled. "Like my dad, you mean?"

"No, no," I said quickly. "Like mine."

CHAPTER FIFTEEN

Our days in Gatlinburg were enchanted. Once our parents were gone, we turned our attention to each other. We'd waited so long to consummate our relationship, I was afraid we would be disappointed when we finally did. Mainly, I was afraid Peter would be disappointed.

Every time I considered warning Peter he wasn't my first, I anticipated the crestfallen expression on his face. I simply couldn't get the words out. Being with Peter was as different as crisp sunlight is from fog and only got better and better with each day that passed. Because I loved him so, I loved his touch, his kiss, his caress. He lifted me to places I'd only dreamed were possible. We settled into blissful days of doing virtually nothing productive and loving every minute. No assignments, no responsibilities, no set time to rise or be anywhere—just glorious days together.

Occasionally, we ventured down the hill into the heart of Gatlinburg and wandered aimlessly along the street, arm in arm, peering into store windows or browsing through little shops. Inside one of the shops, the owner told us of a crafts circle nearby. Later, we made the loop, stopping inside every shop, boutique, or cubbyhole and chatting with each manager or owner, most of whom were local artists. We admired their paintings and photographs, the handmade candles and wood carvings, silver jewelry, and jewelry made from leaves or flower petals. We didn't buy much. Once they learned we were honeymooners with limited funds, they seemed not to mind.

In a small art gallery, I stood transfixed in front of a painting portraying an old Indian woman, her face a map of experience as if everything good and bad that happened in her life had left its visible mark. "It's yours," the owner said. "My wedding gift."

"Oh, I couldn't," I protested. "I love it, but it's too much."

"Nonsense," he said. "I can paint another one. Please. You're honoring me by taking her."

I stared at him, speechless. This man, with his kind ruddy face and blunt-tipped fingers, had not, at first glance, struck me as someone capable of producing even one work of such delicacy. "No, you're honoring me," I wanted to say. I managed only, "Thank you. Thank you so much."

On our last day, we headed to Pigeon Forge, another small town nearby, and frittered away the morning playing miniature golf and riding roller coasters. Until now, I'd resisted the temptation to suggest shopping in one of the two discount outlet malls, but I succumbed at last.

"We do have that money our parents gave us," I said, reminding myself how frugal I had been all week. "I have a feeling my wardrobe is not right for a preacher's wife. Maybe we could just take a look and see if anything grabs us?"

Peter agreed at once, and I thought again of the contrast between our relationship and my parents'. Mom often complained she could never get Dad to go shopping with her, and somehow, I'd expected Peter to be equally resistant. "I could probably use some preacherly clothes myself," he said.

For the next couple of hours, I tried on one outfit after another while Peter patiently offered his opinions. I bought a conservative, one-piece swimsuit—on sale. Then, feeling thrifty, I waffled between two dresses—a yellow linen that would be perfect for summer and a more practical navy blend that could be worn year-round. "Get them both," Peter urged, and I allowed myself to be convinced.

Our resources had dwindled considerably by the time we shopped for men's clothes. Determined to be as generous as Peter had been, I encouraged him to spend most of our remaining dollars on shirts, ties, and trousers. More from necessity than choice, we dined at an inexpensive fifties-style diner decorated with photographs of Elvis Presley, Marilyn Monroe, James Dean, and old cars. I stared at a huge photo of Marilyn. How short her life had been, how sad, too, judging from what I'd read.

We were starving by the time our food came, and I speared a particularly large steak tip. The meat was so full of gristle, I had to chew for what seemed an eternity before I could swallow. "This must be one of those foods where you burn more calories than you consume."

"Yeah? What are some of the others?"

"Celery, I think," I said and Peter grimaced. "You never heard that? They're great diet foods because you chew for so long you can't gain weight on them."

"Maybe we should complain," Peter said. He was still working on his first bite. "This is ridiculous."

I giggled. "I'm trying to look on the bright side. I was afraid I had put on a few pounds this week."

A woman distributing coupons stopped at our table. She handed us a glossy flyer, and I looked at the pictures of Elvis and Marilyn … both in their prime. I thought again of the ephemeral quality of this life—how quickly the famous can return to dust. I shook my head to dispel the unwanted images and took another bite of steak, careful this time to cut the tip in two before popping one into my mouth.

"The coupon's good tonight and tomorrow night," the woman was saying. "The impersonators are terrific."

I motioned to my full mouth, and Peter handed the coupons back to her. "I'm afraid we're leaving town this afternoon," he said. "Maybe next time."

"Too bad. You'd have loved it." She smiled at Peter and moved on to the next table.

When we paid our check, I mentioned that the steak was a little tough. The cashier just muttered a weak apology and made no adjustment to the bill. We were still joking about the steak when we climbed into the Volkswagen.

The car stuttered a little but started up. Peter had purchased it at a bargain after selling his old Plymouth for practically nothing in Malibu. We drove away from Pigeon Forge, laughing about our last honeymoon meal.

"I think I have a crick in my jaw," Peter said.

"What's a crick?"

"You know, like a crick in your neck you get when you sleep the wrong way."

"I never heard of such a thing."

"Trust me, it's a good word."

"Just don't try to use it when we play Scrabble, or I'll challenge for sure." I reached for the selection of cassette tapes on the floorboard. "Creedence? Or Cream?"

"Your choice."

I inserted the Creedence Clearwater Revival tape, and soon we were both singing aloud to "Proud Mary." We jolted when the car suddenly made a grinding noise followed by a series of sputters.

"What's that?" I asked.

Peter's brow furrowed. "I don't know."

"You better pull over."

"I think we can get to the next exit. Maybe we can find a mechanic."

We made it—just barely. As we jerked into a service station, I berated myself for spending all our money on clothes. How could I have been so foolish? I should have had enough sense to save some of our meager funds for a rainy day. I just hadn't expected the rain to fall so soon. As a preacher's wife, I would have to learn to make better decisions if we were to survive, much less to save anything for the future. There would always be unexpected expenditures—furnaces or air conditioning units to be replaced, a refrigerator or washer on the blink. Hadn't my parents often said as much?

What else had they been right about?

Peter climbed out of the car and spoke to the attendant. He was young with short, carrot red hair and a pinkish complexion. He laughed and glanced in my direction.

Peter smiled back, reminding me of the times we'd visited the Malibu Ice Cream Shoppe and of the friendships he'd struck up with the workers.

Peter came back to the car and opened the door for me. "You probably want to get some air while Dale sees what he can do for us."

Dale and Peter looked under the hood. Dale crawled under the car and shook his head when he stood up. I paced, my thoughts spinning. If I phoned my parents, they would take care of things. I hated to come across as still dependent on them, but I didn't see any alternative. I approached Peter. "Where did Dale go?"

"He's talking to his boss."

"What about?"

Peter shrugged. "I'm not sure. I think he needs a second opinion. They aren't really mechanics, you know."

"Where is the nearest repair shop?"

"A few miles."

"Maybe I should call my parents," I said. "They could wire us some money."

"Let's hold off a little longer."

"What other ideas do you have?"

"I'd like to pray about it." Peter took my hand, closed his eyes, and asked God for guidance.

Embarrassed, I closed my eyes and then opened them to find Dale beside us. "It's so nice to meet someone who isn't afraid to do that," he said when Peter had finished.

"What?" I asked.

"Pray—in public," Dale said, and hot shame washed over me ... this time for having been embarrassed. "I hear you two are moving to Sugar Sands to take part in a good work there."

Uncomfortable at being included in this phrasing, I changed the subject. "What did your boss say?"

"He's coming out to take a look at your car himself. He's more knowledgeable than I am." Dale smiled, revealing a gold cap on one tooth.

I resumed my pacing while we waited for Dale's boss. I stopped when he approached, then started again while he assessed our situation. I eyed the phone booth with its slim directory dangling from a chain.

An hour later, our car was ready to go. "Just send us a check when you can," Dale said, shaking hands with Peter. "The boss said it was all right."

As we drove off, I looked back to see Dale smiling and waving while Peter hummed a hymn—a familiar melody though I could not remember the words at first. Suddenly, they came to mind: *God will take care of you. Through every day, o'er all the way, he will take care of you ... he will take care of you.*

CHAPTER SIXTEEN

Sitting straight and tall in my pew, two rows back from the pulpit, I listened as Peter preached his first sermon in Sugar Sands. In the yellow linen dress I'd bought in Pigeon Forge, I felt like a total fraud. I kept remembering a time when my faded jeans and peace signs—in fact my very person—had been an offense to my parents and their friends.

Which was the real Acadia?

I had no idea. Perhaps both were frauds, and the real me was yet to emerge. My left foot was going to sleep. I shifted positions, but the numbness continued. Why was it so impossible to ignore that particular sensation? It didn't hurt, after all. I tried in vain to pretend my foot wasn't driving me nuts. Finally, I gave in and slipped my foot from the stiff high-heeled shoe and stomped my bare foot on the carpeted floor—once, twice, three times.

Peering furtively to my right and to my left, I caught several curious glances just before their eyes darted away. I felt as if everyone in the building was focused on me. I slid my still-tingling foot back into my shoe and kept my gaze on the pulpit. How handsome Peter looked. Suddenly his words captured my attention.

"… Jesus spit on the man's eyes and put his hands on him, and he asked him, 'Do you see anything?'

"The man looked around." At this point, Peter moved away from the pulpit, shifting his gaze in various directions as if he himself were the blind man. I sensed the audience's attention riveted on their new preacher. Audience wasn't the right word … Peter was not a performer, exactly. And yet, I realized that a preacher who could capture and hold the listener the way Peter could was indeed a performer of sorts. Even if he was as genuine and humble as I knew Peter to be. He'd done nothing spectacular, and yet every eye was on him.

In a voice not his own, Peter continued. "The man answered Jesus, 'I see people. They look like trees walking around.'" The amazed voice was that of the blind man now seeing something for the first time in a long time ... perhaps ever.

Then, abruptly, Peter was himself again. "You see, Jesus didn't restore the man's sight all at once. He *could* have, certainly." Peter paused, and he spoke to the audience—no, the congregation—in a personal, intimate tone as if he were speaking to each one individually. "Isn't that the way it is with us? Jesus works on our hearts the way he worked on the blind man's eyes, but we don't see all at once. Spiritual sight comes in stages."

What impressed me was not so much Peter's message as his delivery. The man I loved was a gifted speaker. He could have done *anything* with his life. *What a waste.* As an actor, he could have been famous, the way he gripped an audience. For an instant, I could see Peter taking his bows onstage in an elegant Broadway theater, surrounded by elaborate balconies and boxes ... women in furs and men in tuxes, all standing and applauding. Peter could have been a star.

Instead, here I sat in this little church building with its sign outside reading "Come as you are. You're always at home here." Gazing through the windows to the families passing by on the beach, I knew I could never say these things to Peter. I was ashamed for thinking them. Still my mind drifted to how little money we had and how we were going to manage.

Peter had used a good bit of his first paycheck to reimburse Dale and his boss for their work on our car, even though we couldn't really afford to do so. "They said there was no hurry," I'd reminded him.

"I know," he said, "but I'm afraid I'll forget if I wait."

I smoothed the creases in my yellow skirt, admiring the texture of the linen fabric and thinking things would get better once I began to work and had extra money.

After the service, I faced a steady stream of men and women, either anxious to meet me or merely curious. Even the locals were dressed more casually than I remembered from my church back home. Some of the women wore crisp dresses or summer suits, but many were in cropped pants or capris and only a few wore high-heeled shoes like mine. I gazed longingly at the comfortable-looking sandals as my feet began to throb. My sleeping left foot was wide awake now. The tourists and some of the younger or more adventurous townspeople came in khakis or sundresses. I saw no one over the age of ten in jeans and T-shirts, much less shorts and tank tops.

Introducing myself over and over, the muscles around my mouth grew more and more tired of smiling until I felt my face would crack open. I thought of playing doubles tennis in high school. As comfortable as I'd been at singles, I never really got the hang of doubles. When my turn came to go to the net, I felt more like a misplaced spectator than a true participant in the game. That was how I felt in this moment.

Then Beatrice moved to my side. She was dressed casually in an aqua wrap-around skirt and a soft, short-sleeved shell in a matching shade. She gave me a quick hug and took charge of the introductions. Somehow, when Beatrice said my name, it rang differently, sounding more substantial, as if I really *was* someone, not just a pretender who happened to be married to the new preacher.

When the last of the congregation trickled out, Beatrice said, "Whew! Bet you're glad that's over."

I laughed with relief that she understood and did not judge.

"I could come over to help you settle in later this afternoon, when you've had time to recover," Beatrice offered. "Or is that too soon?"

"No, that would be great." Yielding to an impulse, I leaned into Beatrice and buried my face in her shoulder. Her presence was so comforting, like the mother I still needed.

"Then, as soon as you're ready, we'll get started finding you a job for fall—if you want to." She peered into my eyes through her oversized glasses, as if trying to see inside me.

"I'm ready."

Beatrice nodded. "Gives you something to plan toward. Life needs a structure of some sort, don't you think? Speaking of which, you know they're planning a potluck next Sunday in your honor?"

CHAPTER SEVENTEEN

Looking at the upturned faces, for a second, I thought I might faint. The scene before me was unreal, stranger than most dreams. Unable to find a position at the middle-school level, I had reluctantly agreed to try my hand at teaching high schoolers.

I stood in the front of my first class. I steadied myself by grasping the aged oak desk at the front of the room.

Only a few years ago I was in high school, struggling to project a unique voice in a conventional world. What business did I have taking on a leadership role? I fingered the sand dollar Beatrice picked up, glad to have slipped it into the side pocket of my skirt this morning, glad to have its gritty texture against my skin.

The air conditioner wasn't working, and the backs of my legs were sticky with sweat. Even without pantyhose—thank goodness—I worried that my skirt was clinging to the backs of my damp thighs. I resisted the urge to tug at it.

This class was eleventh-grade algebra, my favorite of all the math courses I took in high school. I told myself I could handle whatever came with ease. Then, with a successful start behind me, the rest of the day would be a breeze.

I introduced myself and spoke earnestly of my plans for the year. I searched the faces—some pimply, some already pitted from previous acne, others tanned and smooth, smug in their high school supremacy. Easy to pick out the popular set. Gazing at the perfect complexions of those girls, I was a teenager again, with all the accompanying insecurity. My voice faded.

Weak-kneed, I forced myself to focus not on my years in high school, but back on my first day of student teaching. I turned my back on the class to scribble a few problems on the board. *Please let this strategy work again*, I prayed.

"Who wants to come to the board?" I asked, my voice squeaky with nerves. Complete silence. "It's all right if you don't solve the problem perfectly." I tapped the board with my chalk. "I just want to find out what you already know."

No response. "Look, I know you're hot." I wiped my brow. "Why don't you just solve the problems at your desk, and I'll come around to see how you're doing?"

The minutes dragged on, and I resisted the urge to look at my watch. Finally the period ended, and I breathed a sigh of relief. *One down.*

For my next class, sophomore geometry, I tried something different. I thought back to the petite girl with the hole in her tennis shoe who had made me feel like a teacher for the first time. With her image in my mind, I waxed eloquent on the beauty, logic, and symmetry of mathematics in general and geometry in particular. I paused for breath, feeling rather impressed by my own discourse ... for about a second. Then, as I sought that special face ... the one who would register his or her newfound appreciation ... chortles of laughter met my reddening ears. I realized a folded note was circulating. I didn't dare demand to see it, afraid to make matters even worse.

Not until fourth period did I find a single responsive soul. Even then, I hadn't noticed her during my sweat-filled effort to spark some flicker of interest in these seniors. "How many of you are planning to go to college?" I asked. A surprising number of the seemingly disinterested students raised limp arms.

"If you do, mathematics is an absolute must, regardless of what you major in. You realize that, don't you?"

A few nods but still no enthusiasm.

"And even if you don't go to college," I added, "you need to be sure you're not cheated in every transaction you enter." Still, not a glimmer of agreement in any direction. By this time, the odor of perspiring bodies lingered in the air. Were the rankest smells coming from my own armpits? I'd read somewhere that fear altered the body's chemistry.

I tormented myself with a string of unanswerable questions as the interminable fourth period class dragged to an end, and the students came to life only to file out of the room. What if I never gained control of these classes? What if I could not earn their respect, no matter how hard I tried? What if I had chosen the wrong career after all?

As the last of the stragglers made their way through the door, a student timidly approached my desk. "I'm not the best in the world at math," she said. "Not by a long shot, though I know you're right about how important mathematics is."

"What's your name?" I asked.

"I'm Sybil." Her face was broad across the cheekbones, flushed with heat and with the effort to express herself. She reminded me of the Precious Moments girl pictured on the cover of a Bible I owned as a child. She had a tiny nose, a flawless ivory complexion, a small mouth, and wide-spaced eyes. She wore little or no makeup, and her blonde hair was pulled back in a ponytail. Several strands escaped and frizzed around her face.

She smiled, and her smile was so sweet it pierced my heart.

Only later, when I knew more of Sybil's story, would I understand why her sweetness was so piercing. She glanced at me with wisdom beyond her years. "Some of these kids can be jerks, but you shouldn't let that discourage you. They're just too busy trying to be cool to show what they're really thinking. When somebody like you tries to help us, well—I just want you to know some of us do appreciate it."

Astonished, I gazed into the guileless, wide-spaced eyes. *From whence cometh my help.* Just when I'd been wondering how I was going to survive one more class, Sybil's words energized me enough to keep plodding ahead. I hadn't prayed for her to emerge, any more than I'd prayed for the girl in my student teaching class. Prayer was not in my nature, the way it was in Peter's.

Nonetheless, I closed my eyes and uttered a quick, silent prayer of thanks. Then, as an afterthought, I asked God to be with these two young women who had, on two separate occasions, saved me.

"See you tomorrow, Mrs. O'Neil." The girl smiled her sweet smile again as she left.

Tomorrow—I'll have to do this again tomorrow. Please let the air conditioner be working tomorrow.

"How do you do it?" I asked Mrs. Harris one day over plates of cafeteria spaghetti. She was an English teacher near retirement, an unstylish spinster who had somehow managed to capture a certain respect and even affection from the student body at Sugar Sands High. Her hair was iron gray, her demeanor severe, and yet the students voted her as their favorite teacher almost every year.

She deftly wound the elusive noodles around her fork and studied me before answering. She made no pretense of misunderstanding my question or needing clarification. "It's fairly simple. really. I can see you care about them. You want them to learn, and you believe this learning is in their best interest. Am I right?"

I nodded and waited for her to continue. Wasn't this equally true, though, for every teacher?

"The trouble is that *they* don't know any of this. You think that since you've chosen a career as a teacher, they know how you feel. They don't. You have to make them aware of how much you care about what you're doing, how much you care about their welfare. It's okay to let them know that because you care, you're not going to be easy on them. You *expect* them to rise to the occasion. Not just the smartest ones, but every single soul."

"And they will?" Her strategy sounded way too easy.

"Some of them will. Not all. Don't expect a hundred percent success, or you'll be setting yourself up for disappointment."

I laughed. "At this point, I can be happy with any non-negative success rate." We had just been doing negative numbers in one of my classes.

I didn't believe for one minute her strategy was going to work for me, but I thanked her anyway. Later, looking back, I would remember this conversation as a turning point for me. Not right away. No, some time passed before I found the courage to follow her advice.

At first, I was incredibly uncomfortable looking for a way to show my students I cared. Maybe their seeming indifference to math told me they would be equally indifferent to anything else I had to say. Not so, I discovered. As soon as I left the subject of mathematics ... even for a moment ... to talk about my life, or their lives, or sports—just about anything besides math—I could feel their ears perk up. The change was so abrupt, I wouldn't have been surprised to see actual physical movement, like the twitch of a cat's ear.

Once I had their attention, the rest became a tad easier too. True, when I returned to the day's topic, a few would zone out. When the glazed, bored, or even sleeping faces became more the rule than the exception, I would try another diversion.

"What's up?" I asked one Friday. "You seem distracted today."

"You wouldn't believe what Old Man Hussing is making us do in American history," volunteered Ed Meadows, a stocky boy who played lineman on the football team.

"What?"

"He got pissed—pardon my language." Ed's squarish face reddened, but he went on. "He gave us this pop quiz which, of course, we weren't ready for. So now he's making us write a five hundred-word essay by Monday on why James Madison was the best of the Founding Fathers. I mean—five hundred words!" He groaned.

"Five hundred words isn't so bad," I said. "That's only a couple of typed pages."

"Who really cares what happened, like, a thousand years ago?" another student said.

"Not quite a thousand," I said. For the next five minutes or so, we discussed their topic. Although my knowledge of history wasn't up to speed, I was pretty sure Madison was involved in writing the Constitution. Once we started, the discussion flowed. I just hoped I wasn't defeating the purpose of the assignment, but at least the students were getting interested. I steered them back to mathematics, and they listened with more enthusiasm than usual for a Friday.

At home that evening, I moved about with a bounce in my step. The weekend lay ahead, and I wasn't even dreading Monday this time. I tried to envelop Peter in my good humor. He'd been unusually quiet at dinner and unresponsive when I suggested an evening stroll.

"What's wrong?" I said at last, when all my efforts fell flat.

"Remember the day we interviewed?" Peter asked.

How could I possibly forget?

"There were hints of division then," Peter went on, "but I had no idea how serious the problem was. Not really."

Of course I remembered. Beatrice's words, my reaction to them, my conviction that this congregation represented too much of a challenge. Peter had been so excited, I'd believed keeping my mouth shut was the noble thing to do. So I'd put aside my concerns instead of warning Peter as I should have done.

"I expect that's the case in most churches," I said cautiously, not wanting to be negative. "Isn't that just human nature?"

"I suppose so." Peter looked more tired than I remembered ever seeing him. "Tell me, Cadi. Why do people welcome change in everything else—in medicine and computers and fashion—and resist it in the church?"

"They don't. Not really, although they may accept the new way eventually. There are plenty of people resisting change in all those other areas too. You should hear some of the teachers I work with whining about changes in curriculum and changes in classroom technology."

Peter's eyes crinkled at the corners, the hint of a twinkle brightening the green eyes. "I bet there are others who complain the changes don't come fast enough."

"How did you know?"

"Lucky guess." He rummaged through the cupboard for a bag of pretzels. I sometimes teased Peter that he was like a cow, wanting to graze constantly from dinner to bedtime. Yet he never seemed to gain an ounce. "Maybe they want the church to be the last safe place. The one place that doesn't change," he said. "So when it does, they feel threatened and fight back."

"They'll come around," I said. I hoped I was right.

Part III

The Honeymoon's Over

Help me outgrow my tears, my sometimes-childish tantrums. The periods of self-pity when I tell myself nobody loves me, like I used to as a little girl. Please rescue me whenever I revert; steer me firmly forward into the calm waters of mature behavior.
Marjorie Holmes

CHAPTER EIGHTEEN

"What's the point of living in a beach town," I said, "if we aren't going to enjoy the sand and surf?" I drained my second cup of coffee and grimaced at the grounds in the last sip. My coffee never turned out as good as my mother's, though I followed her instructions exactly.

A month had flown by, and I'd finally developed enough self-confidence in the classroom to shift my worrying elsewhere. Ever since our brief honeymoon, Peter and I had spent most of our weekends in separate pursuits. He worked on sermons, while I organized lesson plans and graded papers.

Peter hesitated. "I have a lot of work to do." He indicated the stack of books and notes spread out on his desk.

"Oh, there's always work." I leaned over to nibble on his ear. One of us needed to put the spark back into our relationship. With school well underway, the beaches were less crowded. I wanted to spend this Saturday with Peter on the white-sand beach, like the newlyweds we were. "Work will still be there when the water's too cold for a swim. Let's take advantage of these last golden days of summer."

"Summer? It's September."

"September is still summer."

When he hesitated, I added, "Bring your notes with you if you have to work."

I packed a picnic lunch, and we set out. With visions of Peter rubbing suntan lotion on my back and splashing water on me, I hummed all the way from our little house to the public access beach. The water was a lovely teal about a third of the way out, then dark blue to the horizon. White waves crested throughout the blue and green waters in no discernible pattern.

Breathtaking.

I spread a blanket, and Peter settled onto it with his notebook, his Bible, and a couple of reference books. "Get that stuff done," I told him. "I'll be back soon."

I dropped my sunglasses, shed my swimsuit cover-up, and headed to the water. I wore my new one-piece with its dark blue tucks up the front. I didn't even have to suck in my stomach, as the tucks concealed any unsightly bulge I imagined from my donut splurge for breakfast. "You can't be too thin," my mother always said—but I tried to think positively. Peter claimed he liked my curves, and I felt pretty curvaceous in this suit. Thinking back to our honeymoon, I remembered Marilyn Monroe's photo on the wall at the little diner in Pigeon Forge. I peeked over my shoulder as I made my way into the water to see if Peter was watching. He was not.

I'd brought our camera along, and it lay untouched beside him and my cover-up. I sighed and turned back to face the water. The tide was low, and I walked out until I could sink into the embrace of the ocean. Floating on the waves, I felt glorious.

As I bobbed up and down, I recalled the day when Peter and I first saw the Gulf. Construction evidence had been everywhere then while the little community struggled to recover from the effects of hurricane Frederic. Pumps from deep in the Gulf pushed sandy water through pipes, leaving behind great piles of sand as the water drained away to rebuild the sugary white beaches.

They were immaculate again, at least on the surface. I wondered what lay beneath now.

After the interviews that day, Peter and I walked on this same stretch of beach, hand in hand. At places, the sand shifted and our feet sank—as in quicksand. We had been trying to envision the paths—no, the path— our lives would take if we moved here. At least we had been together. So completely together then. How recent that felt, and yet how distant.

The sand stretched its velvet carpet in both directions … pearly white … as far as I could see. Unobservant, I had drifted a distance from where I entered the water. At first, I couldn't locate Peter and our blanket. When I did, he was immersed in his notes. I waved a time or two, beaming my pleasure in his direction. I wanted to share the beauty of the day and the turquoise splendor of the water. He did not look up.

With my back to the ocean, I did not see the large wave approaching. It took me down, dragging me toward shore. I emerged, spitting saltwater and sand. Laughing, I sought Peter's gaze, sure he'd be chortling, sharing this moment with me. His head was still buried in his work. Before I had time to recover, a second wave, stronger than the first, sucked me back under. As I came up for breath, annoyance washed over me, as powerful as the wave that had knocked me down. Why wasn't he out here, frolicking with me like young lovers? Didn't he want that too?

Patience, I told myself. Any minute now he would put down his work and join me, or at least, look up to make sure I hadn't drowned. When he didn't, I decided he was just waiting for me to emerge from the water and drag him away. Yes, that must be what he wanted.

I made my way to shore and ran toward Peter. Laughingly, I shook my wet hair and reached for his hand. "Come on! The day's a-wasting."

He scowled. "Look what you've done to my sermon!"

Indeed, the page of closely written notes in Peter's hand was splattered with water, the paper crinkling in places, the words smeared in others. "I'm sorry … I didn't mean to drip onto your notes."

Peter scooped up his papers and dried them off with his unused towel while I located my sunglasses and stretched out beside him in the sun. I closed my eyes, but his harsh tones echoed in my ears. Images swam across my brain—of the day I had intended, two young lovers gazing into each other's eyes … stealing a kiss in the water … ducking and splashing and behaving like the teenagers they had been—oh so very recently. Where had those teenagers gone?

I removed my sunglasses, opened my eyes, and peered out at the Gulf. Without my glasses, the colors were less vivid. Still a lovely bluish-green, but not the brilliant teal I had seen before.

I turned my gaze on Peter's untanned arms as they spread out his notes and as he tried to rewrite the portions I had smeared. Like an old song whose tune I could not recall, the lyrics played in my head. *Looking at the world through rosy tinted glasses, hoping...* hoping what?

I could not remember. What I remembered were the days I'd spent on another beach with other guys … Dave or Warren … tanned, muscled surfers who had loved the water and still had time for me. Yet, I'd only had thoughts for Peter.

Replacing my sunglasses, I tried to be more empathetic, less critical. Peter wrestled with important philosophical questions, struggled with his new role, felt overwhelmed by his responsibilities. Immersed in my own struggles—in adjusting to my classes and students—I'd failed to pay attention while Peter and I slipped apart. I was stricken to think I might have already lost my foremost place in his heart.

Time for action. I rolled onto my side and addressed Peter. "Talk to me," I said. "Please. Tell me where you are these days."

He looked up from his notes, his brow furrowed, and then put his work aside. Perhaps he had just been waiting for me to ask.

"I know we're not the only church in the country struggling with change," he said. "How do you know when it's broke?"

"Broke?" I echoed. "You mean financially?"

"No. You know the old saying—*if it ain't broke, don't fix it.*"

"Oh," I said, relieved. A congregation that was broke financially sounded particularly ominous.

"We're not doing so hot financially either," Peter said, as if reading my mind. "The real problem is more fundamental. If you think of a church as an organization, then we know that just because something is the best it can be at one point in time doesn't mean it will stay that way. A group that fails to evolve can't survive. I'm caught between the ones anxious for change and the ones fighting against change of any sort."

"Is it fair to put a church into the same category as other organizations?" I asked. When I was a kid and still going to church with my parents, everyone seemed bent on keeping our church the way it had been *forever.* Way back to the first century.

"I don't know," Peter said. "I just don't know."

I rolled over onto my belly. "Could you put some sunscreen on my back while we talk?"

Peter obliged, but his fingers felt distant. He accomplished the task without expressing any interest in the back of my neck or the curve of my back. Still I trembled at his touch. How much I loved this man!

"Other churches are dealing with the same issues, but that doesn't make them any less serious. In fact, I think it's worse here," he continued. "I'm trying to write a sermon that will reach out to both groups—to make them see how much the Lord hates division. At the same time, I don't want to alienate either group. Nor do I want to take sides."

"I see." What I saw was how my plans for the day were being derailed, and I knew he wasn't likely to solve this particular problem in one day or one sermon. "We've been married how long?"

"What?"

"You don't know, do you?" I said.

"Sure, I do, if I think about it. Why?"

"I need you to be here for me too. Not just for your congregation. We're still newlyweds. I don't want to lose that—to lose you."

"You're not losing anything." Peter looked both surprised and frustrated. "What do you want from me, Acadia?"

His use of my full name dramatized our distance. *If I have to tell you, it won't be the same.* I told him anyway, feeling foolish and shallow. "I wanted to frolic in the water."

Peter rose reluctantly from the blanket, and that reluctance was the final straw.

"We might as well just eat our picnic and go home," I snapped. "So you can focus." I waited to see if he would object. He didn't.

Back at the house, I left Peter alone to work on his sermon while I mulled over a strategy to reignite the spark in our marriage. My head spun with the task, and I was still pondering when we went to bed that night. When he reached for me without preamble, I stiffened. This was becoming a habit, and I realized I had to be the one to reverse the pattern.

Surely, I wasn't just being selfish if I longed to be wooed, to be seduced. I craved the dance. Admittedly, the blame wasn't entirely Peter's. I too had been preoccupied, thinking about my classes and my students when I went to bed at night, recalling what I had said and how they had responded. And so when the foreplay had dwindled to virtually none, I had not protested as I should have.

"What's wrong?" Peter asked, stroking my hair.

I took a deep breath. He wasn't a mind reader, after all. I would not make him guess. "I don't want the courtship to be over," I said, tears rolling down my cheeks.

"What are you talking about?" Peter's green eyes were dark in the dim glow of our nightlight. He looked so baffled I almost giggled in spite of the pain in my heart. Did he think I had developed amnesia and completely forgotten our wedding ceremony?

"I don't want us to go our separate ways and then just come together in the bedroom for—for this. Don't you remember how romantic we were when we were dating?" I thought back to the way we looked into each other's eyes, and the thrill when our fingers touched... the tender kisses, the teasing, the whispers. "I want it back," I said, hoping he was remembering too, that he could understand what I was talking about. I peered deep into the sea-green eyes to see if I was reaching him. "I *need* it back," I whispered.

I trembled while I waited for his response. I longed for him to take me in his arms, to press me to his chest, to still my trembling, and shush my tears. Instead he swung his feet to the floor. "I'm sorry," he said. "I've just had so much on my mind. I haven't meant to neglect you." And then he sank to his knees beside the bed. "Won't you pray with me?"

What could I say? I climbed out of bed and positioned myself beside him, close but not quite touching. My heart thudded against my ribs. I scarcely heard the words my husband uttered—something about finding the strength to be both the husband I needed and the servant the Lord wanted him to be. *So this is it, then ... a competition—his wife or his Lord?*

CHAPTER NINETEEN

The next day I continued to consider and discard strategies right up to and into Peter's sermon. I did not try to assess the effect his words were having on the people around me. I was too far away ... back in bed with Peter, then remembering the day he offered to give up this path for me ... when I'd refused to let him. Would I live to regret that moment of generosity? Was I regretting it already?

The inside of my right foot began suddenly to itch just below the ankle. A mosquito bite I'd picked up at the beach, perhaps? The itch grew so intense I had to slip my shoe off to scratch. As I did, I became aware of an intense quietude throughout the congregation. I shifted my focus back to the pulpit. Peter's face was earnest, as he looked out expectantly. For a second, his eyes met mine, and my heart raced as if caught unprepared by a professor in college. Could he tell I'd been daydreaming?

"So," he said, "we're going to try some things a little differently. We won't be doing anything"—he hesitated, either searching for the right words or trying to give them added emphasis—"anything at all that's not scriptural. We're just going to try a few changes to reach out to the younger folks in the community." He paused again and looked around the small auditorium.

I looked too, expecting to see some nods or smiles of encouragement. There were none. On the few younger faces in the room, I saw curiosity. On the older ones, I saw mainly doubt or skepticism. Some scowled with downright disapproval. I knew Peter was seeing this too, and my heart wrenched for him.

He plunged bravely on. "Without its youth, our church—any church—will die. Now, the first thing we're going to try is to put our hymnals down and lift our faces and our voices to the Lord in songs of praise. The words will appear on this screen." Peter pointed as a young man rolled a screen on rollers to center front. I turned around in my seat to locate a second young man next to a projector in the back.

Others twisted in their seats as the screen lit up and the words appeared. Peter led the song, and for a time he was singing solo. A couple of male voices joined in, and I added my never-strong soprano to the mix.

Blest be the tie that binds
Our hearts in Christian love.
The fellowship of kindred minds
Is like to that above.

A woman behind me tapped me on the shoulder. She held her hymnal up in my direction. "What page is it?"

I pointed to the screen. "I don't think he said. The words are up there."

She squinted and mumbled something to her husband. They both gaped at the screen. Little by little, several voices joined in until the rich singing filled the room. Then, suddenly, voices began to drop out until we were left with little more than a quartet. Necks craned, heads twisted, and I followed suit. Two well-dressed men with very short hair, probably in their late twenties, entered. Although they did not hold hands, their shoulders and arms touched in a way that—combined with something in their walk, or their manner, or their dress—spoke volumes. To my horror, men and women shifted in their seats ... purposefully not making room for the men.

Then someone did make room, and the men slipped into the pew. I breathed a sigh of relief. The woman who had moved over smiled a welcome at the men, and I saw who she was. Beatrice. Beside Beatrice on the same pew was another familiar face, one I couldn't place at first. Her mouth opened wide in song, the teenager's face was still round with baby fat. Of course. Sybil, from my class at school.

Beatrice had dark circles under her eyes, as if she had not slept well. But she too was singing. She caught my glance and sent me a thumbs-up sign. For a second, I wondered why. Then I realized she was showing her support for Peter's changes, and her encouragement for what lay ahead. She probably assumed Peter had discussed his plan with me before today. Was it my fault he hadn't?

A sharp twinge of guilt was followed by a moment of sudden clarity. The looks on the faces around me, the jaws clamped shut, said very clearly we were not all one in the Spirit. The young man who had rolled the screen for Peter sat in the front row. He lifted his arms heavenward, and I could sense ... rather than see ... heads shifting their curious gaze toward this young man.

Behind me, the couple who'd asked for a page number whispered audibly to each other, and then I heard the crinkle of a candy wrapper. A second later, the pungent scent of peppermint met my nostrils. I glanced behind me to see the jaws of both the man and the woman moving, almost in unison—not to the lyrics of the song but to shift a candy from one side of their mouths to the other.

My husband needed me, just as I needed him. By being sympathetic to the dilemmas he faced with these people, I would also find the way to reestablish my foremost position in his mind and his heart, my rightful position. Inside my head, I could almost hear the conversation I would initiate.

"Now I understand what you're dealing with," I would say, "and I want to be there for you. But I need you to be there for me too." I ignored a small but insistent voice in my head warning me that I was being manipulative. After all, I was just being honest ... how could that be wrong?

CHAPTER TWENTY

Sybil approached my desk after class on Monday.

"I was wondering if maybe I could talk to you sometime," she said. "There's no hurry."

"I was glad to see you at church yesterday," I said, conscious of playing the role of preacher's wife. "Do you have questions about an assignment?"

Sybil's cheeks flushed a soft peach, a little splotchy as if she had applied blush without looking, though she was wearing no discernible makeup. "No, it's not about math."

I waited for her to explain, and the flush deepened. "It's personal."

"Oh." Was she approaching me in my capacity as her teacher or as her preacher's wife? I cleared my throat. "Sure. If there's no hurry, we could get together next Saturday. Maybe have a picnic. Or would you rather meet sooner?"

She looked relieved. "A picnic Saturday's good. Thank you, Mrs. O'Neil."

"What's for dinner?" Peter asked that night as he did every evening.

My feet ached, and a wave of irritation swept through me that he was making no effort to help. After all, I'd been on my feet all day and had no idea what he'd been doing. Surely, he didn't expect me to be the kind of wife his mom had been when he was growing up, not when I was carrying a full-time job outside the home.

I was a lousy cook, and there had been limited time to teach myself after we married since I'd found a job so quickly. My mother never had much patience with my blundering efforts when I was small. By the time I was old enough to be of some real help, I'd lost interest.

Peter would have to be content with something out of the freezer. I located a package of frozen lasagna I'd purchased on impulse. The picture on the package looked so tasty, with ripe tomatoes and bubbling cheese, my mouth had watered in the store.

I scanned the directions, then ripped the plastic wrap and cardboard top from the package. The congealed mass of brownish-pinkish goop was none too appetizing. I turned the oven to preheat and waited, remembering my mother's wonderful Italian dishes—her mostaccioli casserole and the best spaghetti with marinara sauce ever. I wished … what? What exactly did I wish about my relationship with her? I pushed the wish down deep, the way I always did.

I needed to discuss dividing household duties with Peter, who was currently deep in a phone conversation with one of the young men from church—the one who'd helped him to project the song lyrics on Sunday. How could I talk about bringing the romance back into our marriage, and at the same time, ask him to help out more around the house? He would probably be as confused as I was. First things first, I thought. Which *was* first?

While the lasagna baked, I decided to make a pitcher of tea, sweetened with sugar the way both my dad and Peter liked. Beatrice had shown me how to make the tea. At the time, the process seemed so simple I hadn't bothered to write the steps down. I put water on to boil, then measured the sugar, located a pitcher and teabags and then tried to remember whether I needed two or three family-size teabags for a pitcher of this size. What size was this pitcher anyway—a gallon, a half-gallon, a quart? I had no idea.

Peter popped into the kitchen. "Something smells great."

Indeed the aroma of Italian herbs and spices filled the kitchen. "I hope it will be. I slaved all day." I laughed at Peter's raised eyebrows. "Just kidding. It's a frozen dinner."

"No need to apologize." Peter pulled me into his arms and planted a big kiss on my cheek.

"You seem to be in a good mood." I settled on two teabags—I didn't want Peter to accuse me of being extravagant—and dropped them into the pitcher. I poured the boiling water over the teabags, but the strings to the bags were completely underwater. How was I going to get them out without burning myself?

"I'm pretty excited about the changes we've initiated. Of course, talking about them is the easy part. Implementing them is another thing altogether."

I fished out the teabags and wrapped the strings around the handle of the pitcher. "And getting people onboard is still another," I said.

"How long before supper's ready?"

I glanced at the timer. "Another twenty minutes or so."

"I'm in no hurry." Peter's stomach rumbled loudly.

"Liar."

While we waited, Peter talked about his plans for bringing in tourists, construction workers, and more youth from the community. "Do you have any idea how fast this area is growing?" he asked. "Lots of outreach potential."

"I can see how many high rises are going up. Many of those people are seasonal, aren't they?"

"A lot of them, sure, but retirees too. There's a huge demand for workers to do the landscaping and the cleaning, for servers in restaurants, and clerks in shops."

"These people can't afford the high rises," I protested. "Where do they live?"

Peter shrugged. "Places like ours. As you go inland, the property gets a lot cheaper. There's not enough affordable housing around to accommodate them all." The modest two-bedroom house we were renting was only a few blocks from the beach, but lightyears from the price range of Gulf-front homes. I knew because I'd looked at some real estate flyers a bit wistfully and couldn't help wondering what my parents would think of our small place if they ever came to visit.

"So what does all that have to do with the church?" I asked Peter.

"People who are struggling to make ends meet need the Lord," Peter said. "Of course rich people do too. Still, it's harder for them to see their need."

If they don't realize their need, how can you be so sure they have one? Aloud, I said, "Remember the girl in my class I told you about—the one who was at church Sunday?"

"Sybil?"

"That's the one. She wants to talk to me about something personal."

"Like what?"

"She didn't say. She came up after class today, and I told her we could have a picnic on Saturday."

"Should I come too?" Peter asked.

"No way. She came to me, not you." I laughed. "She's probably having trouble with her boyfriend or mother or something and wants advice. I'm sure it's nothing serious."

"That lasagna ready yet?"

"Another five minutes or so—I thought you weren't in a hurry."

Peter sauntered to the refrigerator and opened the door. After a moment, he turned to me, munching on a raw carrot. "How'd you think it went yesterday?"

I stalled. "Watch out," I said, "or you're going to spew carrots all over the place or me." When he didn't laugh, I said, "Putting the lyrics up, you mean?"

He nodded, and I decided to be frank. "Not that well. Maybe it's just going to take some time getting used to."

"Maybe."

Now or never ... while I had the chance. I sucked in a deep breath and took the plunge. "Look, Peter, I've been doing a lot of thinking lately."

On the inside I quavered, suddenly afraid to put myself out on this long, fragile limb—one that might break and send me plummeting to a hard earth.

"What about?"

My mind went blank for a moment. Then I remembered my rehearsed speech and spoke as if uttering lines in a play. "I understand what you're dealing with, and I want to be there for you. But I need you to be there for me too. I need to feel desired. I need to feel like I'm special to you."

Peter pulled me to my feet, pressed his lips to my hair, to my forehead and eyebrows. "You *are* special to me. The most special thing in the world. Don't you know that?"

My eyes were suddenly wet with unshed tears. He took my hand and led me toward the bedroom. "What about the lasagna?" I protested.

"It'll keep."

"It probably needs to cool a while anyway," I agreed. I pulled away. "I just need to turn the oven off."

Following Peter into the bedroom, I said, "For me, romance isn't just about sex. You know that, right? I want us to be romantic everywhere, whether we're in the kitchen or on the beach, like when we were dating."

"I'm trying, Cadi. Just don't give up on me." Peter's eyes blazed, his focus entirely on me.

Funny, though, that just as I congratulated myself for accomplishing this much of my mission, my own mind drifted away, back to the earlier conversation with Sybil. What did she need my advice about? Something in her tone, or her face, led me to believe the matter might be more serious than I'd intimated to Peter.

CHAPTER TWENTY-ONE

I stared at the girl seated beside me on the beach. I let her words sink in, even as I longed to repel them the way a thick coat of sunscreen might ward off the sun. Gone was the cozy comfort zone in which I'd naively packed our picnic basket—wrapping sandwiches in red checkered napkins … tucking in a thermos of hot coffee alongside a thick wedge of chocolate cake … envisioning myself listening with a sympathetic ear.

My first inclination was disbelief. The things she described did happen, of course, but not to people I knew. Certainly not to this fragile young girl with her soft skin and enormous eyes. Beside me in the sand, her feet were slender and blue-veined, the toes surprisingly long and narrow, more like fingers than toes really. I studied her profile, wondering what perverse streak would cause her to fabricate such a tale. And I saw the blue marks in the pale flesh of her throat, visible through a heavy coat of concealing makeup made all the more obvious because she wore none on her face. I reached out to touch the side of her throat. She turned to face me and pushed her pink tee-shirt off one shoulder, revealing ugly dark blue marks on her tender flesh.

I withdrew my hand as if I'd been stung and sucked breath sharply into my lungs. I inhaled the salty sweetness of the ocean air, suddenly turned sour. "How could you let him do this to you?" I breathed.

I immediately regretted those words. The last thing I should do was to make her feel at fault.

She shrugged and released the neck of her T-shirt, letting it slip back into position. "He didn't exactly ask my permission."

"You've got to break up with him," I said. If she was telling me the truth, the solution was obvious.

"It's not that easy."

Beside us in the sand, a pale sand-colored crab emerged shyly from his hole. I reached for him, and he vanished back into the sand.

Sybil laughed. "My brother Gary and I used to come here at night, shining our flashlights on the crabs and watching them scurry. Sometimes we would bring a net."

"Your brother?"

"Half-brother, really." Had a shadow crossed the soft face, with the baby fat still clinging? Perhaps a cloud had moved in to obscure the sun.

"Are you close?"

This time, there was no mistaking the look in the large, child-like eyes. "Not anymore," she said.

"Why not?"

"I don't think you want to hear this."

I did not yet realize how right she was. I just wanted to shift the conversation away from her boyfriend, Bradley. "Try me," I said.

For a time we were both silent, listening to the sound of the surf, letting the sun warm us. Like the crab, she had to decide whether to shrink back into her hole or to expose herself to an unknown element who might prove hostile or friendly.

"There was this hole in the bathroom wall, see," she said at last, her voice so low I had to hold my breath to hear. "I didn't know about the hole, not for a long time. The house was so small, I thought the bathroom was the one place where I could be alone, be private, you know, and then one day I saw it."

"You saw what?" Fascination mingled with foreboding about what she was going to reveal.

"An eye. Gary was watching me when I came out of the shower."

"Are you sure? Maybe you just imagined he was or dreamed it."

She shook her head. "Nope. He didn't even deny he'd been watching He just laughed and told me he'd been doing this for a long time. He even brought his friends over sometimes to watch."

"What did you do when you found out? Did you tell your parents?"

"I told my mother. Lot of good that did."

"Why—what did she do?"

"Nothing. She just said, boys will be boys. After that, I nailed a block of wood over the hole, but he kept drilling through it. The whole thing was like a game to him, and I could never feel comfortable after that in my own bathroom."

Disbelief washed over me again. This girl had to have been pulling my leg. Surely this was too much ugliness for someone her age, in this God-fearing community, to have endured in silence. She must have seen the doubt in my eyes. Crab-like, she drew back inside herself. "What have you got in the basket?" she asked.

Relieved, I opened the picnic basket to reveal the contents. "Ham and cheese on white bread, or tuna salad on whole wheat?" I offered.

She hesitated. "You pick first."

"No, I like them both. It's your choice."

"I'll take the ham and cheese if you're sure you don't mind."

I handed her the sandwich, and we ate in silence for a time. I searched my brain for a non-threatening topic of conversation, wondering if this girl would find a way to turn any subject into a personal horror story. "What are your plans for the future?" I asked at last.

She brightened. "I want to go to college."

"Really?"

"Very much. That's what I've been saving up for, working at the soda shop, you know."

Here at last was a positive note, something I could sink my teeth into. I swallowed my last bite of sandwich before commenting, "There are loans and grants too. You should apply for as many as possible."

"The thing is … they always expect you to contribute something. They never pay a hundred percent."

"You, or your parents," I pointed out.

She laughed. "Right."

"Your parents—your mom and stepdad, I mean—aren't they willing to help?"

"Nope. In fact I have to help them."

"What do you mean—like paying them rent?"

"That too. I help out every month with the bills. My stepdad is out of work and then he had to go to the hospital for some tests, so I used a chunk of my savings to help pay his medical bills."

"You sure you don't want some coffee?" I unscrewed the thermos as I digested this last shocker. I thought of my own parents, of my resentment toward them over matters so much less... less what? Less painful, less selfish, less *wrong*.

"I don't drink coffee." She blushed, the pink suffusing the full cheeks and down her throat and disappearing behind the pink T-shirt where the dark blue bruises lay. She looked so young and vulnerable in that moment. Suddenly, I knew that every word she had spoken was the truth.

I took a sip of coffee—still warm. I offered her the other thermos, filled with ice and water, and a paper cup. She poured daintily, only splashing a little onto her hands, and drank.

"Let's walk awhile," I said, rising to my feet.

She glanced at her watch—a wide pink plastic band and a dial with a daisy in the center. "Oh, I wish I could. I need to get to work though. It's later than I thought."

"You work today?"

"I work every day." She smiled, and a deep dimple appeared in her plump cheek … as if to say that working every day was a pleasure and a privilege.

I bent to pick up a shell that had washed up not far from our mat. Though it looked perfect from where I stood, once in my palm I saw the shell was only three-quarters whole.

CHAPTER TWENTY-TWO

My conversation with Sybil preyed on my mind. This young woman needed help, and she had turned to me. To me, of all people. Never had I felt so inadequate. The next time I saw Beatrice, she sensed at once something was troubling me. We were driving toward Point Mildred, a narrow peninsula of land to the west of Sugar Sands, less than a hundred yards wide in places and about a mile and a half long.

"I don't know how much I should tell you," I said. "I'm so new to this role—I'm not comfortable with the confidentiality rules."

Beatrice laughed, pushing her glasses up on her nose and making a slight adjustment to the rear-view mirror. I was surprised she would make light of such a serious issue. Of course, she did not yet know the seriousness of Sybil's revelations.

"I'm not laughing at you," she said. "You'd think there might be a code of ethics for being a preacher's wife. Like the code of ethics for a doctor or a lawyer. Ironic that there isn't, don't you think?"

I was not amused, but I saw where she was coming from. "It's like being a parent, I guess," I said. "Any fourteen-year-old can be a parent. It's easier than getting a driver's license." I remembered how out of touch with my feelings my parents had been throughout my teen years. "If I'm going to be a preacher's wife—and I guess I'm one already …"

I stopped abruptly as this fact slapped me once again. "If I am, I want to be a good one. But I feel so—inadequate."

Beatrice did not laugh this time. She glanced at me, brown eyes warm with sympathy behind the thick lenses. She waited for me to continue.

"Look!" she said, pointing to a group of pelicans congregating on the Bon Secour side. She pulled the car off the road, and we watched in silence. The pelicans were brown and white, their beaks disproportionately long but ever so graceful. A number of gulls were here too and a lone heron. One delicate little bird walked along the shoreline, its beak long and slender as were its legs. It seemed perfectly at home here, unperturbed by the absence of others of its kind or size.

None of the birds showed signs of being intimidated by the presence of the others, whether larger or smaller. They shared the small space comfortably, and I thought of the factions in the church that worried Peter so. Why couldn't the different types of people accept each other's idiosyncrasies as easily as the birds did? This harmony would change fast enough, though, if we threw food in their direction. Was that what all this conflict—or, indeed, all conflict—was about? The survival of the fittest or the most obstinate?

A pelican plummeted into the water and emerged, a small fish captive in the long beak. Surely the pelican had no mixed feelings about bringing the life of the fish to such an untimely halt.

The pelicans rose into flight. As they soared overhead, I envied their ease and freedom. Little by little, they shifted positions in the azure sky until they formed a V, as perfect as any marching band trained by hours of rigorous practice.

"Ready to move on?" Beatrice asked, and I nodded. Back in the car, I soaked in the beauty around us. We could see water on both sides for a time, the Gulf on our left and the bayou on our right. Sybil had grown up here, surrounded by all this beauty, yet such ugliness too.

She had not asked me to keep our conversation a secret. "If she didn't ask me not to tell anyone," I said to Beatrice, "do you think it's okay if I tell you?"

"I can't answer that for you," Beatrice said. "But I can promise you I won't tell anyone else, not without your permission."

"All right then." I breathed a sigh of relief and poured out Sybil's story. After a bit, Beatrice parked the car. We took off our shoes and walked, the sand warm beneath our feet.

Beatrice's face betrayed no horror or shock.

"Did she say something to you already?" I asked.

"No, not a word. I just met her on Sunday and sat beside her because she looked sort of lost and a little forlorn. Still, I'm not as shocked as you are."

"You're not?"

"I've heard worse. And so will you over time, sad to say."

Oddly, Beatrice's words struck me as comforting rather than ominous. She made Sybil's problems seem less insurmountable, almost manageable.

After that, a floodgate opened. I poured out my heart to Beatrice's sympathetic ears. She did not say much. A time or two Beatrice's eyes glazed over, and I wondered if something was troubling her too. Mostly she listened while I talked.

"She said breaking up with her boyfriend wasn't that simple, though she didn't say why. I should have asked her."

"It's not too late."

"I need to ask her more questions, don't I? I need to unravel all the mess going on in her head—like whether she blames herself somehow, whether she thinks she deserves to be hit. I've heard of women like that, haven't you? I just never thought they would be so—so sweet and kind of innocent, the way Sybil is, despite everything that's happened to her."

"These are tough issues, Acadia, for anyone. Even a seasoned counselor. If you decide you're in over your head, you can always hook her up with a professional."

"I don't think she'd go for that," I said. "She doesn't have much money."

"There are Christian counselors," Beatrice said, "who work for little or no pay in cases of need. I can try to get some names for you, if you like."

I shook my head. "Not yet."

We returned to the car, brushing off our feet as we got in. I felt better, having figured out my next step. I would get Sybil to tell me why she couldn't break up with her boyfriend. If I could get her to talk to me, the way I had talked to Beatrice, surely, she would see for herself what she should do.

We drove past several pastel-colored houses sitting precariously on trucks of some sort. "What's going on here?" I asked Beatrice. No two seemed to be the same color, with shades ranging from aqua, blue gray, and lavender to peach and a pale gold-tinged yellow.

"A lot of the houses being moved out of Sugar Sands are being brought here. To make space for high-rise condos."

Many of the houses were not in great shape, but they had a quaint charm. One end of the blue-gray house was patched with something that looked like black duct tape. I smiled, thinking of my dad, who often joked that just about anything could be fixed with duct tape. With some repairs, the houses would be lovely, perched on stilts not unlike the small bird I'd seen earlier.

"Shame," I murmured. "For Sugar Sands, I mean." There were still a few of these pastel, single-family dwellings in Sugar Sands but not many. "Do you think the coastline in Sugar Sands will eventually hold nothing but high rises?"

"I hope not," Beatrice said, "but it makes sense economically."

Knowing Beatrice was an active partner in several development deals, I tried to imagine this gentle woman holding her own in negotiations with contractors and realtors. When she parked the car a second time, we got out and walked barefoot on the beach, the vanilla-colored sand warm between our toes.

I asked about her business. As she warmed to the subject, I listened, fascinated. My image of the kind-hearted mentor morphed into one of a shrewd wheeler-dealer, tough as leather when needed. Yet there was nothing two-faced about Beatrice, and I did not think I would ever see her as hypocritical.

Later, Beatrice asked to stop at a small shop where she needed to pick up a gift for a tea. I agreed at once, in no hurry to part from the comfort of her companionship. I browsed while she discussed her options with the salesgirl, a fresh-faced young woman who reminded me a bit of Sybil, and who was apparently well-acquainted with Beatrice. I wandered aimlessly up an aisle crowded with the usual beach paraphernalia and souvenirs.

I paused at a rack of painted plaques. One in particular caught my eye, a landscape of two striped beach chairs under an umbrella. A caption read "May your time be filled with relaxing sunsets, cool drinks, and sand between your toes."

I thought not of the tourists who rented the expensive places, but of those who lived here—people like me and Beatrice and Sybil—and of the time we have on this earth … whether on these glorious beaches or elsewhere. Today, I'd had sand between my toes.

CHAPTER TWENTY-THREE

The following week, I watched for an opportunity to talk to Sybil alone after class. But she refused to meet my gaze, and always there were other students about. By this time, the class had warmed up to me and clattered about—sharing jokes and stories, asking my opinion on issues that seemed trivial just then, or discussing college plans. This would have pleased me greatly the week before, but their clamor interfered with the mission at hand—to find a way to talk to Sybil.

Finally, I resorted to requesting she meet with me on Friday after her last class. Still, she did not meet my gaze. Several other students did, however, their eyes curious, and a couple of boys whistled ominously or called out a low "Uh-oh." But their attention shifted quickly enough.

When Sybil entered my classroom later that afternoon, I had just dismissed my last class. There was still a ring of students surrounding my desk, talking as much to one another as to me. Sybil hung back, shyly, on the fringe of the circle.

"If you'll excuse me," I said in my strictest down-to-business voice, clearing my throat for added emphasis. "I need to speak with Sybil alone."

The boys and girls sauntered off, shooting curious glances over their shoulders. "Do you have a few minutes?" I asked when they were gone. Sybil's face flushed a pretty shade of peach. "I guess so."

"If you don't, we can get together tomorrow."

"No—now's better."

"How's everything?" My carefully planned words dissolved in my mouth.

"Fine."

I motioned to a desk in the front row. "Sit down, please."

Sybil opened her mouth, as if to protest, then closed it. She took the seat I indicated, and I sat in the student chair next to her, leaving us both facing the front of the room rather than each other. I dragged my desk to a different angle so I might look at Sybil when I posed my questions. I wanted to see, as well as hear, her response.

"Are you still seeing Bradley?"

The color drained from her cheeks. "I guess so."

"What do you mean—you guess so?"

"I mean—yes."

"Has he hurt you again?"

She hesitated, just perceptibly, before shaking her head. I scanned her throat and arms but found no new bruises.

"Are you sure?"

"He loves me. He just gets so—upset sometimes. It's not his fault. I mean—it is, of course—but he can't help himself." Her eyes pleaded for understanding.

"He may not be able to help himself," I agreed. "If that's the case, it's just that much more proof you need to break up with him. He may need professional help, but you can't let him destroy your life."

Sybil's voice was so low I could barely hear her. "I know you're right," she said. "But I don't know what he might do if I break up with him."

"What do you mean?" I blanched at the thought of violence.

"I know he would get angry. So angry."

"Nonetheless, you have to think of yourself," I said, not quite so sure of myself now. Was I getting in over my head? Should I advise her to seek professional help? If I took that strategy, she might feel dismissed.

I plunged ahead. "Promise me you'll break up with him."

Sybil hesitated. "I can't do that. I don't want to promise something I might not be able to—to honor."

Honor. The word hung in the air. Sybil's honor ... my honor. Just a word, yet the word implied everything. I had to respect her answer. "Then promise me you'll at least think about what I said."

This time she did not hesitate. "I promise." The dark blue eyes were guileless, as if glad to be able to give me what I had asked. I could imagine her with her brute of a boyfriend, anxious to please him, to give him what he had asked, wanting to make him happy.

Too late, I remembered how Beatrice had let me do virtually all the talking, let me sort things out and come to my own conclusions. I had intended to do the same with Sybil. I had meant to get her to explain to me why breaking up wasn't so simple as I thought. I'd hoped that as she talked, she would come to her own decision to break up with Bradley. Instead I had practically dictated to her what she should do.

I remained at the student desk for several minutes after she left, replaying the conversation. Disappointed in my lame counseling effort, I put my head on the desk and bumped it against the laminated top. A twinge of pain shot through my left temple, the beginning of what might develop into a full-blown migraine.

After a time, I rose, erased the board, and collected papers to take home for grading, while my mind continued to buzz with what I'd said and what I'd failed to say or do. I remained certain of one thing, however. Breaking up with Bradley was the right thing … the only thing, for Sybil.

I waited for her to approach me next. She did not, though there were days when the round eyes met mine. Occasionally, I thought I detected some sign of hope, of self-confidence, even of gratitude … her deep blue eyes filled with relief, as if she wanted to say, "I did it!"

The weeks passed, and the seasons changed so gradually I couldn't say when the transition took place. There was a new crispness in the air, and the beaches were largely devoid of crowds of teenagers or families. The water temperature was still pleasant enough to swim, and a few individuals and small groups dotted the beaches. I loved the beaches in October. I relished the peace and quiet. I could commune with the Gulf in its new mood without being splashed by kids on boards or distracted by couples photographing their offspring.

Peter remained caught up in his plans for the church … like me, learning patience. He wanted to gain the confidence of the congregation before launching further innovations. Every other Sunday, worship songs were displayed on a large screen, hymnals used on the alternate Sundays. Even then more of the worshipers looked up to sing rather than down at their books.

Little by little, the singing became more enthusiastic on the days the screen was used. When several of the older members told Peter they missed the screen on the alternate weeks, Peter took this small victory to heart.

Halloween approached, and he planned a fall festival for kids of all ages from the congregation or the community. Instead of trick-or-treating, attendees could play games, dunk for apples, and spend time in prayer and songs of praise. Because I remembered how disappointed I'd been as a child to approach a dark, uninviting house on Halloween, I offered to stay home and pass out candy to the small trick-or-treaters from our neighborhood who came to our door.

A small, golden-curled girl of about three, dressed in an angel costume complete with halo, approached. "Twicker tweat." Could a child of mine have ever been … ever be … so adorable?

I doled out a generous portion of candy and stood on my front porch, waving goodbye to the little angel until she and her father were out of sight, longing for Peter to share the moment.

The next person to cross the yard was a grown man—a parent, perhaps. He wore a plain black mask covering only his eyes and nose. A sparse, scraggly growth of a reddish blonde hue adorned a weak chin. I glanced past him in search of his child, but none was in sight.

I shivered with foreboding, then scoffed at my fear. His kid was probably just lagging behind. A group of children in the next yard laughed and chased after each other, the contents of a small witch's bag tumbling onto the lawn. None of them appeared to be connected to the masked man.

I shook off my premonition. Surely the general eeriness of the holiday was working on my imagination. When he showed no sign of slowing his pace, I took a step backward and started to close the door. The man caught the door with his foot and shoved it open.

A scream froze in my throat as he pushed inside. He was broad-shouldered and strong. My heart banged in terror. I found a voice, though it didn't sound much like my own. "What do you want—who are you?"

"I just want to talk to you. Give me a little cooperation, and you won't get hurt."

Like a nightmare where my feet felt glued to the floor, I found myself unable to move or even scream. The din of happy children sounded farther away.

"All right." My voice came out in a raspy squeak. "I'll cooperate. Do you want money? We don't have much, but—"

"I don't want your money. I just want you to stay out of my life."

He had mixed me up with someone else, I realized with some relief. I only had to make him see his mistake. "I don't know what you're talking about. I've never seen you before in my life." Although I could see only the lower part of his face, I would recognize him if I knew him … or would I? Could he be someone from church—had he been stalking me?

"You know Sybil, don't you?"

The light dawned. "You're—you're Bradley?"

"That's right. I don't want to hurt you. I don't want to hurt anyone, but I will if I have to." He stood so close to me I could smell his warm breath … something like garlic.

Sudden fury supplanted my terror as I thought of the marks on Sybil's slender throat and shoulders. "Is that what happened to Sybil? Did you *have* to hurt her?" My voice shook only a little as I willed myself to be strong, to get through this somehow and then to find a way to help Sybil once and for all.

"That's none of your business, now is it? Which is exactly the reason for this little visit—to make sure that, in the future, you keep your pretty little nose where it belongs." He pushed hard on the tip of my nose, and Sybil's bruises flashed through my mind. If this man was capable of such cruelty toward Sybil, whom he supposedly cared about... what might he do to me?

Though my legs trembled, I stood my ground. My heart had moved into my throat and pulsed wildly. I would not be bullied by this—this pitiful excuse for a man. With an effort, I faced him as if I were the one in control of the situation. He was only a man—a flawed, fallible man with dirty fingernails.

He railed at me. "Who do you think you are anyway? Putting ideas about college into Sybil's head, making her think she's better than me, making her think she can walk out on me any time she likes."

In that instant, I saw the little boy inside, scared behind the mask, afraid of losing Sybil. Fear engendered violence, though, and I quavered. Summoning the firmest voice I could manage and hoping he could not detect the tremor beneath, I said, "This is a free country the last I heard." As I spoke, I thought perhaps this was the kind of thing he might have said himself, the kind of thing he would understand.

"Don't patronize me." His lip curled. "What you don't seem to understand is that I'm the only one who knows what's best for Sybil. I'm the one who loves her, who's gonna be there for her day in and day out. Not you with your high and mighty words of advice."

"I may not be there day in and day out," I said, practically spitting the words at him. "But at least I'm not putting any bruises on her!"

So fast I could not have ducked even if I'd anticipated what was about to happen, he struck the side of my face—hard. "That's just a taste of what you're going to get if you don't back off," he said. "I'll promise you that." He wheeled on his heel and left me alone.

The trembling I'd been resisting overcame me, and I collapsed into a heap on the floor, shaking so hard my teeth chattered. After a time, I lifted a hand to my face where he had struck me. My cheek was hot and wet, and for a second, I thought I felt blood. I stared at my fingers. Not red. Then I tasted the salt on my hand and realized I was not bleeding. I was crying. I rose and moved dazedly to the telephone. I picked up the receiver to call Peter, then hung up.

I wasn't hurt, not really, and Bradley was gone. He'd only been here a matter of minutes all totaled. I hadn't missed a single trick-or-treater. I went to the mirror to check my face for marks. There they were, bright red fingerprints. I wondered if they would turn black and blue like Sybil's marks. What should I say to Peter?

The truth, of course. After all, he wasn't the type who would feel compelled to go storming after Bradley. If Peter went after him and beat him up, his image with the churchgoers would suffer. If he didn't, his image with me might.

A knock interrupted my train of thought, and I nearly jumped out of my skin. A pair of small trick-or-treaters, both dressed as Wonder Woman, stared at me wide-eyed and speechless while their dad watched from his car. Weak in the knees, I went back to doling out candy, my mind still on Bradley. I would let Peter finish the festivities at church. By the time he got home, the shock would have worn off. I would be able to describe the event with greater objectivity, putting a less hysterical spin on what had happened. I didn't want to push him into doing anything rash.

By the time he got home, the red marks had faded until I could barely discern them myself. He might not even notice, I thought.

I was right. "How was it?" he asked.

"What?"

"You know—the trick-or-treaters."

"Oh. Fine," I said and launched into an overly zealous description of the small angel. "How was the festival?"

"Great." As he talked, his eyes happy, I knew I could not tell him. Not tonight, though the incident continued to dominate my every thought. Peter had enough worries of his own, and I didn't want to spoil this small success for him.

I had trouble falling asleep, dreading nightmares. I lay awake beside Peter, intermittently shivering with the memory and then cuddling against his warm, sleeping body to still my trembling limbs. When at last I slept, I dreamed, not of violence, but of the beach.

Lying in the sand, I watched the hues of the evening sky shift from blues to pinks to deep lavender. And then I was in the water, thinking how warm the sea was for this time of year. Wasn't it October? Waves rocked me gently like a mother with an infant. Floating on my back, I looked up at the clouds. Yes, October, or maybe November already, because I remembered passing out Halloween candy. Yet I was alone here—alone with the warm water and the lavender sky. The clouds changed colors into the pastels like the houses being moved to Point Mildred. One was gray blue, another peach, and still another a golden yellow. The warm waters engulfed me in their embrace.

Suddenly, the waves became tumultuous. Huge masses of prickly seaweed encircled me, caught my hair in their grasp, entangled my legs. I struggled to move away from the seaweed, but it was everywhere. The clouds changed again, their colors darkening to charcoal gray ... their shapes like leering faces ... fuzzy, familiar but not quite recognizable.

The features settled into faces I knew. Sybil's wide-spaced dark blue eyes, her expression one of innocence in spite of everything. In spite of evil. Beside her, Beatrice's eyes were large and nearsighted, exuding wisdom and caring. Next to Beatrice was a face I did not recognize, the features indistinct as though hidden behind a mask and yet reflecting some intense emotion. A larger cloud moved over the face, also wearing a mask. Behind this mask the eyes were just visible ... devil eyes, blood red and intent with hatred. The cloud shifted subtly, revealing the face next to Beatrice. The features undulated in and out of my vision until, with a start, I recognized the face. My own.

CHAPTER TWENTY-FOUR

"I'm sorry about what happened," Sybil mumbled. She stared over my shoulder at the equations on the blackboard. "I didn't mean to get you in the middle." She'd been avoiding me since Halloween, and I finally asked her to stay after school.

"You're still seeing him, aren't you?" I asked. She wore a yellow chiffon scarf. Though attractive, the scarf seemed out of character.

Her gaze was defensive, almost defiant. "I tried to break up with him. That's why he went to your house. Now, you can see why——"

"I see more clearly than ever how much you need to ..."

Why repeat the obvious? I rose from my desk. Before she realized what I was about to do, I unwound the scarf from her delicate blue-veined throat. Even though I'd suspected what lay beneath, I shuddered with fresh horror at the array of purple marks. I caught only a quick glimpse before she hid her throat with her hands.

"You had no right to do that!" Sybil gasped and fled, still clutching her throat, leaving her beautiful scarf behind.

I called after her. "Sybil! Don't go. I'm only trying to help." She was out of sight before I finished the sentence. Staring at the flimsy yellow chiffon dangling from my hand, I was at a total loss. Slowly I moved to the board and erased the day's lessons.

"I'm worried about Sybil," I told Peter at dinner.

"Why?"

"Her boyfriend's beating her."

"What?" Peter's fork remained poised in midair while he listened.

I told him what I knew, everything except the incident on Halloween.

"I'm going after him," Peter said, his right hand knotted into a fist, his face uncharacteristically fierce.

I caught at his sleeve. "Violence isn't the answer. You, of all people, should know that."

He stared at me for a long moment, while the food on our plates grew cold. I watched the emotions passing through his green eyes, all emotions I myself knew well. Then his eyes softened, and this new emotion was one I didn't recognize.

He resumed eating, first the pork chop, and then the lima beans and corn. I tried to follow suit, but I was not hungry. I stared at him, trying to sort out what he was feeling or thinking.

"Aren't you going to eat anything?" he asked, and I shook my head.

When he finished his meal, he turned to me, his intention still unreadable. Was he consuming a last supper before going into combat? Or had he dismissed the problem altogether? Then, unexpectedly, he kissed me and caressed my cheek and neck with his fingers, sending goosebumps down my spine as I sought understanding.

"You're right, of course," he said. "Sometimes you are so wise."

I leaned my head against Peter's shoulder, believing in that moment that together we could solve this dilemma. With his next words, Peter showed himself a stranger. "We should be praying for Bradley." He stroked my hair.

I stiffened and pulled away. I wanted to scream at Peter. Did he always have to operate at such extremes—beat him up or save him?

"Bradley is fighting his own demons," Peter said. "He needs our help. Pray with me, Cadi."

I rose and cleared the dishes from the table, rattling them harshly against each other.

"Stop it," Peter said. "I'll do them." He tugged at the plate in my hand. When I jerked away, the plate flew from my grasp and crashed to the floor, breaking into pieces.

Humbly, Peter bent to pick up the mess. His patience infuriated me further, even as it shamed me. Somehow, I had known that no matter how he reacted, I wouldn't have approved.

"Don't forget the Helper," Peter said. I knew he was referring to the Holy Spirit, a concept I could never quite grasp.

"Don't give me that!" I exploded. "Where was the helper when Sybil needed him? Tell me, where?"

Sybil approached me, much to my surprise, later that week after class. I was alone. "I'm sorry," she mumbled. "I know you were only trying to help."

Her face was swollen, but there were no bruises. She reminded me of a little girl, one who'd been crying over a scraped knee. Sybil was always apologizing to me, and I wondered if this was a pattern in all her relationships.

"And?" I said.

"And you're right. You're right about everything."

"So?"

"So I'm trying to do what you said. I *am*. I'm just trying to find the right way." She hiccoughed. "And the right time. I just wanted you to know."

My heart lifted. Perhaps Peter's prayers were being answered, or maybe my counseling was yielding results. Either way I was glad. And yet a kernel of doubt nagged at me, like a pebble trapped in a sandal.

Two days later, as I walked to the school parking lot, an old jacked-up Chevrolet Impala, tires screeching, shot across the lot straight toward Sybil. I screamed just as the car came to a halt inches away from the girl, her arms loaded with books. For a second, I could see her face clearly, lifted in my direction as if in appeal. However, I was on the opposite side of the parking lot and wasn't sure she even saw me. The smooth brow puckered. Suddenly, I could envision her as an old woman … if she survived that long … the puckers carved into permanence but still wondering, still questioning, what had happened to her life.

She ducked her head, turned away from me and toward the driver. Bradley. I was too far away to hear what they said, but I could see Sybil's mouth moving and forming an "O" or perhaps a "No" of protest. Good for her, I thought. But then, she climbed into the car beside him.

"Sybil, no!" I cried. Of course, she could not hear me. I ran in the direction of the car, but there was no way I could catch up. I turned my ankle and swore under my breath, a habit I was trying to break.

My ankle throbbed and my whole body shook as I ran to the school office. I didn't have a key, so I prayed someone was still there. The door was shut but unlocked. I lunged inside, startling the secretary who was calmly collecting her things as if nothing was wrong.

"I've got to use the phone." Still panting and not waiting for an answer, I grabbed it and dialed 911.

"Police? I need to speak to the police."

I felt as helpless as Sybil as I searched for the right words. "I need to report an incident," I said.

"What sort of an incident?"

"A—a sort of kidnapping. Not exactly, but—"

"What do you mean 'not exactly'?"

"This student of mine—she's been abused by her boyfriend, and she just got back into his car."

"Did he force her into the car?"

"I don't know exactly, but I know she didn't want to get in with him."

"How do you know?"

"She was saying 'no.' I could see her mouth moving."

My account was met with silence. Had I sounded that lame? I needed to make a stronger case. "She was trying to break up with him," I said.

"Did he have a weapon?"

"I don't know."

"Did you see a weapon? Did you see him behave forcibly?"

"No." I sighed with the realization I'd failed.

"In that case, there's nothing we can do. Sorry, ma'am."

The connection went dead. I repeated the words aloud. "There's nothing we can do …"

CHAPTER TWENTY-FIVE

There's nothing we can do. The words continued to echo in my head over the following days and weeks. There was nothing I could do either. Or was there something?

On a rare date with Peter, I stared at the menu, determined to enjoy myself. My eyes took in the delicious-sounding seafood dishes along with the accompanying high prices. No Royal Red shrimp for me, or seafood platter, not even the grilled fish dinner. We were seated in a screened-in porch with the Gulf only a few yards away. You had to pay extra for this kind of a view.

I turned reluctantly to the section of sandwiches. Po'-boys—how appropriate. Around us, couples and groups were drinking pitchers of beer and frozen daiquiris. I eyed them with envy, hearing their laughter and wishing for their light-heartedness.

How had my life become this serious so quickly?

Peter, too, was studying the menu for items in our price range. "A spicy crawfish Po'Boy sounds good, don't you think?"

"I don't think I've ever eaten a crawfish," I said.

A waitress with a blond ponytail—she didn't look old enough to be working, much less serving alcohol—made her way through the crowd to our table. "Can I get your drinks?"

"Just water for me," Peter said.

I sighed. "Water for me too." I looked longingly at a golden colored frozen drink topped with whipped cream at the table on our left. "What's that, by the way?"

The girl followed my gaze. "That's a mango daiquiri. You want one?"

"No, thanks. I was just curious."

Peter didn't think he and I should consume alcohol, for fear of influencing someone with a weakness in that direction. I suspected his feelings arose, at least in part, from his dad's alcoholism. At times I also caught a hint of something else, a deeper fear. Was Peter afraid his dad's weakness might be hereditary?

I reached down to slip my sandal off and shake the sand out. We'd traipsed through a lot of sand on our way into Tenacious Ted's. I was still getting used to the weather here—the fact that you could usually eat outdoors comfortably in November. I'd grown accustomed to year-round warm temperatures in Malibu, but I hadn't expected them in Alabama. Not every day was like this, of course. Some were downright chilly.

From across the porch, a peal of masculine laughter rang out as I sipped ice water. I looked over, and my breath caught in my throat. The guy's hair was tousled, and his eyes crinkled when he laughed. His companion, a young attractive woman, pushed dark hair back from her face, her laughter joining his. Peter glanced in their direction. The couple reminded me so much of us—the way we'd been in college. Longing struck me like a blow to the gut, a wish to turn back the clock. "I wish they'd share the joke," I said.

Silence fell between us while Peter and I each followed our separate trains of thought. At last, I broke the silence. "What are you thinking about?"

"The church membership is falling off," Peter said.

When I had noticed the pews becoming less full, I'd blamed the empty rows on seasonal factors. "Maybe it's just a slow time of year."

The young waitress bounded over to our table, ponytail swinging. "Are you ready to order?"

Peter selected the crawfish Po'Boy, and I chose a grouper sandwich. I debated whether to pay an extra dollar to have it blackened and decided not to. When the waitress left, Peter said, "I know this time of year is slow, but it's more than that. We're also down from the same time last year."

"Maybe the hurricane is still affecting things."

"That should be getting better by now, not worse."

Peter's refusal to accept my positive outlook annoyed me. Apparently, he was determined to ruin our rare evening out. Before I could formulate a response, he continued. "There are a lot of members leaving us for more traditional churches. There are some newcomers too, but many of them are gravitating to the more progressive churches. We're caught in the middle—too conservative for some, too liberal for others."

An older waitress, wearing the same uniform of shorts and a rainbow striped T-shirt, delivered steaming bowls of gumbo to the table on our right. A delicious aroma drifted over. "So, what's to do?" I said.

"I don't know. That's what I'm trying to figure out."

"Do you have to figure it out today?"

"No, of course not." Peter looked repentant, his brow furrowed, his eyes now focused on me. "What's on your mind?"

"Sybil," I admitted, although those thoughts were just as despondent as Peter's.

I'd been trying to push Sybil out of my mind without much success. She hadn't approached me again, but dark rings around her eyes told me she wasn't sleeping well. After the day I saw her and Bradley in the parking lot, I tried repeatedly to make eye contact with her. She always avoided my gaze. I was worried about her but not in the mood to discuss my concerns with Peter. Not tonight.

The young couple across the porch held hands, and this exacerbated my frustration almost to the breaking point. How could I make Peter see that what I wanted, what I *needed*, was to hold hands and laugh? To be young again, while we *were* still young, before it was too late.

"How is she?" Peter asked.

"I don't know. I don't want to talk about her."

Peter cocked an eyebrow. The waitress appeared with our sandwiches, surrounded by French fries. I didn't remember any mention of fries on the menu. I spread mayonnaise on my sandwich and squirted ketchup into the corner of my plate. My weight had been slowly inching up, and potatoes were something I tried to avoid. The fries looked so tempting, though, crispy and hot and fresh. Who cared anyway? Peter was so absorbed in church trauma, I doubted that he'd notice if I gained ten pounds, let alone another one or two.

I dipped a fry in the ketchup and munched. For a time, we ate in silence. Peter, of course, did not hesitate to eat every one of his fries plus the crawfish, which were also fried. His weight never seemed to fluctuate ... so far as I could tell ... no matter what he ate. And he ate plenty.

"Did she break up with ... er ... Bradley?"

Hadn't I just told him I didn't want to talk about Sybil? "You're not hearing me!"

Several heads spun in our direction, their smiles frozen in place, as if no one else ever quarreled in this idyllic setting. I knew Peter was probably worrying that some of his church members were hearing us. I wanted to scream, "What are you staring at?" In that instant, I was a teenager again, dressed in black jeans and peace signs, an embarrassment to my parents.

I waited for Peter to speak. When he did, he nearly whispered. "Are you hearing *me*?"

I rose from the table and pushed back my chair. "I'm going for a walk." I headed down the steps and toward the sugary white sands of the public beach.

Digging my toes into the cool sand, I tried to clear my mind. Why was I so upset? Could a person be jealous of God? And if so, would that jealousy be the unforgivable sin? The concept of an unforgivable sin had struck terror in my soul as a child. Although I could never figure out what the unforgivable sin was, I experienced a wave of anxiety every time I heard the idea mentioned—a fear that somehow, I'd committed that particular sin. A lovely dark bird with a long beak, a fisher of some kind, watched me approach. Maybe, I thought, she would let me walk right up and touch her. At the last instant, she flew. Not far and not from fear … but slowly and gracefully, flying low over the Gulf, searching for prey. Funny, I always thought of birds as female. Birds, like cats, seemed feminine to me. Graceful and yet a little distant, dangerous even.

Not friendly and forthcoming like a dog. Like Peter. His face, not so peaceful as I had once thought, imprinted in my mind. I kept looking behind me to see if he was following. Finally, as I hoped, he was there, hurrying to catch up. Relief poured through my veins, along with a glimmer of satisfaction … a sense of victory. I felt ashamed of my thoughts.

"Did you settle the bill?" I asked when he was at my side, though I was certain he had. There was a predictability about Peter, as annoying as it was comforting. He was not the kind of man to run from a restaurant without paying the bill, no matter what kind of trauma had taken place.

"I did." He reached for my hand. I allowed him to hold it but didn't curl my fingers into his as I usually did. I carried both sandals in my other hand. "I'm sorry if I seemed not to be listening," he said. "I know how worried you are about Sybil."

I *was* worried about Sybil, true enough. Yet I was more worried about myself and whether I could survive as a preacher's wife. Peter always gave me too much credit. "It's not that," I said.

I bent down to pick up a small creamy shell, perfect and fragile and still wet. "I wanted tonight to be about us, the way we used to be. I wanted to feel young and carefree. If we can't feel that way now, what hope is there for our future?"

Peter hesitated. "We are young, but we are not exactly carefree," he said at last.

"Don't you *want* to be?"

"I guess not. The world is too full of troubles and cares for me to ignore them."

I wanted to scream—to tell him he couldn't save the world—that I was sick of his piousness. I forced myself to speak calmly. "Just for one evening … can't we be carefree for one evening?"

"Let's sit down," he said. A couple of beach chairs had been left out overnight, not far from the water's edge, with no one in sight to claim them. We sat, and I dropped my sandals beside my chair.

The moon was almost full, hanging low in the sky, a splendid silvery gold, making me long more than ever to rediscover the romance in our relationship. The water lapped at our feet, and we sat quietly.

"I don't know exactly what set me off tonight," I said finally. "There's something about being a preacher's wife that makes me cautious all the time. Like I'm afraid to wear a bikini because someone might see me and question my morals. I'm afraid to order a mango daiquiri, even a virgin one, because somebody might see me and get the wrong idea. This life is making me crazy. I knew it would—I *told* you it would—and I was right." I was getting worked up now, my heart thumping rapidly. Being right felt so terribly wrong.

"Cadi, Cadi," Peter said. "I know you did, but I was so sure everything would be all right. It's my fault. I forced you into this."

His remorse quieted my emotions. "No, you didn't. You offered to do something different."

"I offered, but you knew what I really wanted."

I stifled a laugh. How could anyone want this—this confusion and stress and disquiet? "And now … do you still want this?"

He hesitated only a moment before answering. "I do."

Somehow, I had expected him to waver in the face of the church's problems and the tension between us. How little we understood each other. Just like any other couple, we were victims to poor communication. Once, I would have quoted from *Cool Hand Luke* "What we have here is failure to communicate." Today, I wasn't in the mood to make light of the matter.

"I thought we were special," I said. My voice broke.

Peter rose and pulled me to my feet and into his arms, kissing me long and hard under the silvery gold moon. "We *are* special," he said.

At these words, which I so needed to hear, my heart sang a little. But the song was more a muted ballad than a joyous tango. Thoughts of Sybil hovered behind the song. She was special too, and she deserved someone so much better than Bradley.

CHAPTER TWENTY-SIX

Snowbirds rolled into Sugar Sands throughout the months of January and February, renting beach homes at off-season rates to escape the cold climates up north. My students recovered from their holiday breaks and settled into a routine of sorts. I resolved to teach them as much as possible before spring fever broke out.

Beatrice and I met regularly for coffee or walks on the beach, and her friendship sustained me. One Saturday, we met for lunch at Poseidon's Fork, a favorite among both locals and snowbirds. Paintings of local artists crowded the walls, mixed in among an assortment of ocean-related memorabilia. Fishermen's nets, charts of fish species, enormous seashells, and an old anchor hung alongside advertisement posters.

"Joe's going to be taking care of you today." The greeter's voice was vaguely familiar. I blinked and took a closer look. Maude Davis.

I shot Beatrice an inquiring glance as we slipped into our seats, and she read my mind as she so often did. "Didn't you know Maude had taken a job?"

I shook my head.

Beatrice smiled in Maude's direction and made no effort to lower her voice. Instead she spoke as if seeing a retired preacher's wife in this role were the most natural thing in the world. "She told me they could use the income and, besides, it got her out of the house."

Just over our heads, a framed clipping from *Southern Living* praised the food and ambiance of Poseidon's Fork. Beside the clipping, a Miller Lite ad boasted a huge fake beer bottle. Above it, a large framed print pictured oysters in the half shell. Glancing to the other side of the room, I spotted an odd woven substance hanging in one corner.

I pointed. "Is that what I think it is?"

Beatrice laughed. "I'd say it's a hornet's nest." A large roll of brown paper towels stood on our table, alongside a variety of Tabasco bottles and pukka sauces. There was nothing fancy about Poseidon's Fork, but I liked the atmosphere. I flipped past the regular dinner selections to the back side of the menu, where the day's luncheon specials were listed. Some were as cheap as $3.50, including tea or coffee and dessert. I considered the Greek grouper, which wasn't a bad deal at $5.95, but couldn't justify the extra $2.50.

Beatrice looked tired, though she was neat and stylish as always in a pantsuit of blended earth-tones. These colors were uncharacteristic for Beatrice, who typically wore pastels. I wasn't sure the new look was becoming.

"I'm debating between the fried flounder and the beans and rice with sausage," I told her.

"Both are good here. I'm not terribly hungry myself. I think I'll just have a bowl of gumbo."

I settled on the beans and rice. Joe—a slender-built man with a dark ponytail, a long goatee, and a sweeping mustache—brought our iced tea. "Their tea is so much better than mine," I said after a few sips. "I never quite get mine right somehow."

Beatrice chuckled. "Who knows if they ever clean out the bottom of the tea pitcher? Maybe that's their secret."

By this time, a line had formed with some would-be diners crowding near the door and others waiting outside. "I guess we got here at the right time," I said.

Beatrice sipped her tea. "You seem troubled today."

I sighed, not sure how much I could share, even with Beatrice. "It's a combination of things, I guess."

"Such as?"

Beatrice's velvet-brown eyes, magnified behind the thick glasses, were so full of compassion I knew I could share just about anything with her. I blurted out my pent-up fear. "I'm afraid of losing the romance in my marriage."

Beatrice nodded, as if she had expected this. "You know, the first year of marriage is often the most difficult."

"Really? I would have thought this should be the best. We are still practically on our honeymoon. Or should be."

"It rarely works that way. No matter how well you know a person before you marry, the reality of living together takes a huge adjustment."

"I suppose so."

Another waitress, carrying a stack of menus, approached our table. Her permed red-blonde hair stood out from her head in clumps. She asked if we minded if she stole one of our chairs. We waved our consent, and she beamed at us as if we'd made her day. I marveled at the talent of some people to thrive in any circumstance. Why couldn't I be more like that?

"I feel like I have to create a scene with Peter to get back the …"

I couldn't think of the right word, half expecting Beatrice to supply it for me. When she didn't, I finished lamely, "You know—the thrill."

"What kind of a scene?"

My cheeks heated. I doubted if Beatrice had ever resorted to such tactics in her marriage. "I just get upset and frustrated sometimes because I feel like I'm the last thing on Peter's mind. I think back to when he thought about me all the time, and I miss that. If I tell him I'm feeling neglected, then we both get upset. He does try for a little while to focus on me instead of …."

"Instead of what?"

"Whatever else is on his mind. The church and its problems, I guess."

Our food arrived, and Beatrice reached for the hot sauce to spice up her gumbo. "You haven't even tasted it yet," I said. "How do you know it needs hot sauce?"

Beatrice smiled. "You can't get too much hot sauce."

Hot sauce was exactly what our marriage needed. I stared at the wicked-looking pepper on the label and then doused my rice and beans.

Beatrice blew on her gumbo and took a small bite. "I'm concerned about the church too," she said. "You know attendance is down—"

"Yes, I know." I took a wary bite of my rice and beans, and the flavor exploded in my mouth. Not too hot—just right. "I don't know how to help though. This whole business of being a preacher's wife is so foreign to me, and I'm awful at it!"

"What makes you think you're awful at it?"

"I feel like I'm being watched. I worry that whatever I do is going to be the wrong thing."

"Acadia, my dear," Beatrice said, putting down her spoon, "you're worrying too much about what other people think. Go with your own conscience. It's a pretty good measuring stick of what's right and what's not."

"My conscience is confused, I guess. There are things that aren't wrong exactly—at least not in my opinion—but might be inappropriate for a preacher's wife. Aren't there?"

Beatrice picked her spoon up and took another bite before she answered. "There are so many real troubles," she said. "Look outside yourself to see them and quit worrying about what is or isn't appropriate."

Her words reminded me of Peter's. "There are too many troubles in the world for me to ignore them," he had said. Then I thought of Sybil, of the troubles she faced, and of my helplessness in knowing how to reach her. Suddenly I felt chastised, both by Beatrice and Peter ... and the feeling made me want to defend myself.

I didn't even care if Maude Davis overheard me. "I feel like some of the people from church are always watching me to see if I'm doing something wrong. Like they want to catch me in the act."

Beatrice nodded. "That's possible. What worries me more is that there may be some people who are trying to sabotage Peter's efforts."

Maude Davis caught my eye. Her conversation with an elderly couple two tables over had ceased abruptly as she stared directly at us. When she caught my gaze, she looked away quickly.

If what Beatrice said was true, Peter's struggles were greater than I'd realized. "What can I do?" I asked, wondering if she had any answers for me. Indeed, if anyone had.

"Just be there for him. He'll figure things out if you're behind him." Beatrice pushed her bowl aside, though it was only half empty.

"You didn't eat much." I scooped up the last bite of my beans and rice and took a swig of my tea.

Joe arrived with dessert—small bowls of bread pudding. He placed one in front of Beatrice as well, although free dessert was not included with her order as with mine. "I thought you could use it," he said.

Beatrice smiled her thanks.

"What else is bothering you?" She spooned a tiny bite of the pudding.

I took my first bite before answering. Despite the plump, soft raisins ... which I didn't normally care for ... the dessert was delicious. I had gone this far, I thought. I might as well spill it all. "One of the things is money. Or the lack of it. Feeling like I have to order the $3.50 special instead of the $5.95, let alone the $10.00 broiled seafood platter. I know what you're thinking—that being able to eat out at all is a blessing. And of course, it is.

And we're lucky to have jobs when so many people don't. I know all that, and it just makes me feel worse. I hate myself for being so petty—"

"You aren't being that petty or that atypical. Why do you think there are so many preachers vying for jobs at the big wealthy churches and so few for a position like Peter's?"

I stared at Beatrice, who'd surprised me once more. The notion that other preachers' wives, and perhaps the preachers themselves, were also human made me feel a little less wicked. "Peter's not like that," I said.

"No, he's not. Peter's special."

We paid our bills and stepped out into the lemony winter sunlight. There was still a crowd waiting to be seated.

"Do you feel like a walk on the beach today?" I asked. "I should try to walk off some of these calories."

Beatrice glanced at her wristwatch. "I'd love to, but I better not. I've got a doctor's appointment."

"What's it for?" I asked, disappointed we weren't going to be able to continue our conversation. I noticed Beatrice's pallor, which was quite sallow. "Do you have the flu or something?"

"No, no, nothing like that. Just a routine visit," she said. "Acadia, keep up your faith. When I'm struggling with something, my strategy is to wear out my knees in prayer." She placed a gentle hand on my shoulder. "Still, I can't tell you what to do. You have to find your own way." She hugged me before rushing off to her car.

CHAPTER TWENTY-SEVEN

"Is Sybil there?"

"Who is this?" The female answering the phone sounded tired.

"This is Acadia Powers. I mean, Acadia O'Neil." I waited. When she said nothing, I added, "Her math teacher."

"I'll see if I can find her."

While I waited, a clattering like dishes falling to the floor was followed by an angry expletive nearby. Was that Bradley? Surely not. I cringed, wondering if my call was a bad idea.

"Ms. O'Neil?" Sybil sounded shy and sweet as usual but also uncertain.

"Yes, I just wanted to see how you're doing. I—"

"Don't ever call here again!" I shivered at the memory evoked by the sound of Bradley's voice. The line went dead.

What was *he* doing there? Did her parents approve? Perhaps they hadn't even noticed his presence. He'd be hard to ignore, though. Goose bumps rose on my arms and legs. I stared at the phone in my hand.

I was debating the pros and cons of paying a visit to Sybil's household when I fell into a fitful sleep that night. In a dream, I forced Peter to choose. "Who are you married to? I want to know. Is it me, or is it your church?"

Peter's eyes filled with pain and confusion and sadness. He said nothing, but his eyes widened. I nearly relented, tempted to feel his pain, to share his confusion.

Instead, I persisted. "Don't you remember our wedding vows? Didn't you promise to cherish *me*, to put *me* first?"

When he remained stubbornly silent, a rage so completely overtook me I was stunned by its intensity. In the next moment, I shrieked at Peter, my voice no longer human. He'd become a sheep, a docile-faced sheep, and I was a wolf—a vicious, ruthless wolf. When he lay bloodied and dying, his insides ripped apart, I was myself again. And I was sorry, so dreadfully sorrowful for what I'd done to this man I loved.

I awoke and bolted upright, my face distorted and wet with tears, my heart thumping rapidly. Relief poured through me that the dream was over—relief mingled with horror that I should have such a dream. Hadn't I dreamed something similar long ago, before we married?

Peter stirred beside me. "What is it, Cadi?" he said, his hand on my shoulder, his voice thick with sleep.

"Nothing. Just a bad dream." I eased myself back down beside him. "Go back to sleep."

Peter's breathing evened, and I knew he had fallen back asleep.

I lay awake as the morning light broke through our window-shades and formed crisscross patterns over the walls and bed. I was afraid to let sleep come, fearful the dream would return. Peter twitched occasionally and let out a couple of low moans.

Finally, I stretched and swung my legs over the side of the bed, gingerly so as not to wake Peter. In the kitchen, I put coffee on to percolate.

Peter joined me before long. "Something smells good," he said, kissing my ear.

Placing my hands on both sides of his head, I drew him toward me for a better kiss. I needed to feel him close and normal.

"Mm, I like that," he said. "Whoa … you're trembling. Dream still bothering you?"

I shook my head, not wanting to talk about it.

"Funny," Peter said. "I had a really sad dream myself, and I don't usually dream. Or if I do, I don't usually remember them. This one is vivid though … so vivid."

With his words, my own dream came back to me in all its bloody horror. With an effort, I repressed a shudder. Sensing Peter wanted to talk more about his dream, I waited for him to continue.

"Is that coffee ready?" he asked.

"Looks that way." I rose to pour us each a steaming cup.

"Do you want to tell me about your dream?" Peter asked, as I'd feared he might.

"I can't. Besides, it's bad luck to tell a dream before breakfast."

I set Peter's coffee in front of him, along with the jar of coffee creamer and a spoon. "You don't really believe that, do you?"

"That's what my grandmother always said but take your chances if you want to."

I took a seat beside Peter and reached for the creamer.

I had guessed correctly. He was ready to open up, and I could only listen in wonder as he expounded. "Dad was in the hospital in my dream. He was dying, Cadi … unsaved. I kept telling him it wasn't too late."

Peter's eyes filled with tears, and he rubbed at them with a knuckle. His voice cracked so much he had difficulty continuing. "Dad said he couldn't accept Christ without faith, and then he had a coughing spasm. He was so frail, Cadi."

In his dream, Peter sank to the floor to appeal to God to touch his dad's heart. As he did, a tunnel opened up in the ceiling. The cool, sterile hospital room faded away. In the distance, the tunnel forked, and Peter saw what lay ahead for his dad. A choice. He still had a choice. One path loomed wide and larger than life, with a thousand figures drinking and dancing and beckoning to the frail soul. Behind them, plain to Peter's sharp eyes but invisible to Gerald's aging ones, the fires of hell burned hotly. A kindly hand reached out from the other path. But the hand was filmy, the angels becoming dimmer by the moment.

Peter lunged toward the tunnel ahead of his father, anxious to lead the way, to silence the party goers. "No, Dad, not that way!" he tried to say. But words would not come. The narrow tunnel shriveled away, leaving his father lost and helpless.

"Oh, Peter," I said when he finished, his face more strained than I'd ever seen. "I'm so sorry. It was only a dream though. You know what I think it means?"

"I *thought* it was just a dream." Peter smiled, but his eyes were sad. He took a sip of his coffee.

"I think we should go visit your parents. Father's Day is coming up, and we didn't go for Mother's Day. We can celebrate both."

"Won't do any good," Peter said.

"You don't know that."

He hesitated before he spoke. "I'm afraid, Cadi. Afraid of failing him again."

Seeing Peter so close to despair awakened something inside me, a real longing to help this man I loved. Not just because I wanted to be a better person, but because I wanted something for him. I was deeply touched that he'd shared the dream with me, even if I couldn't reciprocate.

I wrapped my arms around him. "We should try, anyway."

CHAPTER TWENTY-EIGHT

By the second evening of our visit, Gerald had quit trying to hide his flask. Watching him tilt it up, I felt Elinor's gaze shift from him to me and back to her husband. I turned away quickly, not wanting her to see my pity. This time, instead of waxing eloquent or sentimental as he sometimes did, he became belligerent.

"What are you looking at?" he bellowed at Elinor.

"Nothing."

"Do I look like *nothing* to you?"

She sighed. "I hate when you get like this. At least try to be decent while we have guests."

"Guests? What guests? Are you calling your own son a guest?"

We were seated in the living room, watching *Three's Company*. I tried to focus on the program, wishing I were anywhere else and wondering how I could stand another day here. I reminded myself that my parents' household was not much better, that all families had their problems.

"I asked you a question, woman. Who are you calling a guest?" He took another swallow from his flask.

"You know what I mean." Elinor smoothed her skirt over her knees.

"I know that I'm getting sick and tired of your constant nagging and complaining."

Elinor patted the space next to her on the sofa. "Come, sit down for a while and watch the show. We could all use a good laugh."

"I hate that foolish crap. You know how I feel about those stupid shows, and still shist—" He drew a breath and proceeded more carefully. "You insist on having them on."

"Would you prefer to watch something else?" Elinor asked.

"Would you prefer to watch something else?" He mimicked his wife in a high-pitched voice. "I'd prefer to be treated like the ... the king of my own ... house ... hold. Isn't a man's home supposed to be his castle? Now there's a laugh for you. All I get around here is nagging and complaining. Did you ever hear the like?"

He looked at me, and I shook my head, ashamed for them all.

"See—she agrees with me," he said. "The *guest* agrees with me. I tell you, if that woman's not sp … spending my money, she's whining about past-due bills."

He sank onto the sofa beside his wife. She turned to look at him, a spark of fire in her tired eyes. "I'm not exactly spending your money on party dresses," she said. "What am I supposed to do when the refrigerator goes out?"

Peter reached across the coffee table to squeeze his mother's hand, and he knocked over a half-empty glass of water. Relieved to have something to do, I scurried from the room to find a towel. I suspected he was wishing he had the money to help them out with their past-due bills but also thinking how little we had to spare.

I thought again of my parents' home, where there was always plenty. How unimportant money had seemed to me when I lived with them and how large it loomed now when there was never quite enough.

Evening finally arrived, and we escaped to Peter's childhood bedroom. He apologized for the tension.

"Coming here was my idea." I pulled a brush through my hair.

"And don't think I don't appreciate your motives." He kissed the tip of my nose, avoiding the cold cream I had slathered on my face. "Tomorrow, I have to tell him what I think."

"What do you mean?"

"I have to beg him to turn to God for help. It's the only answer."

Afraid Peter was setting himself up for further disappointment, I said nothing.

"Pray with me, Cadi." Peter sank to his knees beside the bookcase bed. I hesitated, staring at the old Hardy Boys books, the worn copy of a children's Bible, and the paperback classics by Dickens and Steinbeck. Above them, the poster of the Seven Original Astronauts was a little ragged around the edges. Reluctantly, I knelt beside him, convinced I'd been wrong to persuade him to come.

We said our goodbyes the following day and prepared to return to Sugar Sands, Peter's face weighed by despair. He'd made an attempt to talk to his father. Though I hadn't heard the exchange, I knew from their faces the conversation had not ended well. Gerald was asleep in the worn recliner as Elinor walked us out.

Hope glimmered in the tired face when she hugged me goodbye. "Do you think I'll be able to call myself Grandma any time soon?"

I laughed as if she'd made a joke.

"Can you believe that?" I said to Peter as we drove off.

"What?"

"Didn't you hear what she said?"

Peter shook his head glumly, and I knew this was not the time to launch into a tirade about being pressured into becoming parents before we were ready. He drove in silence, his hands clenched on the steering wheel.

"Would you like me to drive so you can relax?" I asked.

He scoffed. "I doubt if your driving would do the trick."

"So you don't trust me as a driver," I teased, trying to lighten the mood.

"It's not that."

"Do you want to talk about what's troubling you?"

He pounded his fist against the steering wheel and turned to face me, green eyes ablaze in the sunlight. "Why can't I reach him when I want to so badly?"

His face was a jigsaw puzzle of raw emotions: longing and frustration, disappointment and confusion. Where was the tenderness ... the love ... the longing I'd read in these same eyes when we were dating? I couldn't think of another soul whose eyes revealed so much of his heart as my Peter's.

Thinking how often and how fervently he'd prayed for his father's soul, I suspected I was over my head. Still, I wanted to comfort him. "You know what you always tell me—that our time and God's time are so different. What seems like an eternity to us passes in a flash for him. Maybe you just need to give God more time to work on his heart."

I put my hand on the back of Peter's neck. He relaxed his grip on the steering wheel and covered my hand with his. "Thanks, Cadi," he said. "You're right as usual."

Right as *usual?* Did he really see me in such an unrealistic light? Before I could recover, he slipped his hand under my denim skirt and stroked my thigh. I flinched. Peter's ability to switch from serious to amorous was as amazing to me as his capacity for eating no matter what mood he was in.

"It's all right," he whispered. "We're married."

I laughed, glad he was coming out of his depression. A sign in front of a fried chicken restaurant caught my eye: *Six-piece chicken bucket, $3.50.*

"Hey. Let's stop there and get some chicken for a picnic."

"Too late," Peter said as he drove past.

"You can turn around. Aren't you hungry?"

He was already turning the car around. "You know better than that. I'm—"

"Always hungry." We spoke in unison.

Soon, the aroma of fried chicken flooded our car, making my stomach growl. "Now that we've got the food," Peter said, "where's the picnic spot?"

"I was counting on you to handle that detail."

Half an hour later, we still hadn't located a park or a picnic table. "I think there's a blanket in the trunk," I said. "We don't need a table. We can just spread out anywhere."

"I believe there's a river around here somewhere," Peter said. "Why don't you look at the map and see how far it is?"

Before I could figure out where we were in relation to the lines on the map, Peter had pulled off the road. A grassy green stretch of land nestled beside a tea-colored stream. "How's this?" Peter asked.

"Perfect."

Hungry, we devoured the chicken and all the trimmings within minutes. "This was a great idea," Peter said.

"The food *was* good, wasn't it? Reminds me, though, of something my grandmother used to say. She had a sister-in-law who was known to be an excellent cook. Grandma's theory was that she took so long getting the food onto the table that *anything* would have tasted wonderful by then."

"Speaking of your grandmother," Peter said, "we should go visit your folks."

"Grandma's dead," I reminded him.

"I know. I was thinking of your parents."

"One of these days."

"I meant now."

"Now? Like today?"

"Yes."

"I don't think that's a good idea at all." Excuses flew around in my brain, all the reasons I could use to dissuade Peter from this harebrained notion. "Don't you need to get back to Sugar Sands?"

"I suppose I do. But work will always be there. There's nothing that can't wait another day or so."

"The house is *way* out of our way. And they aren't expecting us." Too many excuses made my protests seem lame, but I couldn't stop myself. "We don't even know if they're home."

"We'll find a payphone, and you can call them." Peter gathered up the remnants of our meal and crammed the bones and scraps into a sack. "Can't you?"

I said nothing as I helped Peter clean up. Then I folded the blanket, a delay tactic, hoping Peter would drop the idea. When we got back to the car, he reached for the map. "What are you looking for now?" I asked. But I knew.

"Your father deserves a Father's Day visit as much as mine," Peter said. "More in fact."

"I still don't think it's a good idea."

Peter's jaw was set … his mind made up.

"I can't make you forgive them for whatever they did, but I can insist we visit them." Peter squeezed my hand.

I sighed. At least this turn of events had taken his mind off his dad. His next words, however, took me by surprise. "If we're ever going to be parents ourselves, we've got to come to terms, somehow, with our own."

Part IV

Challenges Mount

My mind carries on an idiotic monologue of self-reproach. Or I lie awake bewailing the day's mistakes. I wince before them. I call myself names I would never call other people. I am stung and tormented by self-lacerations.
Marjorie Holmes

CHAPTER TWENTY-NINE

Being at home again—or rather, in my parents' house—with Peter at my side felt at once familiar and strange. I rummaged through the piano bench to locate the music to a song I once played in a recital. I sat down and placed my fingers on the keys, wondering if the patterns would fail me. They did not, though my fingers were stiff from lack of practice.

When I finished, Peter applauded. He stood nearby, looking at the array of photographs my mother had displayed on the baby grand piano. I rose and peered over his shoulder. He held a brass-framed photograph of me and Gracie Winters, the two of us sporting summer tans and white shorts and raising our tennis trophies high in triumph. My trophy was slightly taller than Gracie's.

"She was the runner-up?" Peter asked.

"That's Gracie Winters. She was a better player than I was, really, but she never could beat me. I just played smarter."

"Maybe you wanted to win more," Peter said.

"Maybe I did."

"I was always disappointed," Mom said, "that Acadia gave up the piano when she did."

"I didn't give up the piano. I just quit taking lessons."

"Same thing."

I shrugged, remembering the battles over practicing the piano. I didn't mind the lessons. But the more my mother insisted I practice, the more I resisted. When she forced me to set aside a time every day for piano, I always found a way to waste the time spent or to find excuses to avoid practicing altogether. Finally, when she told me she and Dad were tired of throwing money away, I said, "Not anymore. I quit."

I didn't want to think about the other times I gave up too easily. And I certainly didn't want to face the possibility that quitting was a character flaw, one which might surface again in the not too distant future. Quitting my piano lessons was not a memory I wanted dredged up for Peter's scrutiny or mine, and I shot Mom a look.

Taking the hint, she picked up another photo, one of Dad and me holding a stringer of striped bass. I wore a pair of plaid shorts, a Monkees T-shirt, and a huge grin. "Remember that day?" she asked.

I nodded. I had been about nine, and the three of us spent the weekend camping on Kentucky Lake. All in all, we had a glorious time—despite the mosquitoes and the sunburn. After that, I begged for a repeat. But Mom seemed to remember the bad parts more vividly than the good … and the second camping trip never happened.

She set the photo down carefully. "Tell me about your church, Peter," she said. "And I want to hear about your job too, Acadia." She included me as an afterthought, consistent with her view that the husband's job should always come first.

I listened with admiration as Peter delicately skirted around all the troublesome aspects weighing so heavily on his mind. He managed, without altering the truth, to describe his experience in our congregation using amusing anecdotes filled with fascinating characters. I tried to match his narrative with some anecdotes about my students, but I lacked Peter's flair for storytelling.

By the time we finished our first meal with my parents, I was growing restless. "What's wrong?" Peter asked when we were out of my parents' earshot.

He and I were cleaning up the kitchen, at Peter's insistence and despite my mother's protests. "I don't know." I shut the dishwasher with a bang. "Yes, I do. Everything is so civil—I'm going crazy."

"I thought that's what you wanted."

"What *I* wanted? I didn't want to come here in the first place, if you'll remember." My voice rose, and Peter shushed me.

"All right, all right. I see your point," he said.

I lowered my voice. "They are so superficial. It's like"—I searched for the right words to convey my frustration—"like they've raised me to believe all of life is clean and tidy, and things like Sybil's experiences just don't happen. I'm afraid they've molded me to think that way too. So, when I'm confronted with something truly ugly, I go into denial." I located two more dirty plates and reopened the dishwasher to make room.

"So what do you want from them?" Peter asked. Before I could retort, he went on. "Don't tell me you don't want anything, because I don't believe that's true."

"Maybe I want to talk about what went wrong in my childhood, why I was never good enough for them."

Mom came up then and caught my last words. My voice had risen again, and perhaps I wanted her to hear. I expected her to pretend not to. "Oh, Acadia," she said, running her fingers through her short, frosted hair. "Is that what you think?" She picked up a dishcloth and began to shine the rings around the burners on the stove.

"You were always comparing me to other girls who were more— more appropriate. 'Why can't you act like Sara Truman or dress like Tracy Williams?'"

Mom put the dishcloth down and whirled to face me. "No, I didn't, or if I did, I didn't mean it like that."

"How *did* you mean it, Mom?"

Picking the cloth up again, she moved to the glass front of the built-in microwave, sprayed it with cleaner, and rubbed furiously. "I just wanted you to be happy. And I thought you'd be happier if you—if you were more like the others instead of always having to be so different."

"Is that what you thought—that *I* would be happier?"

"Yes!"

"I don't think so. I think you thought I would be less of a blight on your perfect life." I was trembling now. "Wasn't that why you let me quit going to church without a fight—so that I wouldn't be an embarrassment to you and Dad—to preserve your precious reputations?"

"Cadi, Cadi," Peter said, taking my arm.

I shook him off. "You started this … so let us finish."

"What do you want me to say, Acadia?" A slight quaver edged my mother's question, spoken in a near whisper.

Dad entered the kitchen and stood quietly beside Peter. There was more gray in his sideburns than I recalled, but otherwise he had changed little. He moved to my mother and put an arm around her. How familiar this felt, always the two of them against me. Now, when Peter should have been on my side, I had the feeling that *he* was on theirs as well.

My eyes stung with tears of self-pity, and I spun around to run from the room. Peter caught me and pulled me to him. "I think you should answer your mother, if you can," he said.

"I don't *know* what I want her to say," I said between sobs.

Mom stepped toward us. "I love you, Acadia. Your dad and I have always loved you. Surely you know that."

Oh, to be loved—wasn't that what I always wanted? Then, why did it feel so empty? Had I been wrong all along? Wrong about everything? I looked up into Peter's eyes, and they brimmed with compassion. As clearly as if he had spoken the words out loud, his look told me we shouldn't care who was right or wrong. Still, I wanted to argue. I needed to figure out who was right—whether my parents' view of life and parenting and religion was as hypocritical as I believed for so long, or whether all my rebellion had been for nothing. Even if Peter was right—and there it was again ... was Peter *right*? Why did I always care who was right? More than that, why did I *need* to be right?

My gaze met Mom's, and it was she who spoke first. "I know we've made mistakes, Acadia. Those other girls—the ones I always compared you to—a couple of them have turned out to be a lot more trouble to their parents than you ever were."

"Really?" I had not kept up with Sara Truman or Tracy Williams or the others since I left for college but figured they were thriving as always.

"Sara Truman and Tracy Williams have been in rehab off and on for drugs and alcohol abuse, while you—you always made good grades. Your dad and I have been so proud. We just never knew how to tell you ..."

My mother broke down, and I moved from Peter's arms to hers.

I had no words. Maybe this inability to speak my feelings was something I inherited from them. Dad patted me awkwardly on the shoulder. As I looked up, his face blurred before my eyes, and I saw tears in his eyes as well.

"We hope you'll come to visit us soon," Peter said when we left. "Our place isn't big, but we do have an extra bed."

I thought of Mom and Dad squeezing into the tiny spare bedroom, where they would have to turn sideways to wheel their suitcases through the door. "Yes, do come," I said. In that moment I meant it.

CHAPTER THIRTY

That night I lay awake, tired as I was, for a long time … remembering. In the memory, I was very young, about five or six. I must have started school already because I pleaded with my mother to get me a little sister. Most of my new friends at school had brothers or sisters or both.

To take my mind off baby girls, my parents had taken me to an amusement park. We stood in front of a tracked ride of little cars, with real steering wheels and gas pedals. They were not connected in a circle like the other rides. I could see the difference, and it scared me.

"You can do it," Dad had urged. "It will be fun. You'll see."

Lying in my bed with Peter, for an instant I could clearly see the blue Kentucky Wildcats baseball cap my dad wore that day. How young he had been, nearly as young as Peter.

I had hesitated, wondering how my parents could be so foolhardy as to push me toward certain danger. "I don't know how to drive. I'm not big enough yet."

"Yes, you are," Mom said. "Look at that little boy."

I followed her gaze. Sure enough, a little boy, no older than me, climbed out of one of the cars, unharmed. He had curly hair, and he wore a huge smile, displaying very white teeth with one missing in the front.

I allowed myself to be persuaded, but I was not convinced. I figured the boy understood things about cars I might never know.

"Tell me how," I said.

"How to what?"

"How to drive."

My parents laughed, and I wondered afresh why they were so joyfully sending me off without a second thought.

"Turn the steering wheel to the right to go right, and turn it to the left to go left," my dad said. "Push the pedal on the right to go, and the one on the left to stop."

I had recently learned my right from my left, and I repeated his words over and over in my head as a man in a blue shirt helped me into a little red car. At the last minute, I turned to look for my mother and father. For a second, I couldn't find them. I felt as if they had left me forever. Then I saw them, Dad with a small camera pointed at me and Mom smiling broadly. "I changed my mind!" I called. "I don't want to do this." Before I could get out, the man in the blue shirt had reached inside the car, pushed something, and I was moving down the track.

Cool air rushed against my face, and the thrill of the ride took hold. For a time, I zipped straight down the track, exhilarated at my sense of power, my mouth spread wide in a delighted grin. Then, ahead of me, the track curved abruptly. I couldn't remember which foot I was supposed to use or if I should turn the steering wheel with or against the curve. Panic overwhelmed me as I headed into the curve. I turned the wheel sharply, surprised my car stayed on the track, although for one terrifying moment it jarred against the side of the track, trying to jump off.

Relief washed over me as the track straightened out for a time. At the next bend, I couldn't tell if the curve was the same as the last one or different. Again I turned, convinced for a second I had chosen wrong and waiting to spin out of control. Once more, after a brief jarring, my little red car and I sailed safely around the corner. By the fourth curve, I had discovered that even if I took my hands off the steering wheel, I was still safe. With that certainty, my fear vanished. Strangely, the thrill of the ride had been lessened as well.

My legs trembled when I climbed out.

Mom beamed. "See, that was fun! Wasn't it?"

"Can I have one of those?" I pointed to a girl with long dark braids a few years older than I was. She was eating a pink cloud on a stick.

"That's cotton candy," my mother said. "It's just spun sugar and not very healthy."

"Oh, let the child enjoy herself," Dad said.

I could hardly wait to taste the sweet pink cloud. The reality of cotton candy, however, was a huge disappointment. I wasn't sure what I expected, but the glob tasted a lot like nothing to me. After a time, I offered what remained to my father. He ate it, despite Mom's frown.

On the way home, Dad stopped our car abruptly as a series of sirens pierced the air. For a long, long time, we were able to move only very slowly. When we finally started to move faster, there was a red car with its front end all crunched up like a potato chip someone had stepped on. A man with carrot red hair was being wheeled on a white cot. He didn't move as we drove past.

"Is he dead?" I asked.

"I don't think so," my mother said. "If he were dead, they would cover him up, most likely."

I had let this register and then Dad said, "Of course he could be dead, but they haven't pronounced him dead, yet."

"Pronounced?"

Dad explained—despite Mom's warning glance—"A doctor will look at him, and see if he's alive or dead. If he's dead, they pronounce him dead as of a certain time."

Mom rushed to add, "Of course that may not be the case at all. He may only have minor injuries."

Or he may be dead. Dead, like the little bunny rabbit my father ran over one day on the road. I'd begged him to turn around and go back. There was no point, he'd said. The bunny was dead.

A shiver ran through my body. How strange that in my little car, I could not go off the tracks, no matter how badly I drove. Yet, in this world—in the real world—a moment's poor choice could lead to being wheeled away like this red-haired man.

"Why?" I asked my parents.

"Why what?" Daddy asked. But I couldn't explain my question.

The memories faded into dreams and back into memories until I could no longer separate the two. Another memory ... or dream—I couldn't tell which—haunted me. I was a teenager, old enough to have a driver's license, still questioning God, much like I had questioned my father all those years earlier.

Having given up on ever receiving satisfactory answers from my parents to this question or any other, I lay alone in my bedroom on a Sunday morning. *Why, God? Why are there so many consequences, and why did you design the world this way? You could have made it safe, so that we never make the wrong choice. But you didn't. Why, God, why?*

I listened for his answer. When none came, I stared at the ceiling. My parents were at church. Would they have found answers there? Maybe they didn't ask questions—maybe they simply accepted life as it came. Was that what God wanted us to do?

I drifted in and out of sleep. Suddenly, I was driving a red car, and I was young and inexperienced. In the road ahead, I saw something dark. Unable to decipher what it was—something alive or only a tire or piece of rubber—I veered to the right. Then, on the verge of losing control as the car bumped off the pavement onto the curb, I swerved back to the left. I overcompensated and drove headlong against the flow of traffic. I gasped. *Why was everyone going the wrong way?*

I managed to dodge the cars even as I realized the fault was mine. I was the one in the wrong lane. And then the inevitable. I could no longer control the car. As I prepared myself for impact, I felt strangely calm. In this world with no consequences, I would not suffer. I would not die.

I bolted awake, damp and sticky with a cold sweat. I tried to recall whether I had ever driven in the wrong lane as I did in the dream. There was a familiarity about the experience, as if it had really happened to me, or perhaps I had only dreamed it before.

I struggled to understand the meaning of the dream. The world of safe cars, the unreal world of no consequences, seemed wrong. Hadn't God designed the world with cause and effect? Yet, sometimes God did allow second chances. At other times—like for the man with carrot hair who crashed while I was riding safe cars at an amusement park—there was no second chance.

How unfair, even random, everything seemed. Why, God? The question I had been asking all my life remained unanswered. *Why... why... why?*

How could you design a universe where individuals were free to choose, where choices mattered ... and where, somehow, in the end everything was fair? I couldn't think of a way. I could only feel grateful that God decided, and not me. With this thought, I finally fell into unfettered sleep.

CHAPTER THIRTY-ONE

The next time I woke, I glanced at the clock … past six. I slipped quietly out of bed. I padded to the bathroom, splattered cold water on my face, and brushed my teeth.

My mind replayed my dream, and I pondered its implications. I made a pot of coffee and busied myself frying bacon and eggs. Grease splattered, and the aroma must have worked its way into the bedroom.

Peter emerged, sleepy-eyed but smiling. "Something smells wonderful," he said.

I tilted my head for his kiss.

"What got you so energized today?" he asked.

"I had a strange night." I smiled at him. "I couldn't seem to shut my thoughts off. When I did, I had this crazy dream … several crazy dreams actually … sort of rolled into one."

He poured himself a cup of coffee and listened intently while I summarized my disjointed night. He made no comment but rose after a time to help me with the toast and marmalade, his face thoughtful. I forked the bacon onto a plate, then turned my attention to the eggs. I cracked one, dropping it carefully into the bacon grease. I watched it, testing the edges to see if it was ready to turn.

"Why do you only cook one egg at a time?" Peter asked.

"I'm afraid I'll break the yellow if I get them too close together." I realized my way of frying eggs meant the first one was likely to get cold before I finished. "How many do you want anyway?"

"Two's plenty." Peter reached for the spatula. "Here, let me finish the eggs."

I surrendered the spatula gladly and finished setting out the dishes, napkins, margarine, and hot sauce. Beatrice's penchant for hot sauce had rubbed off, first on me and now, on Peter.

He managed to fry two eggs at a time without breaking either yolk.

"Think you're smart, don't you?"

He shrugged. "What can I say?" We sat to eat, and he offered thanks. "What do you think your dream means?"

"I'm not sure." I unscrewed the top from the hot sauce and shook several drops onto the nearly perfect eggs. "I think I've been struggling all my life with questions of why—why God lets bad things happen sometimes, why some people get better breaks than others, why life seems so unfair."

Peter nodded, sopping the runny egg yolk with his toast. "Like what?"

"Like why some people are born with different urges. You know what I mean?"

"I do. Like alcohol, or being attracted to the same sex—"

"Or being too inclined to question things. Do you think it's wrong—to ask those kinds of questions?" I asked.

"I'm not sure what's right or wrong anymore."

Peter's words and, more than that, his tone of voice took me by surprise. Both had a negative ring I'd only heard from him before in connection with his father. "What's the matter?" I asked.

"The church is supposed to be like a family, with the members encouraging and supporting one another. Not like this." As he talked about the fighting that divided the congregation, I felt ashamed. His problems were so much more tangible than mine. If I was trying to become selfless, like Beatrice, I had a long way to go.

"A lot of families are riddled with infighting and division too," I said, thinking of Sybil's household and the commotion I could hear through the phone. "So maybe it's not so surprising for the church to be like a squabbling family."

"I suppose." Peter pushed his plate back. "Still, I know God hates this kind of thing."

"Why did you say what you did?"

"Which part?"

"About not knowing what's right or wrong anymore."

He hesitated. When he did speak, the crease between his eyes was deeper than I'd ever seen. "I worry I'm the one who started all the contention," he said. "I came here with all these ideas aimed at stimulating growth and attracting young people, and they're all backfiring. Some of the members make a pretty good case against it."

"Against what? Growth or young people?"

Peter offered a half smile—not quite the smile I knew and loved. "Against me, I guess. Against my new-fangled ideas. To hear them talk, you'd think I was Satan's right-hand man. They almost convince me."

"It's that man, Barry Davis. Am I right? Everything is his fault." I crammed a last bite of toast into my mouth and pushed my plate aside. Thinking of the tall, stooped man with his shifty eyes and sly wife, of his taking the mirth and enthusiasm away from my Peter, I wanted to slam my fist into something. I chewed furiously, crying out when I bit the inside of my jaw.

"He is part of the opposition, Cadi," Peter said, "but he makes some good points. What if he's right?"

"I refuse to believe he makes any good points." I massaged the inside of my mouth, checking my fingers for blood.

"He uses Scripture to back them—"

"What points?"

I had to convince Peter of what seemed obvious. He was too decent to see how others weren't always, how they might be self-centered and jealous, and … yes … even malicious. And if their hearts weren't in the right place, they could use—or misuse—Scriptures to prove whatever they wanted. Maybe because I believed myself to be more like Mr. Davis in some ways, I felt sure I could see through his arguments to the agenda beneath.

"I've been planning a camping trip for the young people. I thought we could sing hymns over a campfire and roast hot dogs and marshmallows. A couple of the kids wanted to bring an electric guitar and a drum set. I didn't see any reason to object. When the Davises found out about the plans, they were livid."

"Why?"

"Next thing, they said, we would be bringing them into the worship service."

"Would that be so wrong?" I asked.

"I'm telling you, I don't know anymore. Some think it would be. They believe that if something isn't explicitly mentioned in the New Testament worship service, it shouldn't be added."

"What about microphones?" I said. "What about lecterns? What about air conditioning?"

"I know, I know. I guess they'd say those things are less integral, just tools to facilitate worship."

"Couldn't you say the same of a guitar?"

"You could... but if it offends a brother, should we avoid the change? Isn't that what the Apostle Paul calls putting a stumbling block into your brother's path?"

"Where does it say that?"

I cleared the table, stacking the dishes in the sink while Peter fetched his worn Bible. He flipped easily to the passage, and we bent over it together. We read silently for a few verses. Then he began reading aloud in Romans 14 from the American Standard Version, while I leaned back to listen.

> I am in the Lord Jesus, and I know that there is no food that is wrong to eat. But if a person believes something is wrong, that thing is wrong for him. If you hurt your brother's or sister's faith because of something you eat, you are not really following the way of love.

I could tell Peter had read this Scripture so many times, he knew most of the words by heart. When he finished, he said, "I don't want to destroy anyone's faith. That's the last thing I want."

While I tried to think how to answer, I moved to the sink, ran water, and squirted dishwashing detergent.

"Leave them," Peter said. "I'll do them later."

I knew this conversation was important, and I didn't want to blurt out my first thought like I usually did. At last, I spoke. "Where do you draw the line? You can't cave in on every single change—because, after all, anything that gets changed is going to offend somebody."

"I know, but I don't want the members choosing sides ... lining up with me or lining up with Barry Davis."

He turned impassioned eyes on me before flipping rapidly to the first passage from Romans 14 to read: "So let us try to do what makes peace and helps one another."

He glanced up at me. "Am I doing that, Cadi? Can I honestly say that's what I'm doing?"

"I don't think this means peace at all costs, Peter." I reached for his Bible and scanned the passages he was reading. I read for a while, letting the words and their context sink in until I found what I wanted.

"Listen to this," I said, then read aloud: "Do not allow what you think is good to become what others say is evil. In the kingdom of God, eating and drinking are not important. The important things are living right with God, peace, and joy in the Holy Spirit. Anyone who serves Christ by living this way is pleasing God and will be accepted by other people."

"Sounds simple, I know," Peter said. "Doesn't feel that way to me, though. Not anymore."

"Yes, it is! Peter, you were on the right track when you came here. It's still simple."

"Oh, Cadi, I'm not sure." Then, in little more than a whisper, Peter said, "I'm so confused."

Now's my chance. If I needed Peter to leave the ministry, I had him right where I wanted him.

CHAPTER THIRTY-TWO

I didn't want him to leave like this, and I knew he wouldn't be happy if he did. "What are you confused about?" I said.

"So many things, Cadi, I don't know where to start."

"Start with one. Tell me one."

"All right. Take homosexuality," Peter said.

I gulped. This was a tough one.

"There are people in our church who think we should shun anyone we know to be living in—in a different lifestyle."

"Like keeping house badly? We could be in trouble!" I wandered over to the oven and traced the edge of the hood with a fingertip. I showed Peter the coating of dust, hoping to lighten the mood.

"No, like two men living together as a couple."

"I know," I said, sitting back down. "And they've been doing a pretty good job at shunning. I doubt if the two men who came in late that Sunday will ever come back."

"Exactly!" Peter said. "We chased them away before we even had a chance to reach them. To teach them. To save them."

"Not we. You and I didn't chase them away." I raked the crumbs on the table into a small pile near the edge.

"No, but we haven't chased after them either."

"We don't even know who they are." I brushed the pile of crumbs onto one hand and tossed them into the garbage.

"No, but in a town this size, we could find out if we wanted to. I'm afraid to find out, because I'm scared of creating that much more dissension. And I hate being such a coward—"

"You're not a coward!" I draped my arms around Peter and planted a kiss on his cheek. He felt scratchy—hadn't shaved yet.

"There's so much more pressure about what to preach for and against than I ever imagined. People can be misled by a leader's personality. If someone rubs you the wrong way—and I admit Barry Davis can do that—you may jump to thinking he's wrong about everything. That doesn't make it so."

"What are you saying?"

"I thought we should do anything we could to attract more young people. Offer basketball games, or beach volleyball, or parties or meals, or whatever just to get them to come. It's an opportunity to lead them to Christ."

"And you don't think so anymore?" I was dumbfounded at this turn-about.

"I'm not saying that. But we don't want to become part of the world just to make the world accept us. We're supposed to be different. If they don't come for the right reasons, then maybe—"

I cut him off before he could finish. "Still it has to be better than if they don't come at all. What's the matter with you? Why are you taking their side?" I peered at him, seeking answers. "You *are* confused. You're as confused as I am."

We stared at each other for a long moment, and then broke into laughter. Still laughing, Peter took me by the hand and led me into the bedroom. The thought of dirty dishes flickered through my head, but I didn't look back. Peter said he would do them later, and I believed he would.

Sometime later, after Peter had drifted off to sleep, I drifted back—back in time. To another me, a girl who would have been stunned and more than a little appalled to find herself lying awake and thinking about doctrinal issues. How long ago that was, and yet how close that cool October morning felt.

The trees outside strutted their red and gold wardrobes when I had popped into the kitchen, ready for church with my own new look in place. Tight jeans that flared wide from the knee down and a hot pink and royal blue tie-dyed T-shirt sporting a large patch on the back emblazoned with the peace sign. Another peace sign dangled from a chain around the waist of my Levi's. I had woven a series of brightly colored leaves into my hair that hung in two Indian-style braids. The leaves kept breaking though, so that I had to replace them with less brittle ones, a process taking a really long time. I wore a circlet of bird feathers in my hair, too, having debated for a while if this was too much.

Dad looked up from his newspaper, and Mom nearly dropped her coffee cup. Their expressions of horror mirrored each other. "You're not wearing that," Mom said.

"Why? God doesn't believe in peace? Or is it feathers he doesn't like?"

Dad shot me a warning look, but I ignored it. "I guess it's just me he doesn't love—if I dress like this."

"Of course God loves you, but not—he doesn't love how you're dressing—he expects you to show some respect when you dress for church."

"Fine. Then I'm not going. I don't want to go anyway," I said. Hadn't they learned anything from the Vietnam debacle? Boys not much older than I getting plowed down for no good reason.

Several of my classmates had brothers who died over there and others who came back bitter and confused. One boy in particular. Jimmy Rayburn, so sweet with shiny dark red hair, had always been kind to me even when he was with his friends. He was not afraid to treat a younger girl like she was a real person. I'd had a crush on him for years. Dead now, squashed like an insect with a fly swatter. Other boys were still there, risking their lives and their sanity, while my parents worried about the way I dressed for church.

My father glanced at his watch. "We're too late to have this debate right now." He had always hated being late, and I had waited until the last minute to make my appearance. "Is she going or isn't she?" he asked my mother.

Mom smoothed her gray pencil skirt over her hips and looked me up and down. "Not like that," she said. "Next Sunday, I expect you to look respectable."

"No." I muttered under my breath so softly I wasn't sure whether they heard me or not.

At the door, Mom looked back at me one last time, her exasperation palpable. "Why can't you dress like the other girls—and why don't you ever sit with them anymore?"

"Because I don't want to. I don't want to have anything to do with them." *Because they don't want to have anything to do with me.*

"Well, next week you're going to dress like them anyway."

"No," I said, my voice much louder than before.

Dad whirled around. "What did you say?"

"I said, *no*." I quaked with fear yet resolved to hold my ground. "There's nothing wrong with the way I'm dressed."

"Nothing wrong!" Mom's face turned scarlet. "Everyone would think you're a druggie or something."

"Then they're stupid and ignorant. They're the ones with the problem. Everyone in California dresses like this."

"How would you know what everyone in California wears?" Dad asked.

"What are you so worried about?" By then, my voice had risen to a shrill pitch as I realized exactly what they were worried about. "You don't care about me. You wouldn't care if I *was* a Satanist so long as nobody knew. All you care about is your *image!*"

"That's not true." Mom's voice was uncharacteristically weak. "We care about you too."

"You're absolutely right—we care about our image," Dad said. "I've worked too hard to get where we are in this community to let you just throw our reputations away on a whim."

"A whim?" All the pain and rejection from school collected in my gut, and I clutched my abdomen, feeling so sorry for myself and so misunderstood. Nausea and bile rose in my throat.

"I guess I won't be going to church with you anymore," I said, barely loudly enough to be sure they heard.

"I guess you won't," Dad said. He and Mom exchanged tired glances, and I waited for her to protest.

When she didn't, I slumped into a chair, silent and stunned. "Fine," I said, "if that's how you feel."

I was too proud to change my stance, and I stopped going to church that very day.

CHAPTER THIRTY-THREE

Beside me, Peter stirred, opened his eyes, smiled, and reached for my hand. "What are you thinking about?" he asked.

Was this episode from my past something I could share with Peter? I tried to think of the words to broach the subject. Instead I said, "I keep thinking about faith."

"Yeah?"

"The Bible talks so much about faith … seems like faith is the most important thing of all."

Peter propped himself up on an elbow to look at me, his eyes serious. "And now abide faith, hope, love, these three; but the greatest of these is love."

"First Corinthians."

"Yes."

"All right. But faith is definitely one of the big three."

"So?"

"Believing or not believing seems like something we can't control. If we just can't believe, how can God punish us for that?"

"Faith is more than belief, Cadi. Faith is active."

"What does that even mean?" I stared at him.

Peter reached over to stroke my hair almost absently as he considered his answer. "James tells us that demons believe. Faith is more about trust, about putting your life—your eternal life—in the hands of Jesus and counting on him to save you."

"I see that, I guess." Did I? I wasn't sure.

I curled against him, resting my face on his chest. Fuzzy chest hair tickled my nose.

"I wanted to be a preacher because I wanted to share the good news, but I'm learning it's so much more than that," Peter said.

I pushed away and gazed intently at this man I thought I knew. How could he have been so naïve? I thought back to all the times I worried about being unprepared to be a preacher's wife. I never imagined that Peter might be just as unprepared.

"You can't mean that," I said. "There's no way you could have expected to stand up in the pulpit week after week and do nothing more than deliver the same message every time."

"No, I guess not. But I'd rather talk about the positive stuff, like love and hope and grace and forgiveness—than about going to hell and about what people are doing or saying or thinking that's going to take them there."

"So what *should* be the attitude of the church toward homosexuals, in your opinion?" I asked, truly curious.

"We should love them, of course. And we should let them see our love before we start trying to change them."

"Then that's what you should do." I snuggled a little harder against his chest, wanting to cuddle a bit longer.

He gave me a quick peck on the lips, but his mind was apparently elsewhere. He sat upright. Obviously, he'd forgotten all about the dirty dishes.

"Cadi, am I being cowardly to focus on the easy part? Here's what's baffling me. I keep reading the New Testament ... these passages I know so well ... and everything seems clear to me while I'm reading. There were these religious leaders in Jesus's day, who thought they were so clever. They kept trying to find fault with Jesus everywhere he turned because he was always doing something new and ground-breaking. Something they thought was wrong."

Annoyed because I wanted to cuddle, I wasn't in the mood to listen anymore. Here he was, sitting up and spouting off about something that happened two thousand years ago. Still, Peter studied me as if waiting for a response. So I asked, "Like what?"

"Like healing on the wrong day of the week or failing to wash his hands before he ate." Peter's eyes glowed with an inner light, and I thought ... not for the first time ... what a powerful presence he would make on a stage. I nodded.

"When I'm reading, I feel like I'm just trying to follow Jesus's example and focus on the heart instead of tradition." Peter rose from the bed to pace while he talked and thought.

194

"But?" I pulled the sheet under my chin, stacked the pillows atop each other, and sank lazily into them.

"But when I'm with Barry Davis and some of the others, I start to doubt myself. I see myself through their eyes, and I start thinking I might be a false teacher. I can't know for sure if God sent me to Sugar Sands to shake things up or not."

"You believe God's in control, don't you?" I pushed back the sheet, rearranged the pillows, and began to do leg lifts, hoping Peter would notice and tease me as he often did.

"Of course." He seemed not to think my question relevant to his current train of thought but kept on talking almost as if I hadn't spoken. "So the question is ... are they the same, or not?"

I sighed, still restless, still needy, still longing for him to come back to bed for a few minutes. "Is *what* the same as *what*?"

"Is the situation here in Sugar Sands the same as the one in Jesus's day? Cadi, am I wrong?" He dropped back onto the bed beside me.

Peter's face was so troubled that, this time, when I reached up to pull him to my embrace, I was thinking more of his need for comfort than of my own. After a bit, I went to the kitchen to tackle the dishes.

At church the next Sunday, Peter struggled to find his voice. He preached on love. As this was one of his favorite topics, I was surprised at his difficulty. He stumbled over his words, even the words he read from Scripture, as if inattentive to the task at hand. Perhaps his train of thought had rushed ahead, leaving his voice behind.

Around me, bodies stirred and throats cleared, the way they often do when a sermon has gone on too long. Peter had not even been speaking for ten minutes. I crossed my legs, noticing a small brownish spot just below my left knee. Was that a bruise or a freckle, or a stain? Surely not an age spot. I rubbed at the spot, which did not fade.

I thought of Sybil, of her clear young skin, of the bruises that sometimes marred the tender flesh. She was not here today, and I realized I hadn't seen her at church for some time.

My mind wandered back to our most recent conversation. I'd called her house just a couple of days ago. Sybil answered herself, to my relief. I'd been bracing myself for her mother or … worse yet … Bradley. "I wondered if it would be all right for me to come over so we could talk in person," I said. "Some time when you're not working?"

"No. That's not a good idea."

"Maybe we could meet somewhere instead," I'd suggested.

After a brief hesitation, a male voice boomed. "Who's that? Who are you talking to?"

"I've got to go." The phone had gone dead.

I wondered where she was now, at this very moment. I rubbed distractedly at the spot on my leg again.

Silence had fallen over the congregation. I cocked my head and tried to pick up the thread of Peter's remarks.

"When I decided to be a preacher, everything seemed simple to me," he said. I realized he'd abandoned his planned sermon, and a shiver traveled down my spine at his courage. "I thought preaching was just about sharing the good news of God's gift with everyone I encountered. And who doesn't love to hear about a gift, a free gift, with no strings attached? The gift of Jesus Christ. That's what I thought."

Peter continued. "Then I got confused. I got to worrying about whether I was actually a false teacher myself." A few heads were shaking now, and Peter raised his hand. "There are some who have suggested I might be exactly that."

"I turned to the Word, and I read and read. I read some commentaries too, written by men smarter than I am. I got to questioning things I'd never questioned before, like whether I could cause somebody else to sin even though I was doing what I believed in my heart to be right. I've got to tell you. I'm perplexed by some of the more philosophical issues that have come up since I've been here. I do not have all the answers."

Peter paused for a long moment to let his admission sink in before he moved on. "I do know one thing though. You don't have to understand all the philosophical issues to do the Lord's will for your life. Matthew 18, verse 3, tells us … and I paraphrase … that unless you make yourself like a little child, you cannot enter the kingdom of heaven. The next verse after that one says the greatest person in the kingdom of heaven is the one who makes himself humble like a little child.

"Now we could take that verse, and we could get caught up trying to figure out if this means some people will be greater or more revered in heaven than others. But I don't think that's the point. What I get out of this passage is that whether I have all the answers or not really doesn't matter too much. And the same thing goes for you."

At this point, Peter's gaze seemed to probe my soul. I wondered if they all felt the way I did, like Peter was preaching to each of us alone. "I think it's time we get back to basics here at Sugar Sands. There are some things God hates, and those are the things we need to stay away from. First Corinthians 5, verses 11 and 12, list some of those sins—*sexual sins and greed, idol worship and lying about other people, getting drunk, and cheating people*. I'm using the wording from the International Children's Bible because I'm trying to think as simply and as humbly as a little child."

Peter held up his Bible for the congregation to see. The Bible was bright red with a large picture of Jesus's face, or someone's perception of Jesus's face, on the front. This was not the Bible Peter usually read. I wondered when he had bought this one. The Bible reminded me of the one I'd seen in his bookcase in Kansas, only newer and brighter. Peter was returning to basics.

"There's plenty in this list," Peter said, "for us to worry about without fighting over basketball goals and recreation centers for our young people."

I heard a sharp intake of breath from an elderly gentleman behind me, and I figured he was the one who objected to using camping trips and team sports to reach out to young people.

"Another thing God hates is division," Peter went on. "Jude wrote about this in his letter to all who have been called by God: 'These are the people who divide you, people whose thoughts are only of this world, who do not have the Spirit.'

"Now, I'm not saying we've got anybody like that here. Not at all. When I read this passage, I just look at myself. I ask you to do the same. I ask myself if I'm too focused on this world, and especially I ask myself if I'm dividing you—because that's the last thing I should be doing."

I could hear a rustling, as some individuals behind me and throughout the small auditorium shifted in their seats. One man rose and walked out the door. I cringed, waiting to see if others would follow. Then a man's voice rang out. "Amen!"

Several others echoed, "Amen."

"Another thing God makes pretty clear in his Word," Peter said, "is what he *likes* to see in us. God wants us to love each other. I'm going to

SONG OF SUGAR SANDS

read one of my favorites from all the passages in Scripture." Peter's green eyes shone, and my heart swelled with love for this fervent man who cared so much and believed so deeply.

I had heard Peter recite his favorite passage on many occasions. Yet, somehow on this particular Sunday in Sugar Sands, Alabama, the words reverberated in my soul as if I was hearing them for the very first time.

"'Now we see as if we are looking into a dark mirror. But at that time, in the future, we shall see clearly. Now I know only a part. But at that time I will know fully, as God has known me. So these three things continue forever: faith, hope, and love. And the greatest of these is love.'"

Peter was silent for a long moment, and my heart thumped hard. Around me hardly a child stirred. There was a feeling in the air of waiting and of reverence at the power in these words. I was not the only one who sensed it.

Peter went on. "I know all of you have heard these verses many times before. Do you remember what comes next? The next verse reads, 'Love, then, is what you should try for.' That's pretty clear, isn't it?"

Several folks shouted, "Amen," while a few resounded with a heartfelt, "Yes."

"I want to believe," Peter went on, "that if we focus on loving the Lord and loving each other and avoiding the things we know God hates, we're going to be too busy to get into petty squabbles among ourselves."

"Won't you rise and sing with me?" Peter's voice rang out strong and clear and alone.

Before our Father's throne,
We pour our ardent prayers;
Our fears, our hopes, our aims are one,
Our comforts, and our cares.

I stood and added my voice, not as strong or as clear as Peter's but determined. Throughout the auditorium, a number of other voices joined in. "Blest be the tie that binds ... Our hearts in Christian love."

When we sounded like a chorus, I turned to see the people behind me. Some, their voices lifted joyously, had lost their critical, bored, or politely attentive masks. Among these was Sybil, who was sitting in the back pew. She must have slipped in after the service began.

But there were others. Mr. and Mrs. Davis sat stiffly in their pews, their mouths clamped resolutely shut. Several members stood but were not singing. A few others remained seated, faint frowns on their brows. I knew the war had not ended. Still, perhaps one battle had been won.

When the service was over, the words to the song continued to play in my head. *The fellowship of kindred minds … is like to that above.* As these words repeated, I shook hands and patted baby cheeks and greeted a host of members by name. I realized with some surprise that I'd begun to put most of the names and faces together, a feat I once feared I could never manage.

Several people congratulated me on Peter's sermon, as if I had something to do with his efforts. Beatrice warmly squeezed my hand. Suddenly, I felt a tug on my sleeve, and I turned to face Sybil.

Her cheeks were flushed, and her round blue eyes shone with tears. "I need to talk to you," she said.

CHAPTER THIRTY-FOUR

I bustled about the kitchen assembling the materials for a picnic on the beach, thinking back to my first picnic with Sybil—my initial shock at her confession, the pained expression behind the innocent eyes, the way she jarred me from my complacency with the world. I'd hoped this time would be different, that she'd have good news. Surely, she was anxious to tell me she'd finally broken up with Bradley once and for all.

The day was clear and hot except for some lazy puffs of cloud. A pleasant breeze caressed my bare arms as I left my car at the designated meeting point. Sybil's rattletrap of a car, a blue Ford station wagon whose faded wood side panels were partially askew, was already parked and empty when I arrived. I scanned the beach for her. She perched erect on the sand, a faded pink blanket beneath her, her hands clutched about her knees. How small and vulnerable she looked in the frame of endless sky and ocean and sand.

I called out to her as I approached, picnic basket in hand. A few pails of purple and yellow lay sideways or upside down in the sand, adding a splash of color to the vanilla of the sand. Amidst a row of uniform, dark-green rented umbrellas, an occasional blue and white, or rainbow-striped one, stood out of line, near the water's edge, asserting its uniqueness—much as I had done in high school.

"I brought cookies," Sybil said when I drew near. She indicated a sack to her right. "I hope you like peanut butter."

"They're one of my favorites."

She made room for me on the blanket, and I dropped down beside her. The water was murky with debris, almost brown with just a thin rim of deep blue on the horizon. The sky above was a richer, sweeter blue but no longer clear. The scattered puffs of clouds had gathered to form one huge teardrop-shaped mass, obscuring the sun. Families with kids dotted the beach. Brows puckered as the adults glanced toward the cloud.

I waited for Sybil to speak.

Nearby, a young mother busied herself with four small blond boys, the youngest not yet walking and the oldest no more than seven. A tattoo of some sort, perhaps a butterfly or a flower, was just visible on her lower back above the line of her swimsuit ... still an infrequent sight here in Sugar Sands. The two older boys struggled to manipulate skim-boards, while the two younger ones hung close to their mom. They were all tidy with neatly cut hair in varying shades of blond and knee-length trunks in patterns of dark blue and orange.

"I don't see how she manages," I told Sybil, impressed by the mom's cheerful tone of voice and seeming lack of anxiety.

Sybil gave a tiny sound, like a gasp or a sob. I turned to look at her. "What's going on?" I asked.

Her hair was pulled back in a ponytail with a plain red rubber-band like the first day I saw her in my classroom. Her eyes seemed larger than ever, rimmed with dark circles as if she had not slept well for days. Still, she said nothing. Sybil and I didn't have an umbrella. With the sun behind the enormous cloud, I didn't think we would need that kind of protection. I shivered with sudden foreboding.

I forced myself to remain silent, and finally she spoke. "I don't know how to tell you—I'm so ashamed—but I don't know where else to turn."

I scanned her throat and shoulders and the delicate cheeks for fresh marks but found none. "There's nothing for you to be ashamed of." I thought of all the abuse inflicted on this slight body. "Whatever it is, you can tell me." I squeezed her hand, icy cold despite the warm day.

"I'm pregnant," she said, looking at the sand. She fingered the brown paper sack beside her. "Would you like a cookie, Mrs. O'Neil?"

Stunned, I shook my head. For a second, I felt faint. I dug my fingernails into my palm to stop the world from spinning, to get a grip. I should have known something like this would happen. I should have talked to her about birth control. Deep down, I must have known she and Bradley were having sex, even if Sybil herself had wanted to abstain. He would have been insistent, perhaps more than insistent. I marveled that she would have taken the time to bake cookies.

"There's more," she said, "and none of it's good." Her words rushed out, like wind from a punctured balloon. "I've lost my job, and there's no way I can afford to go to college now. And my mom and stepdad are so ashamed of me, they're likely to kick me out of the house any day. And I don't know what I'm going to do." Her voice trembled, and I knew she was fighting back tears. Still, she did not cry. The pale face, so frightfully young and burdened, was immobile, as if willing itself into a leather mask.

"All right," I said, as calmly as I could manage. "Let's take things one at a time." *Where do I begin?* With the parents or the boyfriend, or the baby itself? I had to be strong, strong enough to keep this tender seedling of a woman from perishing in the harsh elements. But I myself was barely surviving. How could I hide how devastated I was by her dilemma? I couldn't let her see my true feelings, my horror at the path her life had taken, my fear at what lay ahead. I must be stalwart and maybe she would be too.

I had to make her life seem manageable.

I chose the least ominous of the facts she'd presented. "You say you lost your job. How?"

"When I told Mr. Brubaker—"

"Told him what?"

"About the pregnancy." Sybil stared at the sand once more. I followed her gaze. A tiny, nearly translucent crab poked his head from one of the holes near our blanket, saw us, and disappeared back inside.

"Why did you tell him?"

"He's my boss after all. I thought he had a right to know."

"I don't see why," I muttered.

"He's worried about giving his business a bad name. He doesn't want anyone to think he condones that sort of behavior."

"That's absurd," I said.

"He told me he always thought I was a good girl. He could hardly bear to look at me once I told him." A fat tear slid down Sybil's round cheek.

I took a yellow napkin from my basket and reached over to catch the tear. My fingers brushed her face, and the wetness of fresh tears was scalding hot against the cool cheek.

"I think he's living in another age," I said. "Having a baby out of wedlock isn't viewed the same way today as fifty years ago."

"It is by Christians, Mrs. O'Neil," Sybil said.

I felt rebuked. I was the preacher's wife, not Sybil. Still, I was sure she was wrong.

"Please stop calling me that," I said. "Call me Acadia. And I think Christians know we're all sinners. There's nothing *especially* shameful about being an unwed mother. It's a sin like any other."

Sybil glanced toward her abdomen. "Except that this sin—I mean, my sin—will show on the outside."

"How far along are you?" She could, at least, have waited until she started to show before telling her boss.

"Only about a month or so. I just missed my period, and I never miss my period." She looked away from me, tucking a stray strand of blonde hair behind one delicate pink ear.

Hope surged through me at her words. Maybe she wasn't pregnant at all. Maybe she was jumping to conclusions. "Have you been to a doctor?"

She shook her head. "Doctors are expensive. Besides, I wouldn't want anybody to see me there."

"How do you know you're pregnant?"

"I took a pregnancy test, the kind you can buy at the drugstore."

"Oh." My hopes sank. "You should see a doctor to be sure. No one would know what you were there for—I can help with the cost if that's an issue."

"Oh, no. I couldn't let you do that."

Fearing I'd insulted her by offering, I said no more. I was touched by her pride. Some people, I had learned, were more than willing to take help from preachers and their wives. While others, like Sybil, were much too proud.

"Have you told Bradley?"

Her face flushed more deeply, and this time, the effort not to cry was visible in the delicate features crumbling before my eyes. Then, just as swiftly, she relaxed back into the statue-like mask. "I told him," she said, her voice barely above a whisper.

"And?"

"I really thought Bradley loved me. All those times … after he hurt me and begged me to forgive him … he always said how he loved me. I believed him. But now—now he doesn't want any part of me or the baby."

"You're better off without him anyway," I said.

"How can you say that?" The mask was gone now, and the pain was vibrant in her round eyes. "A baby needs a father."

"Not one like Bradley."

"I know you don't like him. But you just don't understand. You don't know how insecure and troubled he is ..."

Understanding dawned on me at last. Thinking she saw Bradley for what he was, I'd believed Sybil was having trouble extricating herself from a relationship she really wanted to escape. Now I realized she did not. "You love him, don't you?"

Sybil nodded, her face miserable. She scooped up a handful of white sand and let it sift through her fingers. "I did. I loved him so much, but I can't love him anymore. Not after what he said."

"What did he say?"

"I'm ashamed to tell you." The hot cheeks paled, and she dug her fingers into the sand, dredging up handfuls and tossing them aside as if to dig a hole deep enough to hide in. "He said I should get rid of it."

I cringed, unable to speak for a moment.

I swallowed hard, trying to sort out how to say what needed to be said. I watched the tide washing in, the white foam reaching almost to our bare feet before sweeping back out to sea. "Not to interrupt ... but we need to move or we'll get wet."

Obligingly, Sybil rose and picked up her sack. I could almost see her as a kindergartener. She would have been the kind of child who always obeyed the teacher and who got upset when the teacher scolded others in the class for being unruly. How had she found herself in this predicament? Where was the fairness in this?

I rose, too, and collected my picnic basket. Together, we picked up the blanket and moved it back a few yards. I dug my toes into the sand, waiting for Sybil to sink back onto the blanket. After a moment, I saw that she was waiting for me. I plopped down.

"I'm sorry," I said at last. "Sorry you have to deal with all this. Sorry Bradley is such a—a cad." I substituted for the word that first came to mind, a word not fitting for the lips of a preacher's wife. "The thing to do now is to weigh all your options."

"What options? You don't mean—"

"Well ... giving the child up for adoption is one."

Sybil's tiny rosebud of a mouth dropped open for a second before she clamped it shut. "Oh, I couldn't!" she said. "I'd die first. I mean, how could I live with myself if I abandoned my baby?"

"Don't think of it as abandonment. More like doing what's best for the child."

"Oh, I couldn't!" she said again. "What would he—or she—think of me when he got older—and found out?"

"There are worse options. Like the one Bradley suggested."

I remembered some of the girls I'd known, some of the stories I'd heard during my years at Pepperdine. "People think abortion is terrible until they are the one in trouble. Then, all of a sudden, it becomes a viable option."

"Not for me." Sybil was firm. "I could never do that and face myself in the mirror. Not even if it's the only way that Bradley will want me again."

"Is that what he said?"

She nodded. Her eyes were squeezed shut, but tears shone in the sunlight on her full, baby-like cheeks. She was disappointed in me, and her disappointment stirred me to defensive anger. Anger with myself for letting her down. Anger with her for being so naïve as to get into this predicament and for having the equally naïve hope that I could produce a silver lining.

The thought flickered in my mind that I might take the baby myself. Peter and I could raise the child as our own. I dismissed the idea at once. We simply weren't ready for that kind of responsibility.

I struggled to collect my thoughts. "There are women who manage to raise a child alone," I said, "and still go to college. It's not impossible." I heard the false note in my voice. The note saying *those* women had a support system at home, something we both knew Sybil lacked.

"I don't see how," she said, her voice suddenly devoid of hope. "I really don't see how."

"There are loans and scholarships and grants," I offered. We'd been over this territory before, when her position was far less complex than now.

"Yes, yes." The note of impatience in Sybil's voice was out of character for the girl and told me more clearly than words how desperate she was feeling. "Even when I had a job and no baby on the way—even then going to college would have been hard enough."

"Think about adoption. You could find a fine home for the baby. I could help you."

Sneaking a look at Sybil's face, I could see the despair deepen with every word I uttered. I was making a horrible botch of this.

"I just don't know how I could go on if I gave up my baby. What if he—or she—ended up being passed from one foster home to another …

or fell into the wrong kind of hands? I know how tough growing up can be with your own blood relatives. But imagine how awful it might be if you didn't even share the same blood … if you didn't even have that bond." This was a long speech for Sybil, and I could tell she'd gone over and over these issues in her mind before now.

The conviction that adoption was her best course of action grew stronger in my mind. "Let's eat our lunch," I suggested. I reached for my basket. "We can talk some more while we eat."

I offered her the ham and cheese sandwich on white bread, remembering this as her choice from our first picnic together. She accepted the sandwich and nibbled. After a few miniscule bites, she wrapped the sandwich up in her napkin and returned it to the basket. "I'm sorry. I guess I'm not very hungry."

I talked and talked, trying to force a tone of optimism into the air between us. I talked about the adoptions I had seen that worked well. I talked about the unfortunate couples who found themselves unable to conceive and longed for a child of their own. I talked about the importance of an education in the world of today. "If a good couple gets your baby," I said, "they'll be able to send the child to college. Maybe even to private school. They'll be able to give the child opportunities you've only dreamed of. Every mother wants her child's life to be better than her own. By giving the baby up, you might be giving him—or her—the best possible gift."

Sybil said nothing, but I felt certain my arguments were helping her to see more clearly the merits of adoption— both for herself and for the child. We collected our things and started toward the parking area. Something crunched under my bare feet. Looking down, I saw a mass of shells washed into a heap by a high current. In their midst, a few tiny round shells shone like pearls. How many girls like Sybil were there in this small community who dealt with these kinds of issues on their own, let alone in the county, the state, the country?

For an instant, I understood Peter's desire to help people find their way. If I could help Sybil, might I help others? I bent to pick up one of the gleaming pearl-like gems, then drew back, afraid its shine would vanish at my touch.

I awkwardly hugged and patted Sybil before we parted. Her slight body clung to mine, trembling faintly, before she pulled away.

"The first thing to do," I told her, "is to see a doctor. Make sure you're really pregnant before you go further. Then, if you are, just try to weigh all your options and all the pros and cons before you decide on anything. Okay?"

She nodded, and I thought she was beginning to look a little more hopeful.

"This isn't the end of the world, you know." I congratulated myself on having successfully hidden my distress at her predicament beneath a veneer of strength and confidence.

"Thank you for meeting me today, Mrs. O'Neil." A faint smile touched the corners of the rosebud mouth. "And for the picnic. And for not being too—too judging of me."

CHAPTER THIRTY-FIVE

The other group in the hospital waiting room had settled in. A middle-aged woman looked as if she could benefit from a bath, a shampoo, and about twenty hours of sleep. Beside her, two boys of approximately the same age, around middle school, were buried in their comic books. With their heads tilted forward, dark bangs tumbling over their foreheads and shading their eyes, I could not distinguish whether they were brothers or just friends. Several empty Styrofoam cups were stacked on a small table on the other side of the boys. Next to the table, a man leaned back in his chair, his neck at an awkward angle, snoring softly.

What was noticeably missing from our group was any member of Sybil's family. Besides me, only Beatrice and Peter had come. I'd called Sybil's mother, but she had yet to show. None of us seemed able to complete a sentence. Several times we tried.

"Why do you suppose ..."

"What are the chances that ..."

"When do you think ..."

We gave up and sat numbly, frozen in silence and dread. A television in the corner droned news stories.

"Did you catch that?" Beatrice asked suddenly.

"What?" I turned to see that both she and Peter were staring transfixed at the small television set.

Peter lifted his hand, and I sensed the other group in the waiting room had also paused in their various occupations to listen. Although certain I didn't care at the moment what was going on outside this hospital, I, too, listened to the news.

A man has been murdered in Mobile, Alabama. Michael Donald was found hanging from a tree with his throat slit. A three-foot cross burned on the Mobile County Courthouse last night may have been the work of the Ku Klux Klan. Speculation is that the two events are connected, both related to a recent jury verdict of not guilty. The case involves a black man accused of shooting a white cop. A KKK official has been reported as saying *If a black man can get away with killing a white one, I guess a white man ought to be able to get away with killing a black one.*

The news reporter went on to indicate that, according to his sister, Michael Donald was on his way to buy her some cigarettes when he was abducted.

"Unbelievable!" the woman in the other group muttered, and her husband jerked awake.

"What?" he said, and she filled him in while the two boys stared. Their stricken faces indicated they were wondering if such a thing might happen to one of them next, like the Hatfields and McCoys … one killing leading to another … and another.

Shock and horror resonated in us all. There were no words, and I could only think how naïve I'd been before moving to Alabama. Ironic … my relocation from Kentucky to California had been what my parents most feared. Yet, somehow, I'd managed to remain largely oblivious throughout my years at Pepperdine to the truly ugly side of human nature—the potential for hate and despair to lead to violence and devastation.

When the doctor appeared in the doorway, Peter, Beatrice, and I rose as one while the other group looked up. "The family of Sybil Blake?" he asked.

We glanced at each other, then back at the doctor. Still as one, we nodded. Beatrice spoke. "That's us."

"Is she going to be all right?" I managed.

Dr. Edmondson drew a deep breath, tilted his head back on his stout neck, and peered at me through the bifocal section of his glasses. My heart stopped as I waited. "I believe she is," he said.

"Thank you, Lord!" Beatrice said. I sank against her, unable to speak or even to support my own weight.

"There is one thing you should know." The doctor removed his glasses and polished each lens with a blue handkerchief.

"She has experienced some problems with her pregnancy." He repositioned his glasses and glanced at Peter. "Are you the—"

"No," Peter said. "I'm not, but you can tell us. Has she—has she lost the baby?" He put an arm around me, and I managed to regain my balance while I watched Peter and Beatrice absorb the news of Sybil's pregnancy. I had not yet told either of them of Sybil's revelation.

"No. It was touch and go for a while, but the baby is okay. She should get more frequent checkups for a while to make sure, and I'm recommending bedrest for the next few days. She should, of course, discuss all this with her regular doctor." He looked from one of us to the next, perhaps trying to figure out our actual connection to Sybil.

"Can we see her?" Beatrice asked.

"She's sleeping right now. You should probably give her a couple more hours. Go home, have some dinner, or at least grab a bite in the hospital cafeteria."

After he left, the frozen dam of our silence broke loose. We all tried to talk at once. "What we—"

"Did you know—"

"I can't understand—"

We laughed with relief. "You first," Peter said to Beatrice with his usual respect for his elders.

I listened to Beatrice describe her plans for surrounding Sybil with a support system so strong she could not fall through the cracks and would never again try to take her own life. I saw my own failings more clearly than ever before. What Beatrice was describing was exactly what Sybil had needed when she reached out to me, when she chose *me* to share her pain. And what did I do?

Nothing. I did nothing.

"What we have to make her see," Beatrice said, "is that she is no more a sinner than the rest of us. The only difference between Sybil's sins and the other kinds—like pride and selfishness and anxiety—is that her kind of sin is easier for other people to see."

I remembered Sybil saying something similar herself. That her sin showed on the outside. What Beatrice couldn't know was how perfectly she was describing me and my sins, the kinds that may be easy to hide from the outside world but are ever so plain in God's eyes. The burden of those sins weighed me down.

"Cadi?" Peter placed a supportive hand under my elbow. "Are you all right?"

"I think I need to sit down." I shook from my toes to the top of my head.

Beatrice rushed to my side, and together, she and Peter helped me into a chair. "Let's take the doc's advice, and get something in the cafeteria," Beatrice said. "You look like you could use some coffee."

I nodded numbly, unable to collect my thoughts enough to protest.

"Do you want to go with us?" Peter asked. "Or should I bring something back?"

"I'll go." I stood quickly. For a second, the room spun into a maze of color, morphed briefly to black, and then came back into focus. I blinked and allowed Peter to take my arm. I leaned against him as we made our way to the cafeteria.

The smell of cafeteria food nauseated me worse than the antiseptic odor of the intensive care ward and waiting room. I sensed the onslaught of a migraine. I had been unable to handle Sybil's level of need. I had longed for escape.

I stared blankly at the cheery-faced woman behind the counter. As Peter ordered for me, I pictured my future without him. As much as I needed Peter, he would be better off without me, perhaps with another partner more like himself. I knew what had to be done, and the blandness of that future—one without hope or failure or spice—left me cold.

"You're still shivering," Peter said. He pulled me against him and ran his hand up and down my arm. "It's a delayed reaction to fear."

I looked at him questioningly.

"The fear that we might lose her," he explained. "Did you know?"

"Know what? Oh. That she was pregnant, you mean." I spoke flatly.

"Doesn't matter," he said, and I knew he was trying to excuse my failing.

"Not at all," Beatrice agreed. She fished in her handbag for her wallet and paid the cashier.

We slid our trays onto a corner table, and I tried to match their neutral tones. "I knew. Not for long, but I knew. She told me a couple of days ago." I pressed my fingers to my throbbing temple. "I should have done something. Maybe she wouldn't have tried—"

"Don't think that way," Beatrice said. She stirred a packet of creamer into my coffee and pushed it toward me. "Peter and I are here now, and the three of us will do everything we can to help Sybil. Have a few sips of coffee. To warm yourself."

My shivering seemed more disturbing to her and Peter than to me. Too much guilt crashed through my mind for me to register such externals. Still I obeyed, sipping on the lukewarm coffee.

"None of us would have known what to tell her," Beatrice said. "A pregnancy at her age, and with her background and her boyfriend, is hardly an occasion for joy. Still, you don't like to treat it as tragic either."

"But it is tragic to her." I pushed the stale coffee away. "I knew that. The pregnancy destroyed all her hopes for college."

"Why?" Peter looked genuinely puzzled. "Plenty of people go to college these days with a baby."

"She has more to worry about than that."

"What else?" Peter asked.

"She confided in her boss, and he fired her. He said he couldn't afford to keep her on because once she started showing, people would talk. He couldn't have his customers think he condoned that sort of behavior."

"That's ridiculous," Beatrice said. "And illegal, if I'm not mistaken. She should be talking to a lawyer if she can't make him see sense."

"That's why she should have told you instead of me. You would have done something. I didn't even think of the legal issues."

"Why did she tell her boss anyway?" Beatrice asked while Peter slurped angrily on his soup.

"She was trying to do the right thing," I said. "She wanted to put some of the stuff from church into action in her life. To be completely honest."

"What we need to be thinking about," Beatrice said, "is how we're going to help her get on her feet and get her life into some sort of order." She talked on and on about how she might help Sybil make something of herself while nurturing a baby.

I tried to listen, but clearly, I was not needed. I nibbled at my sandwich. The toast tasted like cardboard. I noticed that Beatrice's food was untouched, while Peter's soup had disappeared. I was always amazed at how he managed to eat no matter how upset he was. Nothing ever fazed his appetite. Would this be something I would remember or forget in the years to come when we were apart?

"Sybil is making great progress spiritually. This is just a setback," Peter said, his mouth bulging with a bite of sandwich. "We should thank God for giving her another chance in this life. Let's pray …"

Suddenly I was furious with him for always believing that things would somehow work themselves out when I knew they never would. I leaped to my feet and screamed at him and Beatrice. "You're missing the point!"

"What is the point?" Peter asked quietly.

"The point is that she chose me to turn to for help, and I let her down. I was too weak and too stupid to see how near she was to doing something like this. She turned to me because I was the preacher's wife, and the preacher's wife ought to know …"

Not wanting to burst into tears, I whirled away. As I turned, I glimpsed Peter and Beatrice exchanging startled glances. The image of their worried expressions haunted me as I fled.

CHAPTER THIRTY-SIX

I placed the flowers carefully on the only empty space I could find, a narrow counter next to a stainless-steel sink. "How are you feeling?" I asked as cheerfully as I could manage. I hoped she could not tell I was fighting back tears. When Sybil was finally allowed visitors, I'd been unable to face her for several hours. I'd finally summoned all my courage to do so.

"Much stronger." Her face was still pale, and the monitors ticked out the rhythms of her fragile life force. Heat burned my cheeks as I thought what might so easily have happened.

Seeing Sybil hooked up to wires and monitors broke my heart, as if I was directly responsible for putting her in this position. In a way, I was.

I said as much, but Sybil refused to listen.

"I'm the one who's sorry," she said. She smiled with an inner light in spite of the tears streaming down her cheeks, like a day when the sun is shining and it's raining at the same time.

I took her hand. She returned the squeeze, her fingers surprisingly strong. "No, I'm the one," I insisted. "I let you down. You came to me and I ... I..."

"Oh, sweet Acadia. Don't blame yourself. You haven't done anything." I was touched to hear her call me by my first name. Although I'd asked her to do so, until now she had always called me Mrs. O'Neil.

"That's just it. I *haven't* done anything. I should have done—"

"It's all right now. Truly, it is." She patted her stomach, and fresh tears welled in her eyes. "When I think what I almost did, I am so angry at myself. God has given me a second chance. And I'm going to make it up to him."

"To him?"

"To my baby." She smiled at me again through the blur of tears. I saw how much she had wanted this baby all along, and what a fool I'd been to talk to her about alternatives.

Spotting a box of tissues on the table next to the bed, I reached for one. I dabbed at the tears on her face and stroked the smooth cheek. "I'm so sorry," I said again.

"You've got to stop that." Sybil's voice was firm. "You're my role model. You're everything I want to be. I can't have you sad just because I did something stupid. You had nothing to do with that."

"I can't bear for you to admire me!" I trembled with suppressed frustration.

"I'm the one who acted like a coward. I'm just sorry for letting you down." Sybil's chin was as stubborn as her words, and I saw she was not going to allow me to accept blame. Perhaps my need to apologize was just another sign of my selfishness. I might not be capable of helping her, but at least I could shut up and quit trying to win forgiveness for something she would not even acknowledge. So I bit back my protests.

"Sybil," I said, as calmly as I could manage, "What's happened to make you this … this accepting?"

"You're not the first one to visit me, you know." She gestured to a basket of fresh daisies and tiny pink roses. Fear clutched at my breast that her good humor was due to a visit from Bradley, in which case she was setting herself up for further disappointment. "Go ahead. Look at the card."

I read the card aloud. "With love, Beatrice Wood." Relieved, I said, "They're beautiful. When was Beatrice here?"

"A while ago. She's been talking to me about all the services available for women in my condition. And then Mr. O'Neil came, and he prayed with me. And he read some Scriptures. You know the ones about the flowers in the fields? About how God clothes them in glory and how, if he takes care of them, he's sure to take care of me."

She paused, out of breath, while I listened in speechless wonder.

"Oh, I know I'm getting everything all wrong," she went on. "I always do that. The verse is all about how you shouldn't worry about what you will wear, or what you will eat—about how God will take care of you. Of me. Do you know the one?" Her face glowed, and I felt reprimanded anew. Why couldn't I have faith like that myself … why did I always need to worry about everything?

I nodded, still mute.

Moments passed, and I realized Sybil was waiting for me to say something. I feared I would choke on my words or cry out my feelings of inadequacy to her.

"What's wrong?" she said, her voice full of concern, not for herself but for me.

"I'm just … so glad you're alive," I whispered. My tears were flowing freely now.

"So am I," Sybil said. "I'm very thankful. Your husband helped me to see that."

Her eyes met mine, full of hope and love, but also puzzled by my behavior. I had the feeling she was looking for some way to encourage me when I should be the one cheering her. "You're so lucky," she said. "You're so smart and beautiful—and married to a man like that—and with a good friend like Mrs. Wood."

Lucky … and undeserving. Beatrice and Peter were responsible for Sybil's improved spirits, while I was superfluous at best. And, quite possibly, worse than useless. I was harmful. I had to leave before I expressed these thoughts and did further damage. I leaned over to hug Sybil before I left. When our cheeks touched, our tears mingled.

CHAPTER THIRTY-SEVEN

My spirits had sunk even lower by the next morning. I called Beatrice, remembering how often she had pulled me up from the doldrums in the past. "Lunch at Poseidon's Fork?" I suggested.

"Not today. I've got an appointment," Beatrice said.

I wasn't hungry anyway. I decided to spend lunch walking alone on the beach. I was still overwhelmed by the difficulties that lay ahead for Sybil and amazed at how hopeful Beatrice, Peter, and even Sybil seemed to be. As I dug my toes in the sand, an enormous sadness came over me. I was saying goodbye to Sugar Sands.

I had to leave Peter to his work. Everyone would be better off all around. I would start over, find a life for myself for which I was more suited. A tiny green stem caught my eye, and I bent to examine it more closely. How odd. A plant growing in the sand. I recognized it from having often seen such plants in Kentucky gardens. But here in the sand! I pictured a picnicker spitting out a watermelon seed that had somehow taken root.

I thought of Peter and his constant efforts to win people over to his Lord by sowing seeds. Did one occasionally take root? The Gulf today was flat as a lake except for the tide breaking at the edge. The water was apple green with a navy rim near the horizon, the gulls white in the distance, flying in no discernible pattern. One would swoop below the others, then rise above. As I watched, their flights shifted like a kaleidoscope, the birds moving across the pale blue sky, calling out to one another.

Suddenly their calls turned angry, and I saw that one of the gulls had something in its mouth, an edible treasure. The others were in hot pursuit. I watched for a time, then a group of pelicans drew my gaze, their brown bodies flying close to the water. Like a carefully orchestrated marching band, they moved in perfect sync. Together they pedaled for a time, then together they coasted. When they rose high into the sky, they stayed in formation as if bound by an invisible cord.

My thoughts drifted again to Peter and his longing for unity in the church. The pelicans were low now, barely skimming the surface, still in nearly perfect alignment.

I came upon a middle-aged fisherwoman, ankle-deep in the water. In yellow shorts and a white sun visor, she cast her line into the Gulf. She seemed perfectly content, even if she never got a nibble. And then, as I passed, she reeled in a small, silvery fish. I watched as she rushed to show her catch to her husband who sat under an umbrella in a purple and gold LSU chair. They smiled at each other, and my heart ached for what I would never have.

A sudden impulse to immerse myself in the green water gripped me. I ignored the curious glances as I glided toward the beckoning waters in my jeans. Nearby, the woman in yellow shorts threw back the little fish.

The water soothed my flesh as I entered. I floated on my back, noticing how different the birds looked from this perspective. The underbellies of the pelicans appeared white, their wings dark with jagged edges, their beaks long. Two pelicans separated themselves from the others, striking out on their own like rebellious teenagers. Not loners, but a pair. I'd heard Peter once crediting God for their coloring. Their topside was brown for protection from predators above, he'd explained, while their undersides made them invisible to the fish below that served as their prey.

A group of gulls flew above me, their wings flapping steadily as if staying in flight was much harder for them than for the pelicans. From this angle they looked white all over, except for dark tips on their wings. Yet when viewed from the beach, their heads were sometimes gray-speckled or even charcoal. What we see all depends on our perspective. From a distance, Sybil and even Beatrice saw me one way. Up close, I saw myself another. How did God see me?

My thoughts circled as I floated, the weight of my jeans threatening to drag me down. Something bumped my chest, and I jerked. Then, in the clarity of the water, I saw the small fish and relaxed. After a time, I grew accustomed to the gentle bumping. One fish emerged between my legs, silvery white with a band of yellow on his tail. I strained to see him better, but he was gone.

Then, inches from my face, I saw it. A jellyfish, its gelatinous center perfect in its opaque whiteness, the edges scalloped white like an old-fashioned doily. I quickly swam away, fearful of the sting, a sensation

I had experienced often enough. Like myself, the jellyfish poisoned whatever it encountered, not intentionally but merely through contact. I thought about my past, about the secrets I'd kept from Peter. I wondered if everything might have turned out differently if I had told him the whole truth … my war with God.

My swim was over, and I knew what I had to do.

CHAPTER THIRTY-EIGHT

"Acadia! Of course, we're glad you're here," my mother said. "We're always delighted to see you. But—"

"We're just concerned about Peter being alone and worried about you," my father said.

Of course, their anxiety would be more for Peter than for me, I thought grimly. How completely he had won them over. Here I was, trying to start over, trying to forget Peter and accept myself for who I was. And all they could think about was Peter's feelings. Coming home to them hadn't been my first choice either, not if I'd had other options. I had known only that I had to flee before I bumped into any other innocent souls.

At first, I had driven aimlessly, struggling to think logically, trying to lay out my choices the way I'd so errantly laid out Sybil's. I couldn't think straight. I didn't want to take any money from Peter's and my meager bank account, and I didn't have enough money on me for even one night in a motel. I felt more alone than I remembered feeling in many years, if ever. At one point, I thought of Cynthia and how quickly we'd hit it off when I was a newcomer to California. Spotting a pay phone in a gas station booth, I'd pulled in.

I searched my handbag for the worn scrap of paper on which Cynthia scribbled her new phone number at graduation. My handbag was a mess, as usual. I must have handled that scrap of paper dozens of times when looking for something else. Almost ready to give up, I slipped my fingers into one last nook. There was the scrap, the numbers slightly smudged but still legible. I searched my handbag next for change. Did I have enough to complete the call? I wasn't sure but not worried. I could reverse the charges. Cynthia would understand.

"I'm sorry," the operator told me. "That number is no longer in service."

And so, here I was, disrupting my parents' lives, much as I had always done. In my absence, Mom and Dad had developed a closeness in their relationship I couldn't remember being there before. Although Mom was still into her gardening and Dad his news, they came together in the evening almost like lovers, each touching the other's hand or neck. Had they always been like this? Had I been too self-absorbed to notice? I didn't think so.

Something had shifted, and I wondered if I'd been the poison here too … contaminating their relationship when I was around. Was there nowhere I belonged?

Their intimacy made me miss Peter. At times, the void was almost unbearable. I took out my frustrations on the piano. I pounded out classical music and jazz and rock, oblivious to the fact that the piano badly needed tuning. "Could you play a little more softly?" Mom asked. "I've got a headache."

I remembered the days when she'd pleaded with me to practice, and I had stubbornly resisted. I recalled, too, a time when her headaches seemed like nothing more than an excuse to avoid interacting with me. I hadn't developed any sympathy for hers until I entered college and started having migraines of my own.

I switched to ballads, and the gentler tunes spoke to my sadness so powerfully I wept as I played. Mom tapped me on the shoulder.

"Peter's on the phone again. Are you sure you don't want to talk to him?"

"I'm sure," I said, my teeth clenched. How many times did I have to tell her?

"He says that if you won't talk to him, he's coming here."

I jumped up so quickly I nearly overturned the piano bench, then stomped into the kitchen. "Don't come!" I said into the receiver. "There's no point." I hung up before Peter could respond, before I could hear his voice and be swayed from my resolve.

"Who did you say was covering your classes?" Dad asked the next evening at dinner.

"There are plenty of competent substitute teachers in Sugar Sands," I said, certain we'd covered this territory before. Was he that anxious to get rid of me?

I was anxious too. I'd have to find a job and move out. Perhaps I could do some substitute teaching myself.

"When you go back to Sugar Sands," he said, "do you imagine you'll be able to step back into the classroom as if you never left? What if they make the sub a permanent offer?"

Ever the businessman, always thinking about money. What little appetite I'd had evaporated, and I pushed back my chair. "I told you already, I'm not going back." Why did they refuse to believe me?

"Are you sure about that, Acadia?" Mom said.

"I know you don't want me!" I fairly screamed at her. "You're making it pretty clear that I'm an intrusion. I sympathize with your predicament, but can you please deal with the inconvenience a little longer? Not long—just until I can find a job."

Dad sighed. "That's not it at all. We're just afraid you haven't thought this through—"

"Believe me, I have." I cut him off and walked away. I resumed my position at the piano. My playing was improving, and I wondered how good I might have been by now if I had obeyed my mother's admonitions and practiced when I was a child.

I was pounding out a favorite jazz piece when I sensed a presence behind me. I glanced over my shoulder. My heart, undergoing a slow death, sprang to life.

I swallowed the smile that threatened my lips. "I told you not to come."

"I had to come." Peter bent to kiss me, and I turned my head so his lips only grazed my cheek.

In the kitchen, my parents cleared the table, though they were unusually quiet. I suspected they were straining to hear me and Peter. I motioned him to follow me to my bedroom. I closed the door, and he tried to pull me into his arms. As much as a part of me longed to be held, to feel his familiar bulk, I knew I had to be strong.

I stiffened, and his arms dropped to his sides.

"What's going on, Acadia?"

"I warned you. I warned you I wasn't cut out for—your kind of life. I botch everything I try to do." I dropped onto my childhood bed. Peter sank down beside me, making no further effort to touch me.

"That's not true." His emerald eyes heralded his conviction. "Sybil is doing really well. You wouldn't believe how good she looks, almost radiant, in spite of everything. Beatrice has talked Mr. Brubaker into putting her back into her old job, and she's seriously considering starting college next semester. With a little encouragement from Beatrice, the church ladies are actually rallying around her. Can you believe it? They're even planning a baby shower."

He waited for me to react. I *was* happy for Sybil and truly relieved. Yet, I couldn't feel happy for myself. His words just confirmed what I already knew. I wasn't needed. They were all better off without me. Finally I said, "You don't get it, do you?"

"No, I guess not." His jaw tightened.

"Everyone is better off without me! I'm not who you think I am, Peter. I'm no good. I'm poison. I have to get away from you before I destroy you. Can't you see that?"

"No, I can't." Peter's eyes flashed with anger—anger mingled with pain. "You're my wife, Cadi. You belong with me."

"Dessert anyone?" Mom's voice drifted up the stairs, along with the inviting rich aroma of my mother's homemade fudge.

I groaned, and Peter's anger evaporated before my eyes ... at least for the moment. "Smells like your Sodom and Gomorrah, doesn't it?"

"What?"

"Temptation city," he explained. "Can we call a truce long enough for me to sample your mother's fudge? I've heard you talk about how good it is too often to pass up a chance to find out for myself."

My stomach rumbled its agreement. A few minutes later, Peter was licking the large fudge spoon, something I used to do. I watched, amazed, as Peter once again charmed both my parents, hiding the pain and anger I'd seen flare up only minutes earlier. Only when his gaze met mine did I see the solemnity again, the confusion and hurt.

After consuming about a thousand calories of fudge, I was ready to lash out at anyone and everyone. Adding to this evidence of my weakness was the unmistakable realization that Peter was more comfortable with my parents, even when we were on the verge of splitting up forever, than I was.

"Are you leaving with Peter?" Mom asked softly, as if we were alone ... though neither Peter nor my father was out of earshot.

"I most definitely am not." A silence fell over the room.

My parents stared at me, their eyes accusing. I stammered an explanation. "It's not that I don't want to. It's ..."

"It's what?" Peter's tone demanded an answer.

"It's ... that I can't. You should leave now." I turned and ran up the stairs, hoping they couldn't see the tears streaming down my cheeks.

CHAPTER THIRTY-NINE

Beatrice arrived a few days later. The fact that she too hit it off with my parents did little to improve my self-esteem, though I was touched by her effort in coming so far. Her friendship was one thing I would certainly miss.

"I can't believe you're here," I said. "It's so far for you to drive all alone."

"I had to come." She echoed the same words Peter had used. Her eyes were warm and deep behind the thick lenses. "You need to come home, Acadia." She took a sip of the hot tea my mother had prepared upon her arrival. "Your students need you. Peter needs you, and Sybil needs you."

"No, she doesn't. She has you."

Beatrice hesitated for a second, as if weighing her thoughts. Then the brown eyes flashed, and I wondered if I had ever seen Beatrice truly angry. "You think you're the only one who screws up, don't you? What about me?"

"I don't know what you mean." I set down my cup.

"That day at the hospital—you were reaching out for help the same way Sybil reached out to you. All I did was go on and on about what *I* was going to do for Sybil, what *my* plans were. I didn't hear your cry any more than you heard Sybil's. Otherwise you wouldn't be here now."

I stared at her, her words sinking in slowly. Could she be right? "That's not true," I protested. "You tried to include me in your plans, but I could see I wasn't really needed." I turned my back to Beatrice so she wouldn't see the tears in my eyes and walked to the sink. I emptied my cup into the drain.

"That's my point. I let you think you weren't needed—the furthest thing from the truth."

"No, it isn't." I positioned my cup in the top rack of the dishwasher, and Beatrice followed suit.

We sat back down, and I tried to explain my logic to Beatrice. She deserved that much. "I don't want to hurt Peter." I stared down at the table.

"But that's what I'm doing every day that I stay with him. The day I left, after you went to your appointment, I took a swim and saw this jellyfish. It looked so perfect on the outside. But if it touched me, I'd be sorry. That's the way I am. I don't mean to hurt anyone, but you and Peter just don't see me for who I really am."

"And who is that?"

I forced myself to meet her gaze. "I'm poison."

"Why do you say that?"

"There's something you don't know about me. No one does. Not my parents, not my friend Cynthia, and not Peter." I hesitated, wondering if I could tell Beatrice. I'd buried the memory so deep, committing myself to never talking about what I did.

"I'm listening." Her face was serious, waiting.

I couldn't meet her stare, so I veered my gaze once more at the table. I rubbed at an imaginary spot with my forefinger. "I had an abortion, Beatrice!"

"When? Tell me." Beatrice reached out a hand to cover mine, and I managed to look into her eyes. They were kind, gentle, not judgmental.

I struggled to think where to begin. My parents had left us alone to give us space to talk ... so they said. I wasn't ready for them to hear this confession. At last, I spoke in a hushed voice. "Cynthia had fallen in love, and she was spending every minute with Henry. I was trying to fill the void, I guess, by looking for *my* Henry. I was a pre-med major back then, and I met this guy. He was a senior and had already been accepted to medical school. He had his whole future mapped out." I tried to picture Eric and found I could not.

"Did you tell him?"

"I did." I hadn't wanted to tell him, but I'd been so confused, so stressed, I hadn't known where else to turn. I'd hoped he could change the situation, make things better somehow.

"Did you love him, Acadia?"

"Not really. I guess I thought I did. But nothing like the way I love Peter." Hard to believe how I'd once spent practically every waking hour thinking about Eric, and now I couldn't even picture his face.

"What did he say?"

"The abortion was his idea. He talked as if the baby wasn't even a baby, just a tiny pea. He said everything would go back to normal afterward."

Tears sprang to my eyes as I remembered all I had tried so hard to forget. "But of course, it didn't."

Beatrice tightened her jaw and shook her head ... not in judgment of me but of Eric. Still, I couldn't let her think I'd been that naïve.

"I'm not blaming him. He was never serious about me—a fact that became obvious the more he talked about ... you know ... about doing what I did. I was depressed and scared. Still, I believed having an abortion wasn't right for me. What I didn't know was there would hardly ever be a day when I didn't wonder what he—or she—might have been like, when I wouldn't blame myself for not giving my baby a chance." I choked back a sob. "No matter how hard I try to forget, I can't."

Beatrice nodded. "That's why the whole ordeal with Sybil hit you so hard."

The tears were rolling down my cheeks now. I swatted at them in annoyance. I didn't deserve Beatrice's sympathy. "So now, you see why I can't go back to Peter," I said. "Why I'm poison."

"Oh, Acadia," she said. "Don't you think God will forgive you?"

"I don't see why he should."

"Because he is God. And that's what he does. Abortion is serious, but it's not an unforgivable sin."

Beatrice removed her glasses and dabbed at her brown eyes. I peered into them through my tears and saw that hers were wet as well.

"You need to confess to God, and you have to tell Peter," she said. "And you have to forgive yourself."

"What would that change?" My voice rose, and I lowered it lest my parents hear. "Forgiving myself won't bring the baby back."

"No. That's something you'll have to learn to live with, but you need to move past it—to become the beautiful, caring woman I know you're capable of being."

Why does she always give me more credit than I deserve ... even now?

As if reading my thoughts, Beatrice said, "Let's pray for guidance." Then she did.

I remained unconvinced, restless. I rose and moved mindlessly to my new post in the living room, the altar at which I shed my frustration. Beatrice followed me to the piano. She listened, her head tilted, as I pounded out "The Entertainer." I could hear my mother puttering around in the kitchen.

"Play something else," Beatrice said when I finished. The smell of Mom's mostaccioli wafted into the living room. I felt an unfamiliar surge of gratitude toward her for welcoming Beatrice so graciously and for allowing us to be alone.

Beatrice rummaged through a stack of sheet music and assorted books of songs, pulling out a book of Patsy Cline tunes. "Could you play one of these?"

I had avoided that book since I'd been here. Virtually every song on the radio or on television made me think of Peter, and I knew Patsy's lyrics would do the same. Reluctantly, I took the book and thumbed through the pages. I played "Crazy" first. Then, as the lovely melody filled me with sad longing, I turned a page and found "Sweet Dreams." The music consumed me, and I couldn't stop. I played "Walkin' After Midnight" ... "Leavin' On Your Mind" ... and finally, "Just Out of Reach." When I paused to glance at Beatrice through a haze of tears, I saw the moisture in her eyes too.

"Ron loved Patsy's music," she said, her voice unsteady.

I waited for her to tell me more, but she changed the subject. "Peter's a mess. If you had any idea how much I miss Ron, you wouldn't ..."

I could see she was fighting back sobs. "Every day with the man you love is a gift, Acadia. Don't let another one get away."

I flipped through the pages of another book. I stopped at a familiar hymn, "Blessed Be the Tie That Binds." I could see Peter's face long ago, or so it seemed, telling me that family ties were the strongest bonds on earth. Slowly I began to play the tune, thinking of my families—the one with my parents ... the one I'd formed with Peter ... and the church family where I first met Beatrice. Wordlessly, she squeezed my hand. I stopped playing, my fingers still resting on the keys, her blue-veined ones resting atop mine.

The words and melody replayed over and over in my head that evening as we ate my mother's delicious dinner, as I put fresh sheets on the bed in the guest room, and as I handed Beatrice a stack of bath towels.

"Think about what I'm telling you, Acadia. You're not poison. You just think you are." She hugged me, and we parted for the night. "Until tomorrow," she murmured.

"I'm glad you came." Fatigue traced its path across her face as I added, "I hope coming here wasn't too much of a strain on you."

"I'm just tired. I'm glad I came."

I went to my bedroom and pulled back the covers. Sleep did not come. A parade of memories danced across my fevered brain—some of me with Peter, others with Beatrice and Sybil—but mostly the memories of me with my parents. Of a small child, hardly recognizable as myself, afraid of the dark, or playing Scrabble with my dad, his face bursting with delight when the child triumphantly spelled out "quiz" on a triple word score.

Bind us together, Lord, bind us together with ties that cannot be broken. Tears stung my eyes as I headed to my parents' familiar bedroom door. I tapped lightly before entering. Their faces peered up at me as they had hundreds of times before, when I was small and needed them to kiss my hurts or calm my fears.

"I'm sorry," I said. "I'm so sorry."

They reached out and embraced me.

CHAPTER FORTY

I looked back at my parents' house—the house I no longer thought of as home. Following Beatrice back to Sugar Sands, I had plenty of time to think while we drove our separate cars. The engine in my car, which I'd owned since my Pepperdine days (how far away they felt now), had been skipping occasionally on the drive to my parents' house. I'd intended to talk to Dad about probable causes. Instead, in my self-absorption and pain at being separated from Peter, car troubles had slipped from my mind. Dad was slipping too, or he'd have checked the problem out without my asking. With Beatrice's reliable red Cadillac so close, I felt reassured that we would be okay.

I thought back to our honeymoon when Peter's car broke down, and he prayed instead of calling my parents. How silly his prayer had seemed to me at the time, and how silly the Acadia I was then seemed to me now.

I turned on the car radio, wondering if I could pick up anything. "Keep on Loving You" by REO Speedwagon was playing. I automatically pushed another button, having the habit of avoiding love songs. A serious-toned male voice told me I'd stumbled into a news update. I'd never been one to keep up with current events. That was more Peter's forté than mine. He liked to know what was going on in the world, and he often incorporated news items into his sermons. My finger was poised to push another button when the words caught my attention.

President Reagan has been shot in the chest outside the Washington Hilton Hotel. The president's press secretary, James Brady, is severely wounded, and a Secret Service agent, Timothy McCarthy, and a local police officer, Thomas Delahanty, are also shot. The assailant, John W. Hinckley, Jr., was seized at the scene.

I left the radio on the station for a while to see if further updates were coming through, but I kept getting the same report. My mind swung back in time to the assassination of John Kennedy. I was only six, but I could tell from the way everyone acted this was really big news. I was in school when I found out, and our first-grade teacher cried in front of the class. When I got home that day, the television kept showing the car with President Kennedy and his wife. What I remembered the most vividly were the photos of Caroline, who was the same age as me. She looked so forlorn, and I remembered thinking that being the daughter of someone famous wasn't such a good thing.

I tried another station.

Initial reports claim he may have a punctured lung. Vice-president George Bush is on his way from Texas. Until he arrives, it's unclear who is in charge. First Lady Nancy Reagan is on her way to George Washington University Hospital, where her husband is undergoing emergency surgery.

I tried to imagine what she was feeling, and I was glad I was on my way to Peter. Though the engine continued to miss occasionally, we made the trip uneventfully, stopping often to stretch our legs, refill our tanks, and use the toilets. I would be strong for Peter, I told myself and Beatrice. I would be a good wife, if I had it in me. If Peter could forgive me when I told him everything …

"Just turn it over to God," Beatrice said.

"But doesn't God expect something from you? How do you know when you've done your part?" Without closing my eyes, I spoke a prayer aloud as I drove. I talked to God for a long time, and I felt better afterward.

By the time we reached Sugar Sands, I noticed that Beatrice's gait was unsteady, and the strain in her eyes palpable. How selfish of me to put her through this, and how dear she was to me.

Surprising Peter was her idea, not mine. She wanted to see the look on his face. The last few miles were the slowest. A dense white fog had descended on the communities around Sugar Sands. Across the sand dunes, swirls of fog materialized like ghosts.

On entering the house, I crinkled my nose before recognizing the smell. Tuna fish and boiled eggs. If anything, the house was tidier than it had been when I was there. He'd already adjusted to being without me. Beatrice was wrong—he didn't need me.

The joy in his face dispelled my doubt, and an answering joy rose in my breast. Tight in his arms, I forgot Beatrice's presence until I felt, rather than saw, Peter grinning at her over my shoulder. "What happened? Did you—"

"I went after her," Beatrice said. I pulled away from Peter in time to catch Beatrice's bright smile, which didn't quite obscure the fatigue in her face.

"Why didn't you tell me?" Peter demanded. "And what did you say to her that I didn't?"

"Nothing much. I just warned her not to waste another day. Because each one is special."

I reached for Beatrice's hand and squeezed, thinking how fragile her grasp seemed. "Sit down and let me get you something to drink—or eat." A few hours had passed since our last snack. "You could spend the night here. I'm exhausted, and I know you are."

"No, I need to be going. You two should be alone." She shot me a meaningful glance, and I knew she was urging me to talk to Peter right away. I wasn't ready, though. Not this soon.

"Don't rush off," Peter said. "Cadi and I have a lifetime to be alone. Would you eat a tuna sandwich?"

Beatrice shook her head. "No, I'm ready to get home and kick off my shoes."

"You can do that here." I was suddenly anxious for Beatrice to stay. I needed her presence.

"Not tonight," she said.

Peter and I walked Beatrice to her car and hugged her before she drove away, her car disappearing in the heavy fog. Yet, her presence lingered, like a friendly ghost, as we sat at the table with our sandwiches. "She's quite a lady," Peter said

"I wonder if I'll ever be like her. That wise. You know?"

Peter nodded. "Me too."

He wondered if *I* would ever be that wise? Peter must have recognized the hurt in my eyes, because he quickly clarified, "I mean, I wonder if *I* will."

Somehow, I had never felt Peter needed a role model. "You already are," I said.

Peter looked at me for a long moment. When he spoke, the certainty in his voice, almost a bitter edge, took me by surprise. "Far from it."

"Why do you say that?"

"I fell apart, Cadi, when you left." Peter's voice broke, and his hand shook when he reached out for his water glass.

I covered Peter's hand with mine. "I'm so sorry. I didn't think I was needed here. I thought I was in the way."

"You couldn't have been more wrong." He turned his palm up to squeeze my hand.

"Are you sure?"

"It's the only thing I am sure about anymore."

"Why? What's happened?"

He released my hand and reached for the glass again. He gulped down half the contents before answering. "Nothing new. Just the same old problems with the church. The truth is they're worse, but let's not talk about them tonight. Let's just—"

"The problems are worse?"

Peter's face was set in grim lines. He sighed. "People are flocking to the new church in Crystal Bay."

"Why? Who?"

"The Robinsons and the Hartleys. The Thurmonds, too, and Joe and Jill Stanley." He tossed back the rest of his water, like a shot of whiskey.

"Couples mostly?" I tried to hide my dismay.

"Yes. The message I'm getting is they are not so much upset by anything we've done as what they're afraid we might do next."

I refilled our water glasses, wondering if my departure had somehow triggered theirs. "Like?"

"Oh, I don't know. Offering up young virgins on the altar?" His voice was wry, devoid of real amusement. "The most painful thing … apart from my fear of losing you"—his voice cracked a little—"is that when I see these people in town, most of them don't even speak to me. Almost like I'm being shunned or something."

"Oh, Peter." I set the glasses down so hard some of the water sloshed out. I draped my arms around his shoulders.

"I can handle anything now that you're home. I'm sorry for dumping all this on you the minute you walk in."

"Don't be sorry." I sat down beside Peter and picked up my sandwich. Anger washed through me in a hot, tingling rush at these people who were so judgmental and so unlike the Christ they claimed to follow. Giving in to this anger would not do either of us any good. But how could I burden Peter with my revelation when he was already dealing with so much? I would have to wait.

I could hardly believe anyone would shun this kind and loving man who meant only good. Forgiveness, I thought. Gentleness, and love, and forgiveness. Patience too. Patience had never been my strong suit. I'd given up—or nearly given up—on so many things. On piano, on God, on my marriage. How was I to help Peter now?

We ate in silence while I digested what he'd told me. To stall for time, I asked, "Did you add mayonnaise to the tuna salad?"

"No. Was I supposed to?" Peter said. "I thought something didn't taste quite right." He jumped up and headed to the refrigerator, as if he too was glad to be distracted.

"I always do, but it's good this way too. Just different." I chewed deliberately, contemplatively. "Maybe the problem," I said at last, "is that you're trying to solve everything yourself. Maybe you should turn things over—you know—to God, like Beatrice always says."

Peter stirred mayonnaise into the tuna fish salad remaining in the bowl. "I know you're right. I just get so impatient sometimes." He screwed the lid on the mayonnaise and put it back into the refrigerator.

As we headed to the bedroom, an odd restless sensation came over me. I detoured to the bathroom sink for a drink of water, guzzling as if I'd die of thirst. The sensation did not abate. Suddenly I realized what it was. I knelt beside the bed and reached up to take Peter's hand. "Let's pray together."

After church on Sunday, we asked for an outdoor seat at Tenacious Ted's. With chagrin, I remembered my discontent the last time we were here, which now seemed like part of a different life. With my spirits high, I relished the sand in my shoes, the sun in my eyes, the breeze sweeping my face and stirring my hair. Peter and I lunched alone instead of accepting one of the increasingly sparse invitations from the members of the congregation.

We had to wait about a half hour, as the local church goers had already lined up ahead of us. I didn't mind. Glancing around, I saw a number of patrons dressed formally, women in dresses and hose, men in sports jackets or even suits and ties, their attire speaking more loudly than words of the conservative nature of this church-going community. Today, this did not strike me as a bad thing. Once seated, I ordered the grilled mahi-mahi sandwich and substituted broccoli for the fries.

The broccoli was delicious—crisp but not hard, flavorful without a heavy cheese or butter sauce. I did not even miss the French fries. While we ate, we talked about the issues still hovering over the church and the two factions claiming to know the *right* way. The need to be right—and my parents wrong—had once been so important to me. How foolish my rebellion seemed now. I could hardly remember what we disagreed about. Surely, not just the way I dressed for church.

Then I remembered my conviction that they cared only what other people thought of them and not about me. Why had I been so certain the two were mutually exclusive? I shook my head to dispel unwanted memories and focus on the present. Food had never tasted better.

He dipped a French fry in a mixture of ketchup and hot sauce. "The more liberal group—I hate to call them that because I don't like labels—they want to use the land to build a youth center and forget about a new church building for now. The others want to build a new church building and forget about a youth center."

"What are their arguments?"

A familiar-looking couple stared at us from another table—Joe and Jill Stanley. I smiled and lifted my hand to wave. Jill wore a crisp dress—navy blue with a wide white collar—and sheer hose. Their attire indicated they had been to church but not to ours. In spite of Peter's warning, I'd been shocked by the number of empty pews.

I continued to smile in their direction, though my lips trembled. They looked away, their eyes refocusing so quickly I could not be certain they had seen me. Yet, I felt sure they had.

"The main advantage of the new church building is to provide room to grow," Peter said.

"That's reasonable. Isn't it?" I couldn't let the Stanleys dampen my mood, but I was chilled to think they were only two of many.

"Sure, but the thing is—we're not anywhere close to capacity now. And unless we do something to attract more young people, I don't think we're ever going to get there." Peter's voice was fervent, more like the Peter I knew and loved, than the doubtful stranger who had replaced him in my absence.

"If that's how you feel, what's the dilemma?"

"The dilemma is I'm just one person. And there are plenty of others who don't see the situation as I do. Barry Davis, among them."

"He's the ringleader of that sect, I suppose?"

He hesitated for a moment before answering, and I thought he was going to challenge my use of the word *sect*. But he said only, "You got it."

I speared my last piece of broccoli, none too gently. "What do you really think?"

"When a person gets more concerned about traditions than about saving souls, it can't be right."

"We should pray for guidance," I said. Peter shot me a curious glance, and I added, "Now."

"Here?" Peter knew I was uncomfortable praying in public, even a brief prayer at the start of a meal.

"Yep." I reached across the table and took his hands, bowed my head, and waited for his words. I tried not to wonder if the Stanleys were watching. After all, what they thought really didn't matter.

When no words came, I looked up. Peter was watching me, one corner of his mouth lifted in something resembling a smile, his eyes still troubled. "You never cease to amaze me, Acadia O'Neil."

"That's my goal. Don't you feel like praying?"

"I have prayed about this. That's just it. I've prayed and prayed, but nothing is changing."

"You know what you've always told me," I reminded him. "About God's time and our time. How different they are."

Peter pushed his plate away, half his French fries uneaten. This told me more clearly than words how deep his concerns ran. A family with two small children noisily took the seat next to us. The smaller child settled into a highchair, his big blue eyes wise in some unfathomable way, his mouth turned up in a smile of pure, unfettered joy.

I grinned at him, and he grinned back so broadly a coo of delight escaped the rosy mouth. "Look," I said to Peter, and he followed my gaze. "Isn't he precious?"

He nodded absently.

"Oh, Peter, you may not be able to fix this mess. Still, I think you need to get off the fence, if that's where you are. Tell the elders what you think and what you recommend. At the same time, let them know it's their decision, and you respect that. And, of course, keep on praying about everything."

He stared at me for a long moment and then he took my hands in his and bowed his head. He prayed for so long I almost forgot where we were, my relief great at hearing Peter once more pouring out his heart to God. He stopped and I looked up, catching a few curious glances from people at other tables. I smiled at them with only a fleeting twinge of embarrassment. When I caught the Stanleys' stare, I smiled determinedly. This time, she nodded in recognition.

When our waitress appeared at Peter's elbow, I tilted my head toward the mother of the two small children. Her frozen drink had just arrived. "I'll have what she's having... but make mine a virgin one."

The waitress started to move away, and I called after her. "Also, do you have anything that's chocolate?"

Part V

God's Chariots

Don't ever let me stop growing, God.
Spiritually growing. Drawing ever closer to
you, the source of it all: The universe. The
world and the life upon it. The people... the
person... myself.
Marjorie Holmes

CHAPTER FORTY-ONE

When Beatrice tapped her familiar knock, I was making soup. I felt rather virtuous to be caught in this uncharacteristically domestic activity. "Come on in!" I called out.

"You don't have to be an artist in the kitchen," she'd told me once. "Anybody can throw together a pot of soup."

Not that there were a lot of fresh vegetables in my concoction. The empty cans beside the slow cooker were lined up like soldiers. Several cans of tomatoes, a can of corn, two cans of kidney beans, a can of black-eyed peas. On and around the chopping board, carrot ends and slivers of onions and bell pepper seeds provided evidence of the few fresh vegetables I'd assembled. I tossed in liberal handfuls of spices from the cupboard. Although the names were familiar—coriander and cumin and turmeric and cilantro—I had no idea how most of them tasted. Nonetheless, I congratulated myself as I stirred. I might never be able to talk to a struggling teenager the way Beatrice could, but I could put a meal on the table ... or at least a bowl of soup.

I looked up, smile ready, expecting Beatrice's approval. I sensed at once something was wrong. Her face was taut, and deep creases I hadn't noticed before seemed to have emerged overnight. Her eyes darted about the kitchen, refusing to meet mine.

"What is it?" An alarm bell sounded inside my heart. "Has something happened to Sybil—is she all right?"

"Sybil's fine."

"Thank goodness." I breathed a bit easier. "What then?"

"I see you're making soup. Smells great."

"You think so?" My stomach rumbled in appreciation of the smells wafting through the small house, and I realized I was hungry. "Would you like a bowl?"

"Is it ready?"

"Probably not. I don't think there's anything in there likely to hurt us if it isn't."

"All right then. Just a very small bowl."

Ignoring her instruction, I ladled generous portions for both of us. I knew she would tell me what was troubling her in her own time, but a small knot of anxiety tightened in my gut.

Beatrice blew on a small spoonful and tasted it cautiously. "Mmm, it's good," she said.

I took a spoonful and burned the roof of my mouth. "Oh!" I ran to the cupboard, grabbed a glass, filled it with tap water, and took a big swallow. "Hot! Why didn't you warn me?"

"I thought the steam rising from the soup would have been a hint."

"You're giving me too much credit." I emptied an ice tray into a bowl, added a few cubes to my glass, and poured a glass for Beatrice as well. "Would you like something besides water to drink? We have some coke and a pitcher of tea."

I blew on my next spoonful for a long time, then bit into something crunchy. "I don't think the soup is quite ready," I said.

"Carrots take such a long time to get soft. Very tasty though."

"Do you want me to pour yours back into the pot and cook it a few more minutes?"

"No, thanks. Look … Acadia, I don't know how to tell you this except to just come right out and tell you."

"I wish you would," I said. I felt as if my heart had stopped beating. Maybe she was moving in with her daughter in Seattle after all, though she had assured me this would never happen. Maybe she knew something about Peter that I didn't. Maybe …

"I have cancer," she said.

Cancer—the word that had always held such dread for my mother, whose parents both died from the disease. *Cancer*. These days, though, doctors could do so much more. There was surgery, chemotherapy, and radiation. My head spun, remembering the doctor visits Beatrice had dismissed as routine checkups.

"How long have you known?"

"I've suspected for a while. I've only known for certain for a month or so."

"A *month or so?*"

"I'm sorry, Acadia. I just couldn't figure out how to tell you."

"What kind of cancer?"

"The bad kind."

The look in Beatrice's eyes chilled me to the bone, but I replied lightly. "The bad kind? I didn't know there was a good kind."

"The cancer is in my liver and my lymph nodes. It's spreading, Acadia."

"No! Don't talk that way!" I placed my hands over my ears like a rebellious child. "We'll get you the best doctors, and they can operate or something. They can fix this. I know they can."

"I don't think so."

Beatrice's resignation was so out of character for her—for the Beatrice I knew and loved ... for the Beatrice who saw hope in every situation ... for the Beatrice who saw promise in everyone, even me—I was rendered speechless. I rose to refill my water glass, my legs weak beneath me while my emotions spiraled out of control. In a situation like this, I should be a comfort to Beatrice, not an added burden. Still, I couldn't comfort her, not now, not when ...

I turned, glass in hand, to look at her and the room revolved slowly around Beatrice's chair. I reached out a hand to grasp the countertop.

The rotating room stilled. I released my grip and filled my glass carefully. I stepped toward Beatrice, and then she spun with the room, more rapidly this time, blurrily, out of focus. Colors swam before my eyes, and I saw only blackness. As I fell, the image in my head was of Beatrice's kind eyes magnified behind the ever-mottled lenses. The blackness receded, and warm arms and hands supported me. Then Beatrice and I were both falling to the floor—the water spilling over us, and we were laughing. I wanted the laughter to be real, the ominous words Beatrice had spoken vacuumed away like dust bunnies.

Our laughter died. Miraculously, the glass had not broken. Both Beatrice and I were drenched in patches. Her soft yellow cotton blouse clung to one breast so that she looked like a breastfeeding mother with a leak.

"I'll get a blow dryer." I offered and she nodded. While she used the blow dryer, I slipped into the bedroom and changed my clothes. I felt so numb, I scarcely knew what I was doing. Somehow, I emerged in a dry shirt and jeans.

I had to know. "Can't they operate?"

"It's spreading too fast. There's no point."

"Why are you telling me this now? Don't you know I can't—can't handle—"

"I know you *can*." Our bowls of soup lay before us, untouched and unappealing, growing cold.

"You *don't* know that," I said in a strangled voice. "You can't possibly know."

"What are you so afraid of, Acadia?"

I was silent, wanting to answer her honestly but not knowing what to say. I knew only that I was inadequate on all fronts. I couldn't be a mentor to Sybil the way Beatrice could ... I couldn't be the kind of wife Peter needed. I'd only held on this year because of Beatrice's support. Without her, I couldn't possibly go on.

"Remember the preacher's wife who killed her husband last year?"

Beatrice nodded.

"On the news they kept showing photographs of these beautiful little girls." A sob caught in my throat. "They were so lovely, and she and her husband looked so happy in the pictures they showed." Tears spilled, and I could barely get the words out. "I don't want that woman to be me in a few years."

"Oh, Acadia." Beatrice moved to my side and hugged me close. "That could never be you."

"You don't know that. But you do know I've done some pretty awful things in my life."

"God will forgive you. If you ask him to."

"Easy as that?"

"Easy as that."

"I don't see how he could."

"It's hard to understand," Beatrice said. "But that's how he is. And another thing. He won't give you more than you can bear."

Something inside me broke loose, and I pushed Beatrice away. How could she talk about God like this when he let this dreadful thing happen? "I don't want to hear his name," I said through gritted teeth, trying to be calm. Then, abandoning the effort, I burst out, "He let this happen— maybe he even *made* it happen!"

"We have to believe he knows what's best," Beatrice said.

248

"What's best!" My voice rose about ten decibels. "How can it be best for you to die? Leave me alone! Just go!"

Beatrice looked at me, touched my hand once more, and left.

"God!" I screamed, throwing myself on the floor, still slick with a puddle of water we had failed to clean up. I beat the floor with my fists, as if to hurt God. *How could you, Lord?*

CHAPTER FORTY-TWO

I found myself in my car after Beatrice had gone, driving aimlessly, still reeling from her revelation. An enormous void filled my chest, as though she were dead already.

I turned on the radio. "President Reagan went home to the White House today after spending less than two weeks in George Washington University Hospital. He is reported to be doing well."

I thought back to our trip from my house to Sugar Sands … albeit in separate cars. Clearly, I'd made a mistake in returning. Beatrice had deceived me. Without any intent as to direction, with vague thoughts of returning to my parents' house or checking into a hotel or driving into oncoming traffic, I discovered I had instead pulled into the small church parking lot.

On trembling legs, I tried the door to see if it was locked. It was not. I sat on a pew near the back, remembering the day when I perched here for the first time, when Beatrice rescued me from the critical eyes of Maude Davis. My heart ached for the comfort Beatrice's presence had provided from the start, knowing that particular comfort was to be ripped from my life forever.

Anger replaced the ache, and I yielded almost gratefully to the new sensation—a sensation that made me feel alive at least. "Oh, God!" I moaned, my voice echoing in the empty room. "Why?" I dropped my head onto my knees. Then I lifted it slowly upward, my voice softer now. "You let her get sick. You could have healed her, but you didn't. You knew how much I needed her… how much I need her still. Why now—why not later, when I'm on my feet, when I'm stronger? What are you trying to do to me?"

I dropped my head to my lap again and wept. I wept for Beatrice— for her sweet face, for the horrific image of that vibrant life being stilled and cold and unable to do the good for which she was so much better equipped. Mainly, though, I wept for myself—for the hope which had only begun to spring to life and was being squelched now.

I cried raucously for a time, consumed with self-pity. I needed Beatrice in a way God did not. I felt sure God recognized my need and was choosing deliberately to thwart me in my struggle.

My anger shifted abruptly from God to Beatrice. She should have told me sooner. She had no right to lead me on. How could she have kept this truth from me for so long? I thought back to all the clues I'd ignored—Beatrice's pallor when we drove from my parents' home to Sugar Sands. Before that, all the doctors' visits she dismissed as routine checkups. She lied to me. By not telling me, she was a liar.

A sudden noise caused me to whirl around. Realizing my hands were clenched into tight fists, my face blotchy and swollen, I saw my least favorite parishioner. Maude Davis. Worst still, she saw me. I jumped up as if caught stealing the offering.

I froze as she approached, though her touch on my shoulder was gentle. I met her gaze, the expression in her filmy, faded blue eyes taking me completely by surprise. Not harsh or judgmental, not even smug in her recognition of my failures. Her gaze reflected only concern and compassion. Even this woman, whom I'd dismissed as pretentious, envious, and embittered was capable of greater selflessness than I.

I stared blankly at her, unable to speak.

"Whatever is troubling you," she said, "will sort itself out with time."

Will it? I turned to go.

Maude Davis's voice trailed after me. "Take care of yourself, dear."

Beside the image of Beatrice's velvet brown eyes behind thick lenses was implanted those of Maude Davis, pale blue and sympathetic.

CHAPTER FORTY-THREE

Outside, a sharp breeze struck my face. I decided to head to the beach instead of my car. Near the shore a mass of white foam shaped and reshaped itself into concentric circles shifting like amoebas in a biology lab. In the distance, sun glinted off the water's surface, tracing a path of shimmering jewels down its center in an irregular pathway to the sky. Like the jags on a hospital heart monitor, an arrow or two of clarity cut through the muted gems. Three birds flew low above the white foam, their winged bodies dark against the white. Together they pedaled, coasted, and pedaled again.

Barefoot and mindless, I walked along the edge. My feet longed for the cold wash of waves that didn't quite reach me. The bejeweled water path widened and shortened, filling in all the arrow darts except for a single long slender one far in the distance. The shimmering mass continued to sparkle around the edges, while the center of the pathway became almost blinding in its silvery brightness.

Like a torrent of wind ripping through trees, ebbing and strengthening, the sounds of the sea held me. I tried to imagine moving far from its familiar tune. As the clouds around the sun shifted, the path across the Gulf lengthened and narrowed to a point as it approached the shoreline, and then spread once more into the foam of the rolling tide. Within minutes, the pathway to the sky had dissolved into patches, steppingstones to heaven. The stones shifted and moved, making the way difficult, if not impossible, for the traveler to find her way before the most essential stone should disappear altogether.

The magnificence of the Gulf lifted me outside myself, so I could look down on this woman called Acadia. From a distance, I could observe her life and follies as if they meant no more than those of any other human being. Less in fact. The woman named Acadia bent to pick up what resembled a potato chip, knowing it to be a ruffled seashell.

The water reached my feet suddenly, bringing me back. I gasped with the delicious cold of the initial shock. I thought of my life with Peter, and his life with God. I had never been the kind of helper he needed. I'd believed his faith to be so strong it could scarcely be shaken, and I had proceeded to do exactly that. To shake him in his convictions and his priorities—by trying to be first in his life. I had wanted him to love me best—before his God, not after.

By teasing and taunting, by complaining about my unfitness for the life of a minister's wife, deep down I had been pleading with him to keep me ever first in his heart. Even when I took the initiative by encouraging him to pray with me, to turn his troubles over to God, had my motives been pure? Even then, hadn't I been seeking Peter's approval for being the right kind of wife? I could hardly remember a time when I acted in a way that was entirely selfless. Was I even capable of such an act?

Sybil's image floated to my mind, as she looked on the day of our first picnic together. The large eyes, the small rosebud mouth, and the horror of the words coming from those innocent, yet not-so-innocent, lips. My inability to listen, or accept, or believe. All my failings rushed at me, and I was sure I could not go on. Not without Beatrice's strength. Nor could I continue to be tossed about like a potato chip in the tide. I had to release Peter once and for all. His hurt in the short-run—which I knew would be great—would be less in the long-run than the alternative.

Beatrice should have realized this inevitable outcome when she came for me that day. She knew her condition, and she kept it hidden. What could she have been thinking? A dead fish washed up next to me, its cold eyes glazed. I stepped over it, thinking of the brevity of life, of the inevitability of death for fish and fowl and human beings.

In the distance, a large bird flew above a group of gulls. I watched for a time, trying to identify the large bird. His slate-blue wings caught the light as he flew, his head black, his underbelly white. Abruptly he plunged into a swift steep dive and snatched a gull from its peers. He rose again, the helpless prey dangling from his yellow mouth.

I thought of the universe and God's design for us. Why were we humans so much more conflicted than the birds of the air? Was mankind the only species who struggled with this conflict, who was constantly torn between what we wanted and what we thought we *should* want? Why were we so much less sure of our place? The last time I entertained these thoughts,

I'd been with Beatrice on our drive to Point Mildred. Instead of moving toward the mature faith I needed, I was more confused now than ever. What a disappointment I had turned out to be.

CHAPTER FORTY-FOUR

When I returned to the house, braced to tell Peter my decision, Beatrice's red Cadillac was in the driveway. I hesitated and almost drove past the house, then swerved into the driveway. I sat for a moment to prepare myself. The car radio was still on. Leo Sayer's "When I Need You" played, though I'd scarcely noticed until now. I snapped the button to turn it off.

Perhaps I should tell them both together. They were such an integral part of who I had almost become, as well as the reality of who I was.

Entering the house, I smelled the soup I'd made a lifetime ago. Was it really still the same day? I found Beatrice and Peter together in the kitchen.

Peter jumped up. "Cadi—are you alright?"

"I'm fine," I said.

"I'm going to leave the two of you together," Peter said.

"Did she tell you?" I asked. "Do you know?"

They exchanged glances, and I saw that he did. A thought struck me. "How long have you known? Did she tell you before she told me?"

When he didn't speak, I knew the answer. I turned to Beatrice. I had believed her to be my friend, *my* friend, more than Peter's.

"I didn't know how to tell you," she said. "I just didn't know."

I sank into a chair. "Don't leave, Peter. I need to talk to you both."

Peter hesitated. "I think it's best if you talk to Beatrice alone first."

Too tired and too depressed to protest further, I let him leave. I turned to Beatrice. Seeing the pain-ravaged face, I could scarcely believe my stupidity in not figuring something out sooner.

A loud knock interrupted my thoughts, and I left Beatrice alone as I went to see who was there. Bradley pushed his way inside before I had a chance to object. "Look," he said, "you and me don't have to be friends or nothing, but we want the same thing."

"I doubt it."

"Don't get smart with me. Just wait and let me tell you why I'm here."

"All right." I waited, wondering if I should feel frightened.

"Sybil told me what you said to her, back before—you know—and I've done some thinking. I come to see what's as plain as the nose on your face. We ain't so different, you and me."

"I don't know what you're talking about." And now I was frightened, not of what he might do but of what he might say. "I think you should leave now."

"Sybil's all ga-ga over this baby thing, but you and me know what's ahead. Diapers and bills and crying in the middle of the night. My ma had seven after me, and I been through that mess enough to last me a lifetime. Between the two of us, we can make her see that it's no good. That she's better off to get rid of it. Like you told her before—"

"I never said that!" I could see Sybil's face as she had glowed at the mere thought of her son, as she told me how she was going to make everything up to him.

I straightened and faced Bradley, not flinching at the garlic on his breath. "Maybe I did," I admitted, thinking back to my conviction that she should put the child up for adoption. "But I was wrong. Sybil wants to keep her baby, and she will be a good mother. I know she will."

Bradley slumped. "I thought you agreed with me," he said, "but if that's the way it's gonna be, she's on her own. I done told her that." He turned to go, and then he hesitated. There was defeat in his eyes when he looked back at me ... but a pleading too. I wondered if there was hope for this young man after all. "I expect she'll be sorry," he said.

"What was that all about?" Beatrice asked when I returned to the kitchen.

I told her, and she smiled her approval at my handling of the situation. The smile was so weak, though, that my heart wrenched. A measure of strength returned to me in the face of her weakness, and I longed to reenergize this woman whom I loved so dearly. "How about some soup?" I asked.

She nodded. I ladled two small bowls of the broth, then placed a clean spoon and napkin beside each.

She removed her thick glasses and placed her fingers on either side of her nose, massaging the tired flesh and shutting her eyes. The lids were fragile and delicately veined, as thin and crinkly as pale blue tissue paper.

At last, she lifted her head to meet my eyes. Without replacing the glasses, she peered at me as if seeing my soul through a newly acquired spiritual lens. "Oh, Acadia," she said, "I don't want to leave you. Not yet."

"Then don't. You can fight the disease. People do that, you know, when they really want to badly enough. I've heard lots of stories—you wouldn't believe how many times it's just a matter of *believing* you can beat it."

Beatrice replaced her glasses and shook her head. "We have to accept that God knows best. I've never understood why he took Ron when he did, when I still needed him so badly. I just had to accept it."

"I'm not like you," I said. "I'm not a very accepting kind of person."

Beatrice blew on a spoonful of soup and tasted it. "The crunchy vegetables are tender now. What was it, onions or carrots?"

I ignored the question. "What I don't understand is how you could let me become so dependent on you, knowing all along ..."

I couldn't finish—couldn't give words to the horror of Beatrice's approaching date with death.

"You're stronger than you know," Beatrice said.

"No, I'm not. Not without you."

"Haven't we been over this territory before—how you're not the only one who ever messes up around here?" Beatrice put down her spoon. "I messed up that day at the hospital when you were so close to the edge. I didn't even see it. I may have messed up again by not telling you about my illness, and who knows how many other times? It doesn't really matter who messes up or how many times, so long as you keep reaching out to God."

I slurped a spoonful of my soup before I answered, though it had no taste for me. "I can't," I said at last. I rose and moved away from Beatrice, pacing back and forth in the small kitchen. When I spoke, my back was turned to her. "I can't reach out to God unless he's going to heal you. He's the one who let this happen."

I stood still and waited for her to reply. When she did not, I turned to look at her. Her face was so pale, so strained with the pain of her disease and with her concern for me, I ached for her, my love for Beatrice greater in that moment than my need for her. I sank beside her at the table.

She took my hand in both of hers and looked at me again in a new way that made me feel she was seeing inside me. "Acadia, if it weren't for you, I would not even hesitate to go home. To be with God and with Ron. I'm ready to let go, Acadia. And I think you are too." As she spoke, Beatrice's face cleared for a moment … her expression beautiful, as if she was already crossing over.

I'm not ready. I stared at the frail hands holding mine. *I'm not as strong or as good as you think.* I couldn't speak my thoughts. I could not bear to see pain return to her dear, good face. I sensed that she was already departing from me and from the trials of this world. I could do one decent thing before I gave up on my life here in Sugar Sands. I could be here for Beatrice as she passed from this world into the next. I could provide what comfort I was capable of giving. I would not hurt her further.

CHAPTER FORTY-FIVE

During the following weeks, I provided what comfort I could as the disease ravaged Beatrice's body with a shocking lack of mercy. Meanwhile, the distance grew between me and Peter. I knew the distance to be my fault, knew too that Peter was aware of the struggle going on inside my head. I did not want to confront him, not yet. Perhaps in some obscure way, this growing distance would help him come to terms when the time came.

"How's Peter?" Beatrice asked during one of my daily visits.

"He's fine. We're fine."

"Good," she said. I felt sure she knew I was playing a role for her benefit, and still I sensed something else in her penetrating gaze—her belief that the role I played was more real than I suspected. I did not want to shatter her illusion.

I'd grown accustomed by now to the odors of Beatrice's house, so different from the delicious aromas before she sickened. I wondered if she noticed the change. The house was always clean, both then and now. Her daughter, Margaret, who came to stay with her during these past few weeks, saw to that. Several women from the congregation, including me, pitched in to help Margaret. Before her illness, Beatrice's house often smelled of bread baking, or of the sweetness of fresh-cut flowers, or occasionally of the spice of some new recipe she was trying out. Now the clean was a different sort, an antiseptic, medicinal clean.

Yet, despite all the cleaning, the stench of death hung in the air. What I could not grow accustomed to was the change in Beatrice herself. The Beatrice I first loved was already gone. Because she didn't want to surrender her grip on reality, she avoided the drug cocktails as much as possible. And so she hovered between the extremes of physical pain on the one hand and the mental torture of hallucinations on the other. Her face, so pale and strained, was like a muted watercolor copy of the vibrant original. Only the eyes remained bright.

"Sometimes, I get the strangest feeling when I'm with you"—I told her one day—"as if you can see right through me. As if you're gaining some kind of special vision."

"To make up for my nearsightedness, you mean?" Beatrice was in bed on this day, a sure sign of how badly she felt. Even on her worst days, she insisted on sitting up in a chair during my visits. A wry twist of amusement tugged at her lips. We both knew she was nearly blind without her glasses.

"I'm ready, Acadia."

"Aren't you afraid at all?" I whispered.

"Not really. There's a certain fear, I suppose, of the unknown. Mostly, it's a good kind of fear. Anticipation's a better word. I look forward to being reunited with Ron and seeing my Lord." Though out of breath, she looked happy, in a dreamy sort of way.

"Were you ever afraid of dying? When you were younger, I mean."

"I was but less and less over time. I think the worst fear was when Ron was alive, and I was afraid of dying and leaving him alone."

She reached for the water glass on her nightstand, and I helped her situate the straw so she could suck. She drank with effort, her frail throat working, then continued. "There's always one person in a marriage who's better able to go on alone, and maybe I knew down deep I was the one. Ron helped me get ready to go on without him too, you know." She chuckled, a weak ghost of her old throaty laugh. The laugh turned into a cough, and I patted her back gently until she regained her breath.

"As you and Peter grow older, you'll know too. You may be surprised. The saddest times are when the one who's left behind is the one who isn't so able to go on alone."

"Why does God let that happen?"

Beatrice shook her head. I stroked her soft hair, grateful she had been spared the indignity of losing her lovely gray-streaked crop. "That's one of those questions we'll have to ask him face-to-face, I guess. Or maybe we won't have to ask. Maybe we'll just know the answer by then."

I watched as Beatrice drew a shallow breath, and I could tell from the expression in her eyes she was about to change the subject. "I need you to do something for me, Acadia."

I could hear Margaret clanging dishes in the kitchen, and my heart contracted with sudden misgiving as I said, "Of course. What is it?"

"I need you to see Sybil. To see if she needs anything."

I suspected Beatrice added the last phrase more to encourage me to go than out of any real concern that Sybil was in need. Even on her deathbed, Beatrice would know if Sybil were in need.

Beatrice reached for me. I took her frail hand in mine, her grasp surprisingly strong but chilly to the touch.

"Why risk confusing her again?" I protested. "You know she's doing well. You've told me often enough." I did not want to let Beatrice down either by going and messing things up or by not going at all.

Beatrice's eyes, the pupils so large I could barely see the rims of brown iris, burned into mine. "See Sybil. For me?"

I nodded and squeezed her hand.

"You're not alone, Acadia. Lean on the Lord," she said. Her eyes shone as if she could see the pathway to heaven as clear as the shimmering jewels of the sun on the Gulf.

My voice broke. "I love you, Beatrice."

CHAPTER FORTY-SIX

Despite a horrific migraine, I wasted no time in making arrangements to meet with Sybil. If I was going to do this thing, I might as well get it over with. We met at our usual spot. When I saw her, my heart stuttered in anticipation and dread.

With her rounded belly, her condition was too advanced to hide. She wore a short aqua sweater over a brown scoop-necked T-shirt, a wide brown band of some sort on one wrist, and frayed jeans. She had pulled her hair into a careless bun parked high on the back of her head. Wisps of blonde hair escaped around her face, which beamed with pleasure when she saw me.

She flung her arms around me, and I embraced her awkwardly, trying not to press too hard against the baby inside. "I've been wondering when we would get together again," she said. I flinched with guilt at the rebuke in her words.

"How have you been?"

"Great." She patted her belly. "Me and him both."

"Do you feel like walking?" We had agreed not to bring food today, so our arms were free except for a lightweight blanket I carried.

"Sure. The doctor says I should take frequent walks."

I nodded, glancing up and down the beach to pick a promising direction. The weather was lovely ... warm and breezy ... and yet the beach was vacant except for us, the birds, and one couple in the distance.

"Which way?" I asked.

Sybil pointed to the left. I had expected her to ask me to choose. Perhaps her approaching motherhood had shaped a new decisiveness.

We walked in silence for a time. The water was a muted aqua, lighter than Sybil's sweater but darker than the sky, which was nearly white. A gentle lapping soothed my headache. Near the edge of the water, gulls congregated like churchgoers. A larger, browner gull emerged nearby, a mouthful of seaweed and crab remnants dangling from its beak. A second one followed with a dead fish in tow. The circle of life surrounded us.

I relaxed, no longer worried about what lay ahead. Sybil and I would talk, or we would simply share a walk on the beach. Surely, I could not say anything either stupid enough *or* profound enough to make a difference. Nearby a gull strutted her black dotted Swiss frock irrespective of the season, dressing for the weather rather than the calendar, as my mother would say. A lone pelican coasted across the sky.

Seashells lay in clusters along the beach. Among the tiny shells, one larger beauty of a shell lay half buried. I picked it up.

The shell was broken, missing the perfect half I'd imagined buried in the sand, leaving only a jagged edge. The remnant filled my palm, still lovely in its circles of taupe and cream and greenish gold. I flipped it over and caressed the glossy smooth contours of its underbelly, admiring the swirls of marshmallow white. I fingered the broken edge.

"You never finished telling me about your brother." I had not planned to say this.

"My half-brother, you mean. You're the only one I ever told—except my mom, right after the incident."

The wind had picked up, bringing a mist of sand against our faces. "Would you rather sit for a while?"

"Okay."

I spread the blanket and watched as she lowered herself carefully onto it. I dropped beside her. A sudden gust of wind brought a fresh wave of sand, and we laughed as we spit it out. "If we face this way the sand should only hit our backs. Unless the wind shifts."

We rose, and together we repositioned the blanket. As we sank onto it for the second time, Sybil began to talk. "The thing is, Acadia, I've never been very good at accepting change. I don't know why because it's not like I've ever had anything so terrific to hold onto. Not before now." She patted her belly again. "Another thing is, I've always sort of seen everything as black and white. You know what I mean?"

I nodded.

"I had to keep believing Bradley loved me, or I would be broken again … the way I was broken before. When my brother Gary betrayed me, I felt like everything I'd ever shared with him was a big lie."

"And you don't feel that way anymore?"

"I don't. I'm past all that."

"How?" I fingered the broken shell in my palm, amazed anew at the resilience of this woman-child. "How did you do that?"

The slender shoulders, now rounded with extra flesh under the coffee-colored T-shirt, shrugged. "Because I was thinking about the little one here, I guess. There's going to be plenty of rough spots for us, times when he'll hate me and maybe even times when I'll think I should have given him up. No matter how bad the rough times get, I can't let them spoil the beautiful ones.

"I've gone back to work, you know," Sybil went on. "Mr. Brubaker took me back, and—would you believe it?—Mrs. Davis is going to watch the baby so I can work and go to school or whatever. Of course, I may not be going to school here, so I may not need her after all. I know there will be nice people wherever—"

"Maude Davis?"

"Yes, and she says she won't even let me pay her because taking care of the baby would be like having her own grandchild, almost."

I was silent for a long moment, digesting this bit of news as Sybil continued. "I'm trying to put my past behind me now, with Bradley and with my brother, and just dwell on the beautiful parts. And learn from the rough patches."

I mulled over her words. She was so young to be able to see her own flaws and yet to see past them. I thought of my inability to stick with things. Why did I always give up too soon? And I thought with wonder of Maude Davis, who needed money herself. Life was full of surprises.

"You're really okay, aren't you?" I looked at the shell in my palm again and slipped it into my pocket.

"I think so. Maybe for the first time in my life—I really think so." Something in the wide-spaced eyes made me think of the kind of wisdom you glimpse for a second in the eyes of a newborn infant. In the distance, the sun sparkled like white diamonds on the water ... and I realized my headache had lifted.

CHAPTER FORTY-SEVEN

I was anxious to return to Beatrice, to share with her an update on Sybil's progress, and my own. The message on my phone when I returned home was from Beatrice's daughter, Margaret. All it said was "Call me," but I knew.

"She went the way she wanted to. In the bed she shared with my father," Margaret said when I called her.

Beatrice's wish was for Peter to conduct her funeral service at the church building where she had spent so much time over the years. I knew he was struggling over his notes, but I was too distraught to offer much encouragement. Because Beatrice had grown close to a number of preachers during her lifetime, many of whom would be at the service, Peter felt honored she had asked for him.

The day of the funeral dawned bright and fresh, the way I remembered Beatrice before the disease took hold. "You've been waiting, haven't you?" Peter asked me. He stood in front of the mirror as he spoke, making his usual mess of knotting his tie, the one I'd help him select on the last day of our honeymoon. How high our spirits were that day, before the car broke down.

"Here, let me do that." I undid the sloppy knot and started over. "There, that's better. What do you mean—waiting for what?"

"Waiting for Beatrice to—pass on—before you decide about us."

"I suppose I have." I turned away from Peter and made a pretense of fluffing the pillows on our bed.

"And?"

"And I don't know. I'm sorry, Peter. I know how difficult that must be for you to hear, and I promise I won't leave you on the fence. Not for long. Just let me get through Beatrice's funeral." Peter came to me and pulled me close. I longed to yield to his touch, to sink against his body and let him take care of me the way I'd once imagined he might. Instead I stiffened, not wanting to encourage false hope.

Peter changed the subject. "Do you think I should cancel the thing tonight?" he asked.

"What thing?"

"There's a cookout scheduled for the youth group. I told you about it."

I nodded, dimly recalling some mention. Nothing except Beatrice had seemed quite real to me for some time now. "Why would you cancel?"

"I wonder if going ahead might seem inappropriate with the funeral today. Beatrice was popular with the teenagers, you know. They will be mourning her too."

I pondered this while I straightened my hair in front of the mirror. My hair had become uniformly dark, the highlights I'd worn for so long having finally grown out. "Beatrice wouldn't want you to cancel," I said, certain this was true. "She would want everyone to move forward with their plans."

The small church building was crammed to capacity. I glanced at the guest registry. I recognized some of the names from my conversations with Beatrice. Others were from our own congregation, while still others were strangers—none of which mattered, as I was in no mood to play the role of the preacher's wife. Sybil was there, of course, but I could find little comfort in her presence. I sat near the back in the plain navy dress I had also purchased on our honeymoon.

Despite Margaret's request for donations instead of flower arrangements, flowers in every color of the rainbow overflowed the building, their sweet scent permeating the air so that I felt faintly queasy. Peter's voice and face faded before my eyes, and memories of Beatrice replaced them. I would not cry. If I started, I might be unable to stop. The loss wasn't mine alone. God had taken from the world a caring, giving human being. Surely, I was not being entirely selfish to mourn such a loss.

I thought of Beatrice in a peach pantsuit, the shade of the roses on her coffin, her smile, her nearsighted gaze. I thought of the Beatrice of recent weeks, the eyes still piercing but assuming a distant peace, as if she were already leaving me, her body shrinking as she prepared for the next world. I remained dry-eyed, my sadness too great for tears.

Peter's voice cracked, and I wondered for a moment if he would break down completely. "So many people have shared stories with me," he said, gulping back sobs and finding a firmer voice. "Stories of how Beatrice helped them through difficult times." When he fell silent, I knew he was thinking of our troubles, his and mine, and of how Beatrice had brought me back from Kentucky.

"I'm going to read a poem Beatrice shared with me, one written by Alfred Lord Tennyson. It expresses her attitude toward death better than anything I could say."

> Sunset and evening star,
> And one clear call for me!
> And may there be no moaning of the bar,
> When I put out to sea,
>
> But such a tide as moving seems asleep,
> Too full for sound or foam,
> When that which drew from out the boundless deep
> Turns again home.
>
> Twilight and evening bell,
> And after that the dark!
> And may there be no sadness of farewell;
> When I embark;
>
> For tho' from out our bourne of Time and Place
> The flood may bear me far,
> I hope to see my pilot face to face
> When I have crossed the bar.

Peter's voice faded again, and in its place, I saw the Peter of former days, in this same pulpit, speaking as always from his heart.

What was that Scripture he'd read on the day of his first sermon at Sugar Sands? From Matthew, I remembered. I lifted a Bible from the pew in front of me and flipped to Matthew. I scanned quickly but could not find the passage. Peter's words came to me suddenly, nearly verbatim. "Jesus didn't restore the blind man's sight all at once, though he could have. Isn't that the way it is with us? Jesus works on our hearts the way he worked on the blind man's eyes, but we don't see all at once. Spiritual sight comes in stages."

"There were other times when Jesus healed the blind all at once," he'd said. He had read another Scripture, one where Jesus healed two blind men who were immediately and completely healed. And then they followed Jesus. Just like that. For some people, faith comes all at once. For others, faith comes in stages. And that's okay ..."

Beatrice had such faith by the time I knew her. I feared mine could never be so strong, though Beatrice insisted otherwise. "You're stronger than you know, Acadia." I could hear her voice as clearly now as I did when she first said those words to me, as if she were sitting beside me on the pew. And I wished (how I wished!) that she were ... the Beatrice I had first known, so full of energy and life and love.

I turned my attention back to the present and to Peter's eulogy. "We all have different talents," he said. Jesus told us that, and Beatrice often reminded me of this truth. Jeanette Lockerbie once told a group of people that she was a one-talent person, referring to her talent for communicating. After the meeting, one of the women came up to her and said, 'That's not true what you said tonight ... the best part is that you're good at sitting by the fire and being a friend.' Unlike Jeanette Lockerbie, Beatrice was not known for her writing or speaking abilities. But she was phenomenal at being a friend."

Around me, many heads nodded their agreement.

"Each one of us should seek out our own talents, because we may not even recognize what they are—and then find a way to use them. Beatrice would want us to do that."

His eulogy finished, Peter invited the congregation to join in singing some of Beatrice's favorite hymns. I tried to sing without succumbing to the tears welling up inside.

I come to the garden alone,
while the dew is still on the roses.
And the voice I hear falling on my ear,
The Son of God discloses.

And he walks with me, and he talks with me
and he tells me I am his own.
And the joy we share as we tarry there,
none other has ever known.

He speaks, and the sound of his voice,
Is so sweet the birds hush their singing
And the melody that he gave to me,
Within my heart is ringing.

I'd stay in the garden with him
Though the night around me be falling,
But he bids me go, thro' the voice of woe
His voice to me is calling.

My tears finally spilled, and I could sing no more. I cried for Beatrice, who loved roses and gardens and, most of all, loved her Lord. I cried for myself and for my loss. The words of the song echoed in my brain, the change from singular to plural, from "I" to "we." I wanted to be part of the "we," to have the comfort that Beatrice had known, the sureness and certainty of the Lord's presence with me always. "None other has ever known" rang out from the congregation. I was still thinking of these words as we filed toward the front of the room for one last look. Was every relationship with God unique? And, if so, was there hope for me?

In the coffin, Beatrice's face was surprisingly youthful, not shriveled at all but smooth and serene, beautiful even. Her eyes were closed behind the thick glasses. A single peach rose lay across her bodice. Her hands were folded, fragile and lifeless. I reached out a tentative hand to touch one of hers, to squeeze it one last time. Her hand was cold. So cold. My throat caught. "I'm going to miss you so," I said, blinded by the flood of my tears.

CHAPTER FORTY-EIGHT

I spent the hours following Beatrice's burial alone on the beach. With the familiar feel of the sand under and between my toes, I pondered whether Peter had begun to accept the inevitability of our breakup, perhaps even to look forward to the end of the uncertainty.

Something caught my eye, and I glanced down to spot the watermelon plant I'd seen previously. The plant was farther from the water than I recalled, far enough back to be protected from the shifting tide. Still, its survival seemed almost miraculous. Even more astonishing was the growth of an actual watermelon. Green and round and alive. I bent to touch it. The blossoms on the plant were yellow, and they too seemed to be thriving in the sand so far from anyone's garden. I touched one of the blossoms, and the very reality of this life struck me as a gift from God.

Suddenly I needed to talk to him. I began to pray … inside my head at first, then out loud, still stooped beside the watermelon plant. As I rose, I prayed with my eyes open, lifting my head toward the heavens. I prayed as I had never prayed before. I talked to him about Beatrice and about Peter. I talked about my parents and about my faith and about my doubts. "Oh, Lord," I said, not caring who might see me and think me crazy. "I have messed up so badly," I groaned. "I keep trying to take your place in Peter's heart, even though I know how wrong that is. I can't be sure I won't do it again. I have this way of deceiving myself into thinking I'm acting for someone else when I'm really just being selfish. God, I can't blame you if you give up on me."

I could hardly believe the waterfall from my eyes had not dried up by now. After the flood of tears for Beatrice, I'd felt as if I might never cry again. Yet here I was, a few hours later, with tears flowing more freely than ever.

I walked closer to the water's edge, daring the water to reach me, to chill me. When it didn't, I moved toward it until the cold water was biting into my bare feet. I welcomed the cold. I spread my arms to the sea to welcome the wind, to invite the spirit of God to show me the way.

Another sermon of Peter's came to mind—the day he spoke to the congregation about division and unity. About love. The passage that had stirred me so deeply came from Corinthians. I actually memorized the passage as a child, memorized it without really thinking about its meaning.

I tried to remember the exact words—the idea that now we see through a dark mirror. A stronger current brought the salty water over my ankles, but the cold no longer bit into my flesh. The words came to me suddenly as clearly as if spoken aloud.

Now we see as if we are looking into a dark mirror. But at that time... we shall see clearly. Now I know only in part. But at that time I will know fully, as God has known me.

With these words echoing through my soul, the events of my life appeared to me in a new light, as if the mirror had shifted subtly, not yet illuminating the image completely but with slightly greater clarity. My relationship with Peter *could be* part of a plan. My meeting him, loving him in spite of myself, marrying him in spite of my misgivings. The details of my relationship with Beatrice, memories that would be with me forever, blurred with fresh tears like a photograph under water, and emerged with startling sharpness. These too might be part of the plan—our meeting, our friendship, her acceptance of me with all my flaws, my love for her, my loss. Was God's hand in all these things?

I reached into the side pocket of my navy dress and found the perfect sand dollar that Beatrice had given me on our first day together. I had carried it only rarely since that day for fear of breaking the treasure. A premonition clutched my throat that I had broken it today. But holding it before my eyes, I saw it was still whole. I would take it to a jeweler. I would have it encased in a locket of some sort, so I could keep it always.

The lack of comprehension that had haunted and hindered me for so long seemed almost unimportant now. For the first time, I began to *see* with my heart and not my head. It was not necessary for me to understand everything. God had stuck with me through all my doubting and self-pity, even when I lashed out at him.

"How could you?" I asked aloud. "How could you forgive so much? How can you keep on forgiving me?"

I thought again of the blind man who saw in stages. I had seen myself in him from the beginning. All along, even when I was struggling *against* God's will, I was also growing to accept his power. Despite my resistance, my faith had grown. I prayed anew. "Lord, how can I know your will for me? How can I stop resisting you? How can I see and accept? I know you know everything. All the stuff I did before I met Peter. The hate and the drugs and the sex. How can you still love me?"

Even if God could forgive me and still love me, could Peter?

And yet, where better for me to continue my journey than beside someone like Peter? No, not beside someone like Peter. Beside Peter.

A gentle breeze lifted the skirt of my navy dress, and I lifted my eyes to the sky. Must be later than I thought. How long had I been walking and praying? I had no idea. Only the colors of the setting sun told me time had passed. The sky was brilliant with streaks of lavender and patches of gold and peach, as though God was sharing all the colors of his palette with me personally in my moment of need. I felt God's presence so powerfully, so personally, that I cried out.

Peter. I had to tell Peter. I had to tell him everything—past and present. By the time I got home, Peter would most likely have already left for the evening's activities. Peter's face swam before me, as he had looked on the day we met—the long blond hair just brushing the strong, firm line of his jaw, the crinkles at the corners of the green eyes, the grin inviting me in. That Peter faded. In his place, I saw others—Peter, worried and uncertain as he had been this morning in front of the mirror awkwardly knotting his tie … Peter, ablaze with love and tenderness when he spoke of Beatrice … Peter, needing me, loving me, wanting me, but also troubled for me and for himself, for our life together. I had put him through so much, and still I had to put him through more. Was it too late?

CHAPTER FORTY-NINE

I heard Peter's voice before I saw him, the full-throated laughter that always made a person want to join in. I felt like a shy adolescent. The laughter told me Peter could go on without me, and for an instant my doubts were back. Maybe he would be better off, after all, if I left. How could I be certain of God's plan for either of us?

The size of the crowd of teenagers around him surprised me. This turnout was the best we'd had in months. The fire on the beach crackled, and the aroma of charcoaled hotdogs drifted toward me. My stomach growled. In the moonlight, I saw silhouettes rather than individuals. My feet, crunching in the sand, hesitated, turned, ready to run.

The crowd quieted suddenly, and I turned back to watch as the silhouettes merged into a circle. Peter's voice rang out, strong and true, as he began to sing.

"Blessed be the tie that binds our hearts in Christian love."

Amazed, I stood frozen in place. It was the song I had played on the piano for Beatrice, the song that had been, I realized now, running through my head ever since.

Without hesitation the others joined him, their voices lifted joyously. Not everyone there was a teenager. I recognized a couple of the elders from church and a few others, joining hands and blending their voices with the youth. As I stood in the distance, watching and listening, I had the sense that something important was happening here. Something inexplicable, almost magical.

"The fellowship of kindred minds," they sang, "is like to that above."

As if a breeze had swept across the beach, my breath caught in my throat, and my spine tingled. These people—not just the young in age but the young in spirit—their arms locked together, were becoming … what was the word? Becoming more than themselves. Becoming one. The word *rapturous* came to me, and I thought of churches where men and women danced in the aisles, wept, and professed the Lord in dramatic testimony. Always my parents had claimed these displays were melodramatic, their leaders frauds who were only after money.

I had thought so too. More likely, some of these people were truly moved as I was moved now. Joy rushed through me at the realization … here was the future of the church… of Jesus's church. He would have been right here in their midst in his dirty sandals, not judging anyone. He was here now. Not in a closed building in rows of pews but right here on the beach.

I remembered a day I had spent on a beach in Malibu with a surfer I was dating—what was his name? Back then I had told myself the same thing. If there was a God, he was every bit as likely to be with me there as in a church. Yet, I had been troubled by not being in a church beside Peter that day. *Warren*, that was his name. The feel of the sun and the water, the confusion in my brain, all came back in a rush of clarity.

I had been right, and I had been wrong. The setting didn't matter. What mattered was the hearts of those united, bound together in love. I thought of Beatrice, of our first meeting, our walk together on this beach. "There are young people with old minds, and old people with young minds too," she'd said.

As the song ended and the singers drifted apart, I heard my name.

"Acadia!" I recognized Sybil's voice. "You came!"

She hurried to meet me, then seemed unsure of what to do next— throw her arms around me or offer a polite handshake. She did neither. I reached out to take her hands in mine. "I'm glad you're here," I said.

"Me too."

I could see her face now, and she looked radiant in the moonlight. Her eyes sparkled, and her lips curved upward. A faded, oversized T-shirt stretched taut over her rounded stomach. The baby had grown in the short time since I saw her last. She followed my gaze. "Me and him are going to be just fine," she said, and drew my hands toward her belly.

For an instant, I almost pulled back, as if my very touch might injure the unborn child. Then I relaxed and let her guide my hands. "Feel," she said.

A tiny flutter, a movement like a wave and then a firm little kick met my touch. I gasped in delight. "My goodness, he's a feisty one, isn't he?"

She nodded proudly. "Thank goodness, he naps sometimes."

I grinned, realizing she was already taking on a maternal role. I wondered if I would ever feel ready myself. Maybe you just take the plunge and then the appropriate feelings come along, as they had with Sybil.

While Sybil and I chatted, I caught Peter's form out of the corner of my eye. Engrossed in conversation, he gestured with his arms and talked with an earnestness I knew so well. He had not seen me yet. Or had he? Maybe he knew I was there, but he had written me out of his life already. Now I was just another struggling soul, one he would make time for in turn.

Four or five teens who had finished their hotdogs began to toast marshmallows over the fire. Sybil and I watched as the marshmallows went from rubbery white to golden brown. A plump, sweet-faced girl named Morgan laughed as her marshmallow caught fire. One of the boys grabbed her stick and blew the fire out. Their eyes met, and their hands touched on the stick. The way she looked at him made me think of Peter. My heart lurched again, echoing the way I imagined Morgan to be feeling. Her marshmallow was completely charred.

The boy moved his hand away ... reluctantly I thought ... and the pair eyed the burned marshmallow. "Ugh!" Morgan said.

"No, they're delicious like that."

"You can *have* it."

The boy bent his head and sucked the marshmallow off the tip of the stick. "Hot!"

Nostalgia swept through me. I thought of the party where I first met Peter. How recent that evening felt, and yet how much had happened since. We had eaten popcorn, and Peter had seemed to me all sunshine and light in his views of religion and the world in general. Now I knew he had his dark side, his black moments. At the center, he was so soft and tender, so nearly liquid that I longed to merge with him finally, to be truly one with this sweet, sweet man who was my husband.

I turned to find him looking at me, discovering my presence. Somehow, I had known I would. Peter's joy, which always echoed through my own veins, radiated warmth as he moved toward me.

At my side, however, his face darkened. "Are you back for good?"

"Can we go somewhere and talk?" I trembled suddenly at the enormity of what I needed to say.

"Okay." He took my hand and led me into the night away from the group.

At a distance of several yards, he stopped and turned me to face him. "It's bad news, isn't it?"

How did he know? Then his meaning dawned on me. "No!" My heart thudded at the despair in those beautiful green eyes. "I mean, yes, but not what you're thinking."

"What then?"

"Peter, there are things about me that you don't know. Things I should have told you a long time ago." I had rehearsed these words in my head so many times, they came out robotic sounding.

"Okay." Peter's eyes were level, his tone steady.

"I experimented with stuff when I was in high school. I couldn't bear to tell you because you're so good, and I'm so—not. Drugs, I tried drugs. And then my freshman and sophomore years, before I met you... I was so happy to have guys willing to date me, to feel popular for the first time... but that's no excuse."

"What are you saying?"

I was stalling, trying to find the right words. There were none. "I'm sorry, Peter."

"I don't understand."

"I wasn't a virgin on our wedding night."

I watched his Adam's apple move when he swallowed. "What bothers me the most isn't what you're telling me. It's... what have I done to make you think you need to hide things from me? Am I so judgmental?"

I tried to think how to answer, how to tell him what needed to be said without hurting him beyond recovery.

"You're not hearing me!" he said suddenly. "You're trying to think what to say, aren't you?" For the first time he sounded truly angry. "Why don't you try the truth?"

I was crying now. The truth. "The truth is ... I had an abortion, and I'm so ashamed."

The anger drained from Peter's face, leaving him paler than I'd ever seen him. The absence of anger was somehow harder for me than its presence. "Say something," I whispered.

"Tell me everything," he said at last. "Help me understand."

If I didn't understand myself, how could I hope to make Peter do so? Still, I had to try.

I told him everything I'd told Beatrice, and I waited for him to tell me it was over ... *we* were over. We sat at the edge of the sea and let the water wash over our ankles while I talked. And talked. When I finally paused for breath, Peter enfolded me in his arms. "I'm so sorry you went through this, and sorry you have been keeping it bottled up inside you for so long."

He patted my back, and I sensed pity in his touch. Suddenly, I was certain pity was all he had left for me, and I couldn't blame him.

"I understand if you can't forgive me," I said. "I know I did a horrible thing, and I should have told you so long ago."

"Of course I forgive you, Cadi. If God forgives you—and I know he does—who would I be to refuse?"

He still felt distant, and I realized with a shudder that forgiving me and loving me were two entirely different things. Of course Peter would love me again because he radiated God's love toward everyone. That wasn't the only kind of love I needed from him.

In a very small voice, I asked, "But can you love me again? Like a wife?"

His fingers tightened on my back. "Oh, Cadi, I never stopped. Surely you know that."

Gratitude washed through me. Gratitude toward this wonderful man and gratitude toward God for bringing him into my life. I gasped. "I didn't, I didn't know, Peter!"

"There's something else that bothers me," he said. His eyes revealed all too clearly the pain I had caused, and this, too, echoed through my veins.

My heart sank. Peter had always seemed too good to be true. For him to let me off so easily was not only more than I deserved, it was too much to hope for.

"How could you have thought to leave me?" he asked.

My relief was so profound it staggered me, literally. I leaned against him to regain my balance. "I thought ... I wanted ... what was best."

"Best for who?"

For you, I almost said. But I was learning to be honest about my motives, not to deceive myself. "I don't know. For everyone."

"And now—what do you think now?"

We walked away from the kids, toward the edge of the water, while I struggled to find the words. I stooped to pick up a sand dollar. It was whole, like the one Beatrice gave me that first day here. Between that day and this, I had not found a single one that wasn't broken. I held it in my palm.

Peter reached out to take the sand dollar from me. He turned it gently from one side to the other. "I think there's life here," he said, and I watched as he returned the creature to the sea.

A couple of snowbirds, a silver-haired woman and a distinguished looking man with thinning white hair, walked past, hand in hand. They wore matching sweatpants and sweatshirts. "I want that to be us someday," I said.

I saw the tears on Peter's cheeks and felt the answering tears on my own as he pulled me into his arms, bringing me home.

ABOUT THE AUTHOR

DEBRA COLEMAN JETER has published both fiction and nonfiction in popular magazines. Her first novel, *The Ticket*, finaled for a Selah Award and Jerry Jenkins's Operation First Novel. Her nonfiction book, *Pshaw, It's Me Grandson: Tales of a Young Actor*, was a finalist in the USA Book News Awards. She holds a PhD from Vanderbilt University, and a BS and an MBA from Murray State University. She and her husband live in Tennessee.